MIKE SANDERS

THIRSTY 2

A Novel by
Mike Sanders

This is a work of fiction. Names, characters, places, and incidents either are the product of the author's imagination or are used fictitiously, and any resemblance to actual persons, living or dead, business establishments, events, or locales is entirely coincidental.

Wahida Clark Presents Publishing, LLC
60 Evergreen Place
Suite 904
East Orange, New Jersey 07018
973-678-9982
www.wclarkpublishing.com

Thirsty 2
ISBN 13-digit 978-0-9828414-7-1
ISBN 10-digit 0982841477
Library of Congress Catalog Number 2011905656
Urban, Charlotte, NC, Street Lit, African American – Fiction

Cover design by: Baja Ukweli
Interior layout by: Nuance_Art.*.
nuanceart@gmail.com
Contributing Editors: Intel Allah, A. Bracey and R. Hamilton
Printed in United States

DEDICATION

It has been two loooong years since anyone has read a new Mike Sanders novel and I truly appreciate the patience of every one of you! Without you (my readers), writing wouldn't be as fulfilling! Thank you all for supporting my work throughout the years! I know my last novel was dedicated to myself for all my hard work but without further adieu, I would like to dedicate this book to YOU, the reader!!! Much Love!

ACKNOWLEDGMENTS

First, I would like to thank the most high for blessing me with the ability to breathe life into words. Without Him, failure is imminent!

My beautiful daughters, only God knows the love I have for you!!!!!

Special shout out to Wahida Clark and the entire staff at WCP! Thanks for overseeing this project to completion and thanks Wah for the conversations that put the fire under my ass to get this joint done! Lmao!! Love you girl!

Thanks to Nita Thomas, Jarold Imes, Al-Nisa Bracey, Crystal Payne, Sheba Morris, Selina Dozier and everybody who read advanced copies of this project and gave me the corrective criticism that I needed to mold this novel into what it is today.

My fellow authors and friends, Freddie Simmons, Mike Jeffries, Cash, Marcus Massey, TN Baker, Danielle Santiago, and many others.....Let's keep pushing that pen and make *them* realize that black people DO read!!!!

To ALL my fallen soldiers (There's waaaaaay too many to name) Keep ya' head to the sky and stay walking in faith! It does get greater later. I can attest to that!!!!

Special shout to YOU, my loyal reader!!! Thanks for supporting me from day one with the release of my first novel "Hustlin' Backwards"!!! Wow, I still can't believe this is number four for me!!! I look forward to seeing all of you soon while on tour. If I'm not coming directly to your city, I am definitely coming to a city near you! Add me on Facebook by name or email (Mike Sanders or Queencitysbest@yahoo.com)!! And follow me on Twitter (@NeverThirsty704) for cities and dates of my signings! SEE YA' SOON!!!!!

THIRSTY 2

A Novel by
Mike Sanders

THIRSTY 2

A Novel by
Mike Sanders

PROLOGUE

"Are you ok?" Justice's father, Tyson asked her while looking at her as if she'd lost her mind. Her shrill screams echoed throughout the room and he had to cover his ears to keep from bursting his eardrums. Unbeknownst to him, he had just revealed to her that the man she had been living with and had ultimately gunned down was her long-lost brother!

Justice couldn't focus. Her throat felt as if it were closing up and her eyes were clouded with tears of shock. Never in her life had she felt such pain. She sat on the edge of the hotel bed with her head buried in her hands, shaking uncontrollably. Her father had rushed to her side to try to console her but he had no idea of what was going on. "Justice…baby, are you ok?" He cradled her head in his arms and tried to pry her hands away from her head because she was ripping out clumps of her beautiful tresses. "Baby, please talk to me. What's going on?"

Justice could not respond if she wanted to. She felt the contents of her stomach rush to her throat as she shook free from her father's grasp and made a mad dash for the restroom. She barely made it before vomiting all over the toilet. Tyson stood in the doorway and continued to try to get Justice to respond but it was to no avail. He decided to give her a few minutes to get herself together. However, there was no way he was leaving her alone in the state she was in. He closed the bathroom door, leaving a small crack so he could keep a watchful eye on her.

After a few long minutes, Justice finally emerged from the restroom, looking pale and disheveled. It seemed as if all the blood had drained from her face and her hair was in disarray. She looked nothing like the woman that had let him inside the room hours earlier. Justice walked past her father and plopped back down on the bed still in disbelief from what he had just revealed. After all of the frivolous pleading, Tyson came to the conclusion that Justice was not going to talk to him any further until she was ready to confront whatever was disturbing her. He stayed with his daughter for another hour, trying to comfort her and catering to her needs but she still refused to discuss the issue.

After promising to never lose touch again and making plans for dinner in a few days, Justice watched Tyson walk out the door. Once the door was shut, she lay upon the large bed and covered her face with a pillow. She vowed not to tell Tyson or anybody else about what she had done. It was a secret in which she would take to her grave . . .

CHAPTER ONE

Justice, we got a problem in the dressing room." Toni's high-pitched voice broke her train of thought for a moment. She was standing in the doorway to Justice's office with the heavy oak door half-open, allowing the loud music from the club to pour in. Justice was seated at her desk tapping away at the keypad on her laptop. The office had expensive looking cherrywood furniture with photos of Justice's family and her best friend, Sapphire, adorning the walls.

The thing that stuck out the most was the wall directly behind her desk adorned with a large family portrait of her, her deceased mother, and her deceased younger brother, Monk. Absent from the portrait was her father, Tyson, the only living member of her immediate family. Tyson had been estranged from her life since her early teenage years, but they had subsequently made amends two years ago in that hotel room when she'd first returned to Chicago from Charlotte, North Carolina. Tyson's photo sat alone on her desk next to the floral arrangement he'd sent two days ago for her birthday.

"What is it now?" Justice asked without looking up from her computer. She wasn't the slightest bit surprised at Toni's statement. There was always some sort of problem or another in the dressing room. Twenty-five girls running around in a confined area clad in nothing but bras and G-strings, sometimes even less, *would* cause occasional problems.

Toni shifted her voluptuous five foot two frame through the door. Her honey-blonde dreadlocks and apple-bottom ass swung in unison with every step. She closed the heavy door behind her, muffling the roar of Luda's latest stripper anthem, "Thicka than a Snicka." Leaning across Justice's desk, Toni huffed, "The girls you flew in from Memphis are complaining about Virgin and Precious."

Justice finally looked up from her monitor and sighed deeply as she pushed away from the desk and sank back further into the leather Queen Anne. Purely out of habit, her toned arms went up over her head and her slender fingers intertwined before coming to rest atop her silky mane of jet-black hair.

"Toni, if I ain't mistaken, you're the manager here last time I checked." Her sarcasm was hard to miss. She looked at Toni with a frustrated scowl. Sometimes dealing with Toni made Justice feel as if she was dealing with a child instead of a grown ass twenty-eight-year-old woman. Toni rolled her eyes at her boss and folded her arms across her ample bosom without replying.

"How many times have you had trouble with Virgin and that bitch Precious?" Justice asked, her jaw clenched tight and her eyebrows knitted.

Toni hesitated as if she was actually trying to calculate the numerous times those two had caused problems at the club.

Without waiting for a response, Justice ejected, "Exactly. Too many times to count. Every time I bring in new girls from outta town to dance, them two bitches start. You know what . . . fire them bitches." Fire rose in Justice's tightly slanted eyes.

"Just like that?" Toni asked as if she couldn't grasp the finality of Justice's statement.

"Yeah, *just* like that. Tell them to keep their tips from tonight, gather their shit, and get off my property—better yet, go get 'em. I'll do it myself."

Justice was fed up with Virgin and Precious. Those bitches were nothing but troublemakers.

Toni left Justice's office with an "ooooh, somebody's ass is in trouble" expression glued to her face. For the same reason, she was also relieved that she didn't have to be the one to give the girls the boot.

Justice untied her ponytail and shook out her long tresses while exhaling a deep-rooted sigh. She rubbed her temples to relieve the slight migraine that was gradually building. For the past two days Justice had been under tremendous stress because the anniversary of her brother's death was quickly approaching. Every time Justice thought about her brother it brought about a brain-throbbing headache.

As she watched Toni's thick frame sashay its way out the door, Justice mumbled, "I need to be firing *your* incompetent ass." Then on second thought, Justice surmised that Toni had been there with her from the beginning of her legitimate endeavor. She had been there from the very moment Justice had first decided to legally invest some of the blood money she had almost lost her life over.

When she arrived back in Chicago she had no idea what she was going to do next, and that was when she confided in Toni. Toni had been a childhood friend that Justice stayed in contact with over the years. Toni had went to school, majored in

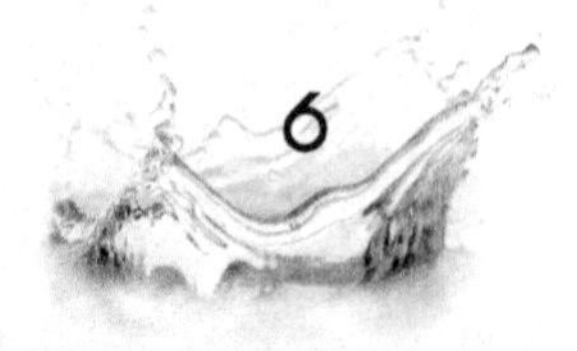

business but could not find a job in her field. When she found out that Justice was looking to start her own business, Toni had been the one who suggested she open the strip club. Ever since Justice's return, she and Toni had become as close as sisters. Toni was an only child who had been raised by both parents and to be labeled as spoiled was an understatement. She was used to getting her way and usually complained like a child when she didn't get what she wanted. Justice always got a kick out of seeing Toni's uppity ass try to act hood around her just to fit in. Justice never understood why a person would go to extreme measures and even dumb down just to be liked. Although she and Toni were like night and day in the aspect of personalities, their business marriage worked . . . most of the time.

Initially, Justice cringed at the idea of a strip club because she had never gotten along with other women, much less strippers with their asses on their shoulders. On top of that, she could not think of another woman who owned a strip club—that was always considered a man's world and Justice didn't see herself a part of it. Nevertheless, to her astonishment, Justice discovered that dealing with the girls who had come through the doors of her establishment for auditions had been easier than she had imagined. Mainly because she realized most of the girls were just as fucked up in the head as she was. Each and every one of them had a story and sometimes, Justice took pleasure in listening just so she could keep her own sanity in check.

Justice had always prided herself on being a good judge of character, so with the girls who had come to her for an opportunity to work she looked beyond the surface. Beyond all the D-cup titties, twenty-two inch waists, and porn star asses,

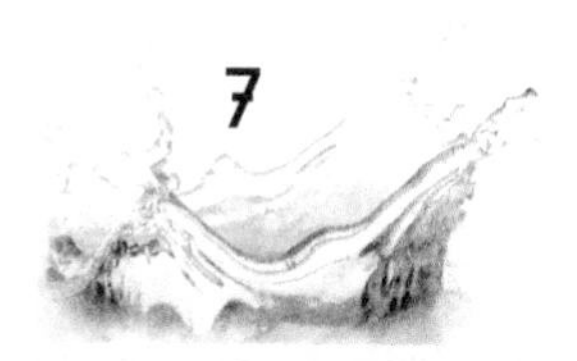

lay insecure opportunists who were willing to bear it all for a quick buck. Justice looked for girls who were not just in it for the money, but enjoyed being on stage and entertaining an audience. She wanted girls who were of decent moral character—meaning they didn't have a dick in their mouths every time she turned her back.

When Justice first opened Phire & Ice downtown on Michigan Avenue in the heart of Chicago, she had no idea it would become one of Chi-town's premiere spots for nightlife. The elite adult entertainment club attracted ballers from all around, especially local rappers and professional athletes. It was not unusual to see Twista or Derrick Rose in the VIP area; sipping Rosê and making it rain on a weeknight.

Most of the time Justice's business ran smoothly without any problems. However, there were times when the estrogen level was at a boiling point and catfights were inevitable. Sometimes Justice felt like she had it all together and other times she felt as if she were running a circus like the late great Bernie Mac as Dollar Bill in the movie *Player's Club.* At those times, if it were not for a caring staff, especially Toni, she felt like she would lose it.

"Boss lady, here they go." Toni's voice brought Justice out of her lingering thoughts.

Justice rose from her chair and watched as Virgin and Precious entered her office reeking of weed and fruity body oil. *I know these bitches ain't been in the dressin' room smoking again*, Justice thought. Looking at the two reminded Justice of why she used birth control. They were definitely a waste of sperm. Grimy bitches!

Precious was the taller of the two. She towered over Virgin by at least eight inches. Nevertheless, Precious's height did not intimidate Justice in the least because if it were not for Precious's heels, she and Justice would have been eye to eye. Justice had no idea where the pair had come up with their names because everybody in the Chi and the surrounding Metropolitan area knew the girls were anything *but* precious and virginal. It was even rumored that the two had used the VIP for occasional tricking. Turning tricks was a definite no-no in Phire & Ice.

After Toni left the office and closed the door, Justice stated, "Sit down." She glanced back and forth between the two girls with equal amounts of animosity, so there would be no mistake about whom she was speaking.

Virgin took a seat on the leather sofa near the door while Precious remained defiantly standing for a few seconds. Finally, she sucked her teeth and reluctantly sat her Amazon-ass down next to her partner.

Precious adjusted the garter on her thick thigh, which was stuffed with bills—tens and twenties, only a fraction of the tips she had earned for the night. Both girls were dressed in bras and matching G-strings along with expensive pumps. Virgin was wearing her signature color of all white, which symbolized purity. Her auburn-dyed hair was fixed in tight cornrows, which made her defined cheekbones even more pronounced. Her creamy, peanut butter complexion was flawless without a trace of make-up. However, the glassy look in her eyes made Justice wonder if she was rollin' on X or jacked up on coke. There was no mistaking that she was high on something.

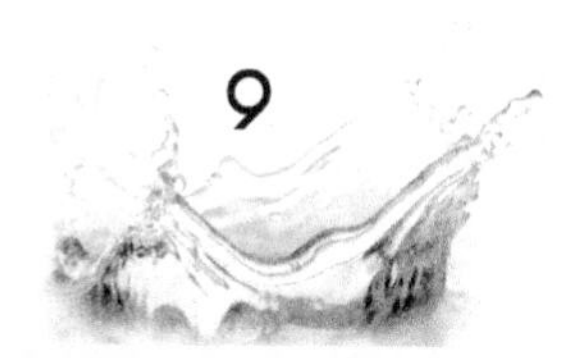

Precious wore fire engine red with gold-colored rhinestones decorating the nipple and crotch area of her two-piece outfit. This night she had her naturally short hair styled into a throwback Halle Berry number. Her ebony skin glistened with a thin sheen of perspiration from the lap dance she was so rudely pulled away from.

With the bodies both Precious and Virgin possessed, Justice hated to admit that they were two of the baddest bitches in the club. Between Justice and the dancers, the confidence level in this room was at a record high and so thick you could taste it. Justice strolled over to the picture window and glanced out over the crowded, well-lit parking area before addressing the girls.

"Do y'all know the definition of the word *insanity*?" She had her back to them and could feel their eyes boring into the back of her head.

"What?" Precious asked with a hint of attitude and slight frustration, as if she hadn't heard Justice's question correctly.

"You heard me," Justice said. She turned to face the girls, disdain evident in her exotic features. "If you don't know, lemme enlighten you. Insanity is when you constantly do the same thing, but expect to get different results, different outcomes."

Precious and Virgin exchanged heated looks and rolled their eyes while twisting up their mouths as if they were sharing the same thought: *Yeah we know what insanity is. This Chinese looking, Kimora Lee wannabe bitch is the one insane. Sittin' up here lecturin' a bitch when it's niggas out there spendin' that dough.*

"I said that to say this: Every time I spend my hard-earned

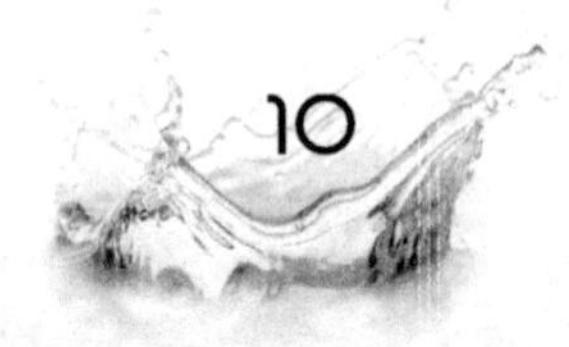

money to bring new faces up in here so my customers won't get sick from seeing y'all same tired ass faces every night, you two always seem to be in the way. Tryin' to do all you can to make the featured girls as uncomfortable as possible. I don't understand you two."

Justice pointed toward the door. "It's enough money out there for a hundred girls to eat and y'all wanna fuck that up every chance you get. You are the only two that hate like that! Y'all are just like cats pissin' on a spot to try to claim turf!"

Justice's slanted eyes bored into the girls.

"I'on know what you talkin' 'bout 'cause I ain't—" Precious started, but Justice cut her off.

"You know *exactly* what I'm talking about, Precious! And I can do without your funky ass attitude right now." Justice's voice rose. "I got eighteen girls who dance here nightly, along with ten I fly in every weekend from different cities. Tell me why I need you two?"

Precious and Virgin looked at one another, dumbfounded. Justice calmly sat back down and began tapping her French manicured nails on her desk awaiting a response. Silently she waited to see what type of justification the girls could come up with that would keep her from banning them from the hottest strip club in Chicago.

After a long uncomfortable silence, Precious responded, "So, you wanna play *that* game, huh?" She arose from the sofa and slowly approached Justice's desk with a devious grin.

She and Justice locked eyes, then Precious stated in a whisper, "You think a bitch don't know how you used to get your money back in the day in Carolina?" She waved her arms around as she looked about the spacious office. "A bitch know how you ended up with all this. Bitch, a hustle is a hustle and I ain't knockin' that. But I guess *nothing* was outta your realm when it came to gettin' dough, huh? Maybe not even murder."

Precious smiled devilishly as she read the look in Justice's eyes.

"So, Lucy Lu, you might wanna be mindful of who you threaten the next time you open your mouth 'cause you neva know who might know what you think they don't know, feel me?"

Justice stammered, "I—I don't know what you talkin' about. You need to get outta my office and outta my building before—"

"Oh, I think you do know what I'm talkin' about. But that's gonna just be between the three of us . . . for now." She looked back at Virgin and winked. "But right now, me and Virgin got a couple of VIPs lined up out there. So we gonna finish out the rest of this night . . . and tomorrow night . . . and the next night . . . and the night after that, and . . . well, you get the idea." Precious scowled at Justice, then turned to Virgin. "You ready to finish gettin' this money?" Just that quickly, the tables had been turned a whole 180 degrees.

"No doubt," Virgin replied as she arose from the sofa and headed for the door with Precious right behind her.

When Precious reached the door she turned to look at Justice and winked. She joked "Holla at 'cha later, Killa." The sarcasm was thick.

Then they were out the door.

Toni was standing outside the door waiting for the girls to

exit. As soon as they came out, Toni went in.

"How much time you give them to get their shit and get out?" she asked Justice. Then she noticed the look on Justice's face. "Girl, what happened?"

Justice buried her head in her desk and ignored Toni's question. After a few moments, Justice raised her head and stated a weak, "They're staying."

"What?"

She looked at Toni. "Lemme think for a minute. Come back in thirty minutes and we'll talk."

Reluctantly, Toni left the office. As soon as the door was closed Justice's mind began reeling. She tried to come up with scenarios as to how the two girls could possible know her secret.

After about ten minutes of pondering over this, she came to the conclusion that the two girls couldn't possibly know what they were talking about. They had to be speculating on rumors. This wasn't the first time Justice had heard about her past of setting niggas up to be robbed, but it was the first time the word "murder" had been mentioned.

Speculation or not, Justice decided that she couldn't take the chance of letting those two bitches keep that secret dangling over her head. She opened her desk drawer and looked down at the .9mm she kept stashed there for protection. She picked it up and had flashbacks of the day she'd killed J. T. Never in a million years would she have thought that she would have to pull the trigger again to take a life, but the way she figured it, she had no choice.

CHAPTER TWO

"Girl, don't you know these bitches tried me last night," Justice spoke candidly into her Bluetooth earpiece. She was sitting on the sofa in her spacious living room talking to her best friend, Sapphire.

"Who was it this time?" Sapphire's voice blared in her ear.

"That Amazon bitch, Precious and her lil' sidekick, Virgin," Justice replied while reducing the volume. "Bitches aiming at my pedestal . . ." She paused for a moment because her other lined beeped. She checked her phone and saw Toni's number. Since Toni was running the club tonight, Justice decided she should take the call because it may have been about something important. "Lemme call you back in a minute. That's Toni."

"Okay, but make sure you call me back so we can plan your trip. My mama is so lookin' forward to seeing you and I am too. Girl, it's been like forever."

Sapphire's mother had recently been hospitalized because of her cancer recurring and her health was slowly deteriorating by the day. Justice had promised Sapphire she would come to visit for a week or two while her mother was incapacitated.

"I know, right. Tell your mama I said hey and I'll see y'all soon. Luh you, girl."

"Luh you too, sis."

Justice clicked over and listened as Toni spoke. After a few minutes into the conversation, Justice realized the call wasn't about anything important. She scowled as Toni let the latest gossip fall from her lips with rapid speed. "Giiiirl, you ain't gonna believe what happened at the salon today . . ."

For the next five minutes Justice was held hostage by Toni's gossip and fruitless information. She tried several times to end the conversation, but to no avail. Toni didn't get the hints. Finally, frustration overwhelmed Justice. "Is everything okay at the club?" She cut Toni off.

"Everything is fine, I got this," Toni stated with confidence.

Justice sucked her teeth and shook her head as if she were standing before Toni. If anything, she knew that Precious and Virgin were up to some fuckery and Toni was too passive to check their asses if need be. She contemplated on going to the club to check on things for herself but tonight she was just too tired to do so.

"Good. But listen, I gotta go. Call me if you need me. *Only* if you *need* me." Justice put emphasis on her words to drive her point home.

"Oh, okay boss lady. I'll holla at'cha later. Enjoy your night off."

"I'm trying to," Justice replied with the greatest amount of sarcasm. Then the call ended.

Justice sat on the sofa and looked around her home. Her residence was on the ground floor of a large turn-of-the century home in the southeast section of Hinsdale that had been transformed into a series of quaint condominiums. A nice fireplace with a large Victorian-style mantle dominated the living room. Bookshelves filled one wall. Every urban novel ever published resided on those shelves. She was an eclectic reader, if her collection of literature was any indication.

She rose from the sofa and went to the window to look out at the night. Ever since she had moved back home from North Carolina, Justice had become a person of the night. Her daylight hours were few and she often utilized those hours for sleeping. For some reason, the darkness seemed powerfully soothing to her, like a gentle cascade of warm water on a brutally freezing night.

She walked into her spacious bedroom and sat on the large Renaissance bed. She picked up a frame from her nightstand with a photo of her mother in it. As she observed her mom's full-blooded Filipino features in the photo, she put the picture down and then glanced into the mirror and noticed how much she resembled her. Only Justice was darker and more voluptuous. She was beautiful, intelligent, and now legally successful. There was no reason for her to be single—yet she was. Suddenly she felt a sense of loneliness wash over her.

Justice thought briefly about a quote she had recently read in a book of poetry by her favorite poet, Shakim. The quote read: "*To find riches is a beggar's dream, but to find LOVE is the dream of kings*!" Like any ordinary woman, Justice too longed for love and happiness. But those two aspects of life just didn't seem to exist in her world anymore. While pondering over Shakim's quote, wet clusters began forming in her eyes. As she lay back and closed her eyes, her mind once again journeyed back two years to the last man she had given her heart to, and the events that caused her to flee Charlotte, North Carolina.

Justice and her brother, Monk had the perfect set up. She'd scope out the potential victims, using her female wit to get information she needed and used just about any way to get it. She targeted ballers, athletes, entertainers and other rambunctious niggas that didn't know how to keep their mouths shut—the more they blinged, the harder she went after them.

After getting the pertinent information that she needed, she'd help Monk, along with his boys, D. C. and Cross set up the victims and then the four of them would split the dough. She made enough dough doing that for years without having to have a regular job—hell, she was a boss.

The only regret that Justice had was introducing Sapphire to the game. Justice loved Sapphire with all of her heart and she treated her as if she were a little sister. Sapphire was the type of woman who was impressionable—had low self-esteem and always made a bad choice with men. Justice had put her on with her first chance to run game and things ended up going sour because the women who Monk, D. C. and Cross tried to rob remembered that Justice and Sapphire were the ones who rang the doorbell.

Meanwhile, Justice and Monk had been accused of participating in the robbery of her ex-boyfriend, Carlos, a major drug dealer in Charlotte. Because of Justice and Monk's treacherous ways, their MO's fit perfectly with the crime they were accused of. Although they were innocent, Justice couldn't get Carlos to listen to reason. Therefore, Monk and Carlos had gone to war and Justice was forced into hiding. In the crossfire, Sapphire was brutally beaten and left for dead and barely lived to survive the ordeal. It was then when J. T. entered Justice's life. He came along like a breath of fresh air and whisked her away from the streets and the madness that came along with it.

Justice let her guard down and ended up falling in love with J. T. She thought she had finally met her knight in shining platinum, until one day she unveiled an ugly truth! By sheer coincidence, Justice discovered that J. T. had actually been the one who robbed Carlos! Not only had he participated, he had also been the mastermind behind the whole scheme. He even knew that Carlos blamed Justice and Monk for the stick-up. After putting together the pieces of that crazy puzzle Justice realized that she had been sleeping with the enemy the entire time!

Subsequently, Justice planned her revenge and carried it out to the letter. When it was all said and done, eleven bullet holes decorated J. T.'s torso and Justice was the one who held the smoking gun. She cleaned out J. T.'s large safe and fled the vicinity. She and Monk were supposed to meet up after J. T.'s murder so they could go back home to Chicago and start a new life far away from the streets of Charlotte.

Unfortunately, Monk was murdered in Rock Hill, South Carolina, only fifteen minutes outside of Charlotte, on the same day they were supposed to have left. Monk's murder went unsolved, but Justice was pretty sure she knew who had been responsible for his death. That Dominican drug dealing bitch named Tan who they had robbed shortly before his demise. Justice made a vow to make that bitch suffer the same way her brother had. Even if Tan hadn't actually committed the murder herself, Justice was sure that she had her hands in it because she was the last person Monk had been with when Justice last spoke with him on that fateful day. Either way, Justice knew that Tan would have to pay!

On that same day, Justice found out that she had carried J. T.'s child, which she wasted no time aborting.

Justice arrived back in Chicago with a trunk full of money, an urn full of ashes, and a heart full of despair. Once back in the Windy City was when she was paid a visit by her estranged father, Tyson. After having a long-needed heart to heart talk, Justice learned that her father had sired a son out-of-wedlock shortly after she had been born. When Tyson told her who his son was, Justice suffered a minor breakdown. That long-lost sibling had been none other than J. T.! The man she fell in love with, the man whose seed she'd carried, and the man whose life she had taken had been her own brother!

Justice wiped her wet eyes and shook the thoughts of her past as she continued to lay upon the large bed in the fetal position. She briefly thought about Carlos and remembered the many phone calls and text messages he had sent her after he found out the truth about the robbery. He begged and pleaded for her to try to understand his position, but his apologies went unanswered. He even paid Sapphire's hospital bills and gave her fifty thousand dollars for getting caught up in the tangled web that had been woven.

Deep down, Justice actually understood that the whole ordeal had been one big ass deadly misunderstanding. She also knew how Carlos's temper was and she couldn't have expected him to handle the situation any other way. Part of her wanted to kill him for putting her through all of the trauma she had gone through while running from his hitmen. Nevertheless, another part of her wanted to thank him. If she had never endured that drama, she would not have gone back to Chicago and found herself.

Her upcoming trip back to Charlotte caused an internal debate on whether or not she would see Carlos while she was there. He already knew she was coming because of Sapphire and her big mouth, but he didn't know exactly when she would arrive. Justice decided she would cross that bridge when she came to it.

Dwelling on her past brought Red, J. T.'s cousin and crime partner to mind. Red was the only one who could have made the connection between her and what had happened to J. T. Last she had heard, Red had been picked up by the Feds. Out of all the places on earth, he had been arrested in Chicago. Apparently, he had followed her there after she had killed J. T.

Justice rolled over and picked up a picture of her and Sapphire that had been taken a few years earlier at Club Prevue in Charlotte. She appeared youthful and so full of life in the photo. Looking away from the picture and into her mirrored reflection, gave her the impression that someone had double-tapped the fast forward button on her life. She was still undeniably beautiful, but if one were to look deeply enough into her eyes they would see her entire story. A smile can masquerade at all times. However, the eyes? They *never* lie!

"I need a break!" she huffed as she had difficulty thinking about the last time she had time off. When she couldn't think of an answer, she decided a vacation was definitely needed and her trip back to Charlotte would serve as just that.

She concluded that she would deal with Virgin and Precious as soon as she returned from Charlotte, but for the time being she decided to let sleeping dogs lie. However, it was without a doubt they were definitely going to be dealt with.

CHAPTER THREE

It was a little after 6 P.M. and the evening sun was shining bright enough to blind the naked eye. An old school two-door Chevy, gleaming like a beacon in an empty desert was parked in the empty lot of Mama Jeannie's Restaurant. The candy-painted box Chevy sitting on twenty-six inch Ashanti rims looked like something straight from a showroom floor. Crystal clear windows and a snow-white leather interior complemented its ice-blue exterior. Its two occupants sat silently; relishing the effects of the weed they had just finished smoking. ". . . I think I'm Big Meech—Larry Hoover—Whippin' work—Hallelujah!" They nodded their heads in unison to Rick Ross as he spit that raw shit on the CD they were listening to. They had the AC blasting, yet the heat from the beaming sun was still almost unbearable.

"Yo, I ain't know this shit was pink," Supreme nonchalantly commented as he glanced out the window, observing the funny-colored building. The long, thick dreads he had grown for the past few years made him look like a wild islander. He exhaled a thick cloud of Black & Mild smoke from the passenger's side before offering the cigar to Carlos.

Carlos looked across 62nd Street at the five-story building that Preme was referring to. He declined the cigar and responded, “Yeah, they hidin’ plenty niggas off in that joint.” This was the notorious Dade County Jail, home to some of the most vicious criminals in Miami and the surrounding Metro-Dade area. This was only one of several county jails in Miami.

“How much was that nigga’s bond?” Preme asked as he toyed with the long, wood-carved walking cane with the gumball-sized ruby embedded in the handle. Ever since Monk had shot him two years earlier, Preme had walked with a limp and he used the custom-made walking cane to help him get around.

“Priceless,” Carlos answered and left it at that.

They fixed their eyes on the entrance to the jail’s intake area as two Hispanic men exited. One older, one younger. It was apparent that the younger man had just been released from custody because he toted a black trash bag, which was presumably full of his personal property. As soon as the young man stepped on the curb near the street, he turned and threw up gang signs toward the top floors of the jail. The older man pulled him along as if he were pissed.

The two occupants of the Chevy turned their attention away from the Hispanic men because they were not whom they expected to see. Minutes later, Preme nodded toward the intake area again and stated, “There our boy go.”

Carlos looked across the street at the man exiting the building wearing Lucky Brand jean shorts, a beige T-shirt and Air Jordan sneakers. “’Bout damn time they let my man, Dave up outta there.”

Dave had added thirty pounds of muscle to his five-foot-six frame and was a far cry from the skinny nineteen year old that

Carlos had first put on years earlier. Dave had just turned twenty-one a week earlier in the county jail and hadn't even had his first legal drink yet. His clean-shaven head gleamed in the bright Miami evening sun while he raised his hand to his forehead as a makeshift visor to block the glare of the scorching sun. He looked about as if he were searching for someone.

Carlos saw that Dave had not noticed them, so he stepped out of the Chevy and raised both arms so Dave could see him. Preme wasn't too far behind as he limped to the driver's side where Carlos stood. "What up, nigga!" Carlos yelled across the street.

Spotting his boss across the street standing near the tricked out Chevy, Dave let a broad smile splay across his face. *I knew my nigga wasn't gonna leave me in that bitch*, Dave thought as he waited for a break in traffic before crossing the main street. He walked up to Carlos and was greeted with a pound and a brotherly hug. Preme greeted him the same way.

"What up, nigga? You good?" Carlos asked his partner as he opened the driver's side door and pushed the seat forward so Dave could have room to get in.

"Hell nah, I ain't good! A nigga was up in that shit for two months. You know these niggas down here don't like niggas from outta town," Dave complained while climbing into the rear seat.

Carlos let him vent a bit before responding, "You know I was waiting for your bond to get cut. What a nigga look like posting a seven-figure bond?" Once Dave was in, Carlos pushed the seat back and climbed back under the wheel.

Dave responded to Carlos's comment, "True dat. But all dat

shit coulda been avoided." He settled into the soft leather, relieved to be out of that hellhole.

Carlos pulled out of the restaurant parking lot and turned right on 62nd Street heading toward the highway. As if he had forgotten to mention it, Carlos turned down the stereo and told Dave, "Oh, by the way, I gotta make a stop before we head back up the road." He handed Dave the blunt, which had sat in the ashtray and Dave took it.

"Y'all some crazy ass niggas, comin' to pick a nigga up from jail smelling like a pound of weed." Dave laughed. "Go 'head and make your stop, it ain't like I got shit to do," he stated. But what he *really* wanted to do was to get on I-95 North so they could make it back to Charlotte, North Carolina. He was homesick as hell! He had only been locked up for a little over eight weeks, but to him it felt like eight years. He was in dire need of a shit, shave, bath, and a home-cooked meal. Not to mention the birthday pussy that had been waiting for him. The thought of fucking his girl for the first time in over two months had him hyped.

Carlos glanced back at Dave "By the way, happy belated birthday my nigga. I wish we had time to take yo' barely legal ass to King of Diamond but we gotta hit that slab as soon as possible. All good though because we gonna get it in when we get back to the Q.C."

"Yeah, happy birthday, nigga" Preme chimed in.

"Hell yeah, we gonna get it in. Nigga, you already know. After I fuck my bitch, we goin' straight to Onyx!" Dave replied

Both Preme and Carlos laughed. "That's what's up" Carlos replied.

"Who Donk?" Dave asked as if he were just noticing the car they were riding in, "I like this shit right here." He ran his hand along the leather of the empty seat next to him. Preme handed Dave a lighter and Dave fired up the weed. As he exhaled his first cloud of smoke in weeks, he almost coughed up a lung and passed the weed back up front.

"You aiight?" Carlos asked, taking the weed from Dave's fingers.

"Yeah, I'm good. You know a nigga ain't smoked nothin' in a minute." He was still coughing with tears in his eyes.

Preme and Carlos laughed at him again. Carlos said, "You asked whose whip this is? It's mine. Big Rob 'posed to be puttin' a box in it for me. We need another stash, ya' dig. Matter of fact, that's where we gotta stop at. I gotta holla at him before we dip." Carlos was referring to his man who owned a stereo installation shop, which also doubled as a spot for installing stash boxes in vehicles.

"If that van y'all had a nigga drivin' was boxed up, a nigga wouldn't be in this situation," Dave mumbled under his breath, but both Carlos and Preme heard him.

Carlos and Preme exchanged inquisitive glances before Carlos looked into the rearview mirror at Dave. He stated, "Yeah, you right, but I felt like you'd be okay for a one day trip. It was a fuck up, but we gonna make it right."

Easy for you to say. You ain't the one who got caught with them keys. And you ain't the one who gotta wear this case, Dave thought. He stared out the window at the passing landscape while rubbing his still burning throat.

Carlos peeped Dave's silent reflection and asked, "You

didn't get no visit from none of them alphabet boys, did you?" ATF, FBI, DEA, it was all the same to Carlos.

Without hesitation, Dave cleared his throat and responded, "Nah, just the regular Jakes askin' the normal questions but you know I ain't give 'em shit. I kept them crackas on they toes like a midget tryna piss in a urinal. Left the mutha-fuckas mo' confused than Fantasia with the S.A.T. test," They all laughed. Dave added, "I'mma soldier. I'mma ride this shit out, my nigga. Fuck dem crackas."

"Yeah, I know you a soldier. Dat's why I fucks wit' 'choo." Carlos smiled into the rearview mirror at his partner. After he had heard what he wanted to hear from his man, he cranked up the volume on the sound system and settled back into the soft bucket seat. Getting on I-95, Carlos punched the gas, making the Chevy float like a speedboat riding the waves.

Twenty-five minutes later, they were entering Opa-Locka. They drove south toward 132nd Street and entered an industrial area. Carlos slowed as he approached what looked like a cluster of warehouses all bunched together. The Chevy came to a stop in front of one of the smaller buildings and Carlos killed the engine. Both Carlos and Preme opened the doors to exit. Preme closed the door behind him and headed toward the rear entrance of the warehouse.

Carlos held the front seat up so Dave could get out. "Damn, Big Rob sho' do be in some low-key ass spots," Dave commented as he climbed out of the back seat and looked at the warehouse.

"He told me to meet him here. He got some scratch for me. Fat ass nigga owe. If I ain't mistaking, he still owe you a lil' change from that ceelo game, don't he?" Carlos asked while closing the door behind Dave.

"Damn, sho' do. I almost forgot about that. A nigga fucked up right now too. I'm shootin' bad as a broke dick dog. I needs that lil' bit." Carlos laughed at Dave's reply before assuring him that his pockets would be back on swole in no time. Dave followed Carlos toward the warehouse with his mind on the money Big Rob owed him from the dice game just before his arrest.

The back door was open as they approached. Carlos entered with Dave in tow. As soon as Dave entered the building, he called out to Big Rob, "Yo Rob! Lemme get me, my nigga!" His voice echoed throughout the warehouse. He laughed and yelled again, "Fat ass Rob! Pay da piper!"

Preme appeared in the doorway to one of the offices down the hall and yelled, "He said come on back."

Carlos and Dave proceeded toward the office where Preme was standing. Once they reached the office, Dave brushed past Preme, almost knocking him off his cane and entered the room, ready to press Rob for his dough. "Yeeeeah, you ain't think a nigga was gettin' out this soon, huh nig . . ." He didn't even finish the sentence because he instantly knew something wasn't right.

Just then, it occurred to Dave that the entire warehouse was empty other than Carlos, Preme, and himself. As soon as Dave turned to face Carlos and Preme he was met with the barrel of Preme's chrome Desert Eagle. His eyes widened in astonishment as he opened his mouth to speak.

"Nigga, close yo' muthafuckin' mouth! That's what got yo'

soft ass here in the first place," Preme spat with venom in his voice.

Without an expression, Carlos stood silent in the doorway as Preme held the menacing pistol sideways, aimed directly between Dave's eyes.

"Man, what da fuck, Los? Fuck this nigga talkin' 'bout?" Dave asked Carlos through trembling lips, stunned as if he had no idea why this was happening to him.

"Them alphabet boys," Carlos replied with a dreaded sigh as he turned to leave the office.

Once Carlos was out of the office, Dave's lips trembled as he stared down Preme's barrel. "Bruh . . . bruh . . . lemme just explain. First—"

Preme cut him off. "First? Nigga, the only 'first' you need to be concerned about is *The First 48*. 'Cause them the mutha-fuckas who gonna scrape yo' ass off this flo'."

Dave's mouth opened to say something else, probably a plea for his life. However, the words were not formed in time as a hot, molten slug from Preme's pistol exploded into his brain! He jerked backward from the impact and then collapsed forward on the cold floor. Blood and brain matter decorated the wall of the empty room. Preme watched Dave's lifeless body spasm and jerk for a few seconds before becoming eerily still.

The thunderous roar rang loudly in Carlos's ears and the sickening thud of Dave's body hitting the floor affirmed that the deed had been done. Carlos never looked back as he exited the warehouse and walked back to the Chevy, gravel crunching under his feet. Once back inside the vehicle, he started the engine and waited for Preme. Moments later, he saw Preme rounding the corner, limping as casually as if he had just finished taking a piss. Just by looking at him, no one would ever guess he'd just blown a nigga's thoughts out of his skull.

As Carlos watched his loyal hit man approach the car, he thought back to the conversation he had three weeks earlier with his good friend, Lyle Jordan, the attorney whom he'd hired to represent Dave.

"Yes, agents from the department of Alcohol, Tobacco, and Firearms visited Dave on yesterday," Lyle had told Carlos over the phone.

"Did he give them anything?" Carlos had asked.

"I'll let you see for yourself. I'm faxing the paperwork as we speak."

Minutes later, Carlos was reading what one of his most trusted soldiers said about him in an interview with the ATF agents. Carlos couldn't believe it! He was angry and hurt all at the same time. Without a doubt, his hurt outweighed the anger by untold volumes. It didn't take much thought about what had to be done. He arranged for a crackhead to sign the bail bond documents for Dave to be bailed out. The bondsman never questioned the skinny, baldheaded guy with the bag full of money as he filled out the necessary paperwork. No paper trail could lead back to Carlos because six hours after the guy signed his John Hancock, he was found in an abandoned apartment with his throat slit.

Carlos had given Dave a chance to come clean with what he had done when he questioned him about getting any visits from the Feds, but Dave had said "no" and that was all Carlos needed to hear. No pleading his case, no explanation for his actions—Nothing! Dave just flat out denied it. In addition, that fueled Carlos's anger even more.

Once Preme was back inside the Chevy, Carlos pulled away from the warehouse and headed to Big Rob's stereo shop located behind the U.S.A. flea market to return Rob's Chevy. The ride was silent and uneventful. Carlos was somewhat torn between the feelings of dread and that of satisfaction. On one hand, he hated to have had to send the young man he had taught the game to dance with the devil. However, he felt as if what he'd done had been absolutely necessary.

After a short drive, they pulled into Big Rob's parking lot. They exited the car and entered the building. "My shit ready?" Carlos asked as he and Preme entered Rob's office. Big Rob was seated behind a large desk eating a sub sandwich dripping with mayo. His long dreads were tied back into a ponytail and his platinum grill was gleaming in between bites of the sandwich. Rob's humongous frame and dark complexion made him resemble a silverback gorilla.

"Where my Donk at?" Rob asked.

Carlos tossed Rob's Chevy keys on his desk. Happy to have his keys back in his possession, Rob smarted off, "Your shit *been* ready hours ago. Fuck y'all been? Shootin' da shit and flossin' my shit all over M-I-Yayo?" He was talking in between bites of the sandwich.

"Yeah, shootin' some shit," Carlos responded as he and Preme glanced at each other. He retrieved his own keys from Rob's desk. "My shit better be proper or I ain't paying," he teased.

Big Rob followed Carlos and Preme out to the parking lot

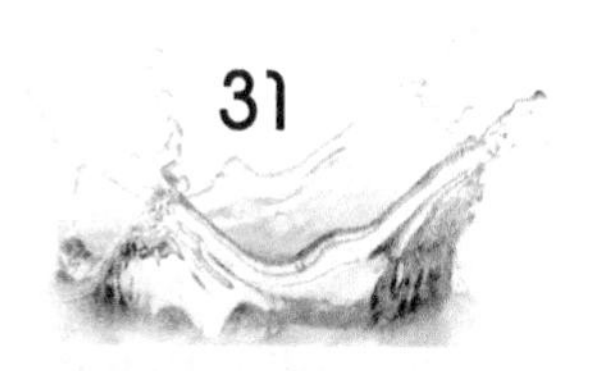

where Carlos's 2012 Tahoe was parked. Carlos started the truck and followed Rob's instructions on how to open the concealed stash boxes, which were in the back floorboards. He nodded his head and smiled in satisfaction once he saw the two large empty compartments. Carlos noted that each hollow box could accommodate at least six keys.

After paying Rob for the installation and tipping him for the use of his Chevy, Carlos and Preme exited the lot in the Tahoe blasting Rick Ross ". . . I'm not a star . . . Somebody lied, I got a choppa in da car. . ."

Rob had no idea that his car had just been used in the commission of a murder; he was just glad to have been tipped so generously.

Carlos headed to the Embassy Suites in Miami Lakes to pick up the two girls they had left there earlier that morning when they arrived in town.

An hour later, Carlos and Preme stretched out along the rear seats as the girls took turns driving back to the Queen City. As they rode, Carlos's thoughts turned to what Sapphire had said about Justice returning to Charlotte for a visit. He was more than ready to see her again. On numerous occasions he had started to go to Chicago to find her, but after his calls and texts went unanswered he figured he'd just wait her out and let her come around when she was ready. He thought about all the drama that surrounded the misunderstanding of the robbery of his stash house, and he sincerely regretted his past actions. He had tried so hard to make amends, especially with Sapphire. He had gone above and beyond to do all he could for her and they had become close over the past two years. However, he still felt as if he hadn't done enough. He would not be satisfied until he could speak with Justice personally, and know without a doubt that she had forgiven him.

Carlos also reflected on the real robbers that had caused all the animosity between him and Justice. J. T., Cross, Joy, and Red. All were dead except one. Red! No one in Charlotte had seen or heard from him since the Feds had arrested him in Chicago. Carlos was more than certain that Red had been following Justice at the time to body her for slumping his cousin J. T., but he never got the chance to carry out his plan. Lucky for Justice, the feds nabbed him before he could get his revenge.

Carlos vowed to one day handle Red, but he had no idea how close he was to that day coming to fruition.

CHAPTER FOUR

On 14th Street off the notorious Peachtree Street in the heart of Atlanta, the Sheraton Suites hotel was quiet on this Thursday night. Just after 9 P.M. Hotlanta's nightlife had yet to begin. On the 3rd floor, no one would ever guess what was transpiring. In room 313, Loon, one of Atlanta's biggest hustlers, in size *and* status, was being duct taped and gagged along with his lieutenant Jo-Jo. They were both just as naked as the day they had entered this world. Soiled condoms dangled from their limp penises and the smell of sex lingered in the air. The two had literally gotten caught with their pants down!

"A bad bitch is always a nigga's downfall," Red, the taller of the two robbers mocked. He smiled broadly behind the ski mask while taping Loon's thick ankles together. Red was dressed in black jeans, all black Nike's, and a black T-shirt along with black driving gloves. After securing the tape around Loon's ankles and wrists he looked over at his partner and stated, "Tell them broads they can come out now."

After taping Jo-Jo's wrists and making sure he couldn't budge an inch, Chris, the shorter robber with dreads, smacked him in the mouth with the pistol, immediately drawing blood. Chris stood up and kicked Jo-Jo in the stomach with the toe of a black Timberland boot and left him lying on the carpet squirming in pain. Red looked over at his partner in crime and shook his head with a smirk because he had already anticipated Chris doing something to cause the victims pain. Chris was by far, the more violent of the two.

As Red watched Chris, he silently hoped Chris's dreadlocks hanging well beneath the ski mask wouldn't later become an identity issue. For that very reason, Red kept his wavy haircut low. But just as abruptly as the thought of identity had entered his mind it left. This was not their first jack and they had never had a problem with someone identifying them before.

The dreadlocked robber stepped over Jo-Jo, walked out of the bedroom area, and tapped on the bathroom door with the butt of the pistol. Chris heard whispering voices and shuffling beyond the door.

"Y'all go 'head and bounce, shawty," Chris commanded in a syrupy southern drawl mixed with Atlanta slang.

Moments later, the door slowly opened and out stepped one of the finest specimens of ebony femininity God ever created. Sasha's onyx skin was accentuated by a mane of satiny black hair that hung down to the middle of her back. Her stomach was flat enough to iron on and the waist she possessed was so tiny it looked as if it was straining to carry her gigantic ass. Directly on her heels was an exact replica. It was her identical twin, Tasha. Both girls were still naked and made no attempt to hide their bodies as Chris stepped aside and allowed them to pass.

As they entered the bedroom area, eight eyes watched in silence as the naked twins collected their clothes and accessories, which were scattered about the unkempt room. A thong was carelessly thrown on the floor between the two queen-sized beds. A bra was strewn across the lampshade above the nightstand. Stilettos were lying on the dresser. Sasha, the eldest twin by five minutes, reached down to pick up her Chanel skirt lying only inches from Loon's face. As she and Loon locked eyes, Sasha winked at the obese hustler with a devilish grin.

Loon couldn't believe the audacity of this scandalous bitch! Only minutes earlier he had dug her back out while she clawed at his shoulders, screaming his name. Now here this bitch was assisting in having him robbed. Or was it Tasha? It really didn't matter if it was Sasha *or* Tasha because as far as Loon was concerned both bitches were as good as dead. He wrinkled his brows and stared at her with pure hatred. If looks could kill . . .

Minutes later, Sasha and Tasha exited the room dressed just as they had entered hours earlier. As soon as the twins left, Red and Chris began rifling through their victims' possessions. Several thousand dollars were retrieved from pockets of trousers and iced out platinum jewelry was snatched from necks and pulled from wrists and fingers. Once they had relieved the men of all their valuables, they placed the takings inside a plastic hotel bag that had hung inside the spacious closet.

The robbers were about to exit the room when Red waved his pistol in Loon and Jo-Jo's direction and taunted, "A lil' piece of advice for you niggas. *Never* let a friendly fox into your hen house 'cause one day that fox is gonna get thirsty and hungry and have'ta eat." Red laughed.

Hearing this, Loon closed his eyes and thought about the two friendly foxes who had just exited the room minutes earlier wearing Chanel and Prada. He felt like kicking himself in the ass for falling for the banana in the tailpipe as he had done.

With that said, both robbers exited the bedroom area and headed toward the front of the suite. Once they were out of Loon and Jo-Jo's sight, they simultaneously removed their ski masks and gloves. Red's light brown face glistened with a thin sheen of perspiration as his hazel eyes sparkled in the light. He looked over at his partner as she shook out her dreads, untangling them. Christina then removed the oversized sweatshirt she had been wearing along with the super tight sports bra that had struggled to conceal her ample breasts. The shirt she now wore hugged her so tightly it looked like a second skin and her braless nipples looked like miniature erasers fighting to cut through the thin fabric.

She saw Red gazing at the imprint of her nipples and playfully elbowed him in the ribs while stuffing the sweatshirt and bra into the bag along with the money and jewelry. She wiggled out of the baggy jeans she wore to reveal a pair of skintight jeans that clung to her thick thighs, wide hips, and round ass. Since she had no change of shoes, the boots had to remain.

Red had seen this sight a thousand times before, yet Chris's beauty never ceased to amaze him. After she stuffed the jeans inside the bag, they opened the door to the suite, stepped out into the hallway, and out of Loon and Jo-Jo's lives.

Minutes later, Red and Chris were strolling through the lobby of the hotel hand-in-hand as if the robbery in room 313 had never taken place. They strode past the front desk chatting away like any ordinary couple, instead of the two vicious robbers they actually were.

CHAPTER FIVE

"You know I'm leaving next week for Charlotte. You sure you gonna be okay?" Justice asked Toni.

"You already know I got it," Toni responded.

Toni and Justice were seated inside Justice's office going over the checklist Justice had given Toni. Justice was reluctant about leaving Toni alone to handle the club, but she semi-satisfied herself with the realization that she wasn't going to be gone that long. What could go wrong in a week or two? But then again, this was Toni she was talking about and she was not convinced that she could handle whatever challenge Precious and Virgin threw her way.

"You know the liquor order gotta be in Monday before noon and make sure the girls that's coming from Atlanta know about the tip out and— "

"Yo … you know I already know all that," Toni cut her off. "How long I been doing this?"

"You right. But . . ."

"But nothing. You need to stop worrying so much. You were gone for *three* weeks when you went to DC. And when you got back, what had happened?" Toni asked with confidence.

Justice could not help remembering her trip to DC and when she returned home she came back to a remodeled office and a substantial profit. Toni had done well and Justice had no complaints whatsoever. It also helped that Precious was sick and that Virgin had decided to be MIA at the time. She just hoped that this time would be no different.

After their discussion, they exited the office and walked toward the club area. While doing so, they passed the dressing room. The dressing room door was cracked and Justice glanced inside and was met with the sinister smirks of Precious and Virgin. As if in slow motion, Justice rolled her eyes and kept it moving. She was silent, but if someone could have read her thoughts, she would have been arrested on the spot.

Toni peeped the exchange, but didn't say anything until they were in the club area. They took a seat at the bar and ordered two apple martinis. "Why you still lettin' them bitches work here?"

Justice ignored Toni's question and turned around on the barstool to look out at the scenery of the club. Phire & Ice was two levels of pure enticement. Justice looked toward the entrance and saw Twin, her door security guy doing a thorough job of searching the two young cats that had just shown their ID's. She glanced over at the stage area and noticed how crowded the club was on this night. The featured dancer, Black Stallion was on the mirrored stage working the pole like a pro, and she was getting tipped very well by the dudes crowding around trying to get a better look. Black Stallion was 6'1" without heels, stacked like a Quarter horse with the complexion of smooth milk chocolate. Her ebony skin was glistening with oil as she dropped to the floor in a full split and began making her voluptuous ass cheeks bounce one at a time. Ones flooded the stage and niggas were tossing more as she twerked to Travis

Porter's "Make it Rain."

Hostesses wearing boy shorts and bikini tops were serving drinks and making rounds, making sure the customers were satisfied. Justice noticed that there were just as many women as there were men in the crowd. Women had become more open to frequenting strip clubs than they had been in the past. Some bisexual and others just looking to have a few drinks and enjoy the scenery. Nevertheless, more than not, most were there checking for the big spenders.

Justice looked up toward the second level where the VIP and DJ booth were located. The DJ gave her a salute. "Boss Lady is in the house tonight," he announced over the mic. Justice raised her drink at him in recognition. Just then, she had a thought. She told Toni, "Let's go upstairs for a minute."

They both got up and walked over toward the stage and edged their way through the crowd and back to the stairs that led to the VIP. Justice wanted to make sure that there was no tricking going on upstairs. She knew how Precious and Virgin got down and she wanted to be sure none of the other girls were following their lead. They climbed the stairs, drinks in hand, and asses swaying harder than most of the strippers. The VIP was decorated with plush couches sectioned off with individual tables lit by candlelight. As they walked through, Justice and Toni greeted a few regulars. There were also a few new customers who they didn't know. They all had stacks of ones on the tables in front of them. That's what Justice liked to see . . . Niggas spending that cash!

After leaving the VIP area Justice and Toni headed back down to the bar.

Once seated, Justice observed the room again and saw three of the new girls she had flown in from DC sitting at the opposite end of the bar talking.

Toni gawked at the one who looked like she was Hispanic and Justice chuckled. She knew Toni secretly liked girls, but Toni had no idea she was on to her. Justice was glad that Toni had never come off on her the wrong way because that would have been the end of their friendship.

Justice took a better look at the Hispanic-looking girl and noticed how much she resembled Tandora, the Dominican drug-dealing chick that had been responsible for her brother's death. Her mind reeled for a moment as she was taken back to that fateful day once more. She vowed to get revenge on Tan. Through Sapphire she had learned that Tan had moved from Rock Hill, South Carolina and was now living somewhere in Charlotte, but she wasn't sure exactly where. Yet she knew it would not be hard to find her. Justice turned back to the bar and told one of her bartenders to fix her another apple martini while she contemplated the torture she wanted to inflict on that bitch!

CHAPTER SIX

While ending a phone call with her father, Tan pulled up to a circular driveway of a mini-mansion in the Southeast Ballentyne area of Charlotte with a sprawling manicured lawn. She parked her copper-colored S-Class Benz behind a platinum-colored Jaguar. After parking, she retrieved her briefcase from the backseat before exiting. As she climbed out of the Benz, the short skirt she wore rose high up on her thick, bronze colored thighs, almost revealing her thong. Her long, beautiful legs glided like those of a gazelle as she walked toward the large double-doors. Her heels click-clacked on the pavement with each confident step she took. Before she could reach the doors, one of them swung open. An African-American woman in her mid to late twenties, the same age as Tan, stood in the doorway wearing a wrap-around short skirt and Louboutin pumps.

Rudely, Tan whisked right past the woman without even speaking. The woman watched dumbfounded as Tan bustled her way through the foyer and disappeared into the spaciously elegant sitting room. The woman was still standing in the doorway with her mouth agape, unable to believe Tan's audacity. She closed the door and followed Tan into the room. Now posed in the doorway to the sitting room with her hands glued to her wide hips, she watched Tan plop down on the eggshell white circular leather sofa. Tan lay the briefcase on the glass top of the expensive mahogany coffee table neatly decorated with magazines such as *Essence, Don Diva and The Robb Report.*

Tan proceeded to kick off her heels and kick her feet up on the table next to the briefcase. She turned her head to the left and finally asked, "Why are you looking at me like that?" She had felt the woman's eyes on her.

"You a fuckin' trip. You know that right?" The woman spoke with a Northern accent, which gave hint to her New Jersey roots.

Tan sucked her teeth and motioned with her index finger for the woman to come toward her. Reluctantly the woman approached with a slight attitude. Tan reached for the universal remote a foot or two away from her on the large sofa. With the remote in hand, she clicked on the surround sound system and selected a CD. Moments later, the room was filled with the voice of the late great Gerald Levert crooning "Baby I'm ready." Tan closed her eyes and swayed her head slowly to the rhythm as she sang along with the Velvet Teddy Bear. When she reopened her eyes, the woman stood so close that their legs were touching. Looking the woman up and down, Tan then reached out and caressed her caramel skin. Starting at the woman's toned calves Tan worked her hands up the woman's thick thighs. When her hand disappeared beneath the woman's skirt, Tan heard her sudden intake of air through her parted lips.

The woman placed her hand on Tan's and caressed it gently. She then bent down and met mouth-to-mouth with Tan as they explored each other's tongues. Tan's hand continued to snake its way through the woman's pantyless crotch area, slipping and sliding in wetness.

After a minute or two of frolicking, the woman broke the kiss and slowly removed Tan's fingers from her dripping wet vagina. "Like I said, fuckin' *Trip*," the woman retorted.

"Sit," said Tan while patting the spot on the sofa beside her. "Sit? What am I, your dog now?" the woman replied sarcastically.

"Let's start over from the door, okay? Hi To'Wanda, how was your day today?" Tan spoke to her roommate and lover with scripted sarcasm.

"Bitch please I ain't beat. I'm not your mother nor your kingpin ass father, so don't run that bullshit on me. Fuck I look like?"

"You too sexy to have all that attitude." Tan said as she placed her hand on To'Wanda's thigh while looking in her eyes."

"Don't try to patronize me." To'Wanda shot back as she removed Tan's hand.

"I got your *patronize.*" Tan looked up seductively.

To'Wanda smiled, then picked up a pillow and playfully swung it at Tan's head. "You so silly."

They both laughed.

"Take a seat, ma." Tan stated and patted the spot next to her on the sofa.

To'Wanda took a seat next to Tan "Anyway, how is *our* daddy doin'? And how did the conversation go?" To'Wanda was referring to the conversation Tan was supposed to have with her father on her way home.

"*Our* daddy?"

"Oh, he still don't know I'm 'bout to be his new daughter-in-law one day?" To'Wanda asked, not expecting a reply. When no response came, she changed the subject back to the phone call and asked, "Did you call?"

"Yes, I did and it went well. I told him about Loon and how I think he's tryna fuck me outta my money. I don't doubt he got robbed, but that shit ain't adding up. He said they came up in the room and robbed him and Jo-Jo and then they took him to his house and made him give up the nine keys I fronted him." Tan looked over at her girlfriend who had a 'he may be telling the truth' look in her eyes.

"At the Sheraton? Hell naw! All rooms are inside and you *have* to pass through the lobby to get to and from the rooms. Picture this—two muthafuckas with ski masks ushering Loon and Jo-Jo through the lobby of the Sheraton Suites at gunpoint!"

Now To'Wanda was starting to get the picture.

"That muthafucka's tryna come up on some free birds. He thinks shit's sweet over here. But I got a pie baked for that fat ass though." Tan spat with venom in her voice. Her Spanish accent was coming to the surface, something that happened whenever she was pissed off. If Loon wasn't pushing so much dope so fast, she would've been cut his ass off. But that fat ass nigga was moving keys in record time!

"Calm down, calm down. We'll handle it," To'Wanda spoke in a soothing tone as she ran her fingers through Tan's silky curls.

"I also told Papa I'mma little low on funds and that I needed a loan."

"Low on funds? Hardly that!" To'Wanda replied, gesturing for the briefcase on the table.

Tan slid it to her and watched her open it.

"How much?" To'Wanda asked, staring at the stacks of one hundred dollar bills staring back at her.

"Two-fifty."

"Did you get to see everybody?"

"Everybody except Carlos. I'll see him tomorrow," Tan replied while yawning. "Oh yeah, Papa says he has another twenty kilos for us. The drop will be in the same spot as usual."

To'Wanda whistled. "Twenty more, huh?" She looked sideways at Tan. "Did you have to beg for that?"

"Nah, just put my 'baby' voice on him. Can't resist when I do that."

"Neither can I." To'Wanda stated seductively as she closed the briefcase and slid closer to Tan. To'Wanda stood up, hiked up her short skirt and straddled Tan's lap with the precision of a hungry panther. Tan normally hated it when To'Wanda was the aggressor because that was her role. She reveled in being the head of the house—she wore the pants in this relationship. However, at that moment, Tan was just as hungry and didn't mind To'Wanda's advances. As To'Wanda nibbled on her neck, alternately biting and kissing on her as if she were marking her territory like an immature schoolgirl, Tan's slender fingers found her lover's wetness and two digits easily slipped inside her hot creamy hole. She took her fingers out quickly and licked them as if she were getting the last dribbling from an ice cream cone—she loved the way To'Wanda tasted and didn't mind showing her. To'Wanda went closer to taste her sweetness on Tan's lips and Tan relaxed and allowed the sensation to consume her as To'Wanda slipped her tongue in her mouth.

To'Wanda came up for air, their kiss temporarily binding their souls and she returned to Tan, leaning forward and licking her ear while moaning her delight. Tan's pussy began purring and throbbing for attention. To'Wanda whispered in Tan's ear, "Let's go upstairs so I can finish what I started before you had to leave me in bed this morning. I've been fantasizing about fucking you *all* day."

To'Wanda seductively slid from Tan's lap and found herself aroused at the thought of Tan taking her in the bedroom. Tan wasted no time in getting up and leading her up the spiral staircase that led to their master bedroom on the second level of the large house. Tan caught To'Wanda off guard when she pushed her against the wall. She reached up tore off To'Wanda's button up shirt as if she were tearing the wrapper from a Christmas present and roughly discarded it on the floor. She was happy that To'Wanda was bra-less and wasted no time swirling her tongue around To'Wanda's hardened nipples like the motion of the Rabbit vibrator. Tan felt To'Wanda's hands rubbing her head and massaging her, lightly pulling her hair with just the right amount of pressure to continue her arousal.

"Yes," To'Wanda whined as Tan pulled her short skirt roughly as she made her way down from her breast to her neatly Brazillian-waxed pussy. This time, To'Wanda had it shaped like a star. Tan stuck the tip of her tongue in—teasing her as she darted in and out of To'Wanda's moistness in rapid succession.

To'Wanda pulled the top Tan was wearing over her head and Tan worked to squeeze her way out of her skirt. To'Wanda, being impatient, swiftly reached down and pulled off Tan's thong—quickening the undressing process. Tan and To'Wanda's lips met for another passionate kiss before they continued their hike upstairs. In their mid-way wrath, they both decorated the staircase with expensive garments. By the time they reached the bedroom they were both completely nude.

Tan gently pushed To'Wanda on the bed and resumed her spot between her legs, enjoying the shivers that went from To'Wanda's legs to her spine as she bit To'Wanda's clit, giving her the first of many orgasms that were to come. She reached under her mattress and pulled out the leather belt with the famous porno star's impression on it and quickly wrapped it around her waist. After applying the appropriate amount of strawberry-flavored lube, Tan swiftly crawled on the bed like a snake and she watched as To'Wanda eagerly and hungrily did her job sucking on the plastic candy man.

Tan slowly and gently penetrated her with her favorite toy and for the next hour the large house was filled with sexually induced moans, groans, and passionate screams from the two women as they pleased one another with tongues, fingertips, and toys.

After administering multiple orgasms to one another, the two women fell asleep in one another's arms the way two satiated lovers do after a tiring bout of mind-numbing sex.

CHAPTER SEVEN

A few days after the robbery at the Sheraton, Red found himself on Cleveland Avenue sitting in the VIP section in Club Pleasers, Atlanta's hottest strip club, getting a personalized freak show from a girl who called herself "Always." As Red sipped a glass of Rosé he admired the girl's physique while the small overhead strobe light illuminated the dim room. His eyes scanned her thick body like a bar code. The thickly built redbone standing before him had a body most women would kill for. Round, full titties that stood straight up with chocolate-colored nipples the size of thumbnails. An ass that was killing the hottest video vixen complemented her tiny waist.

As Always swayed and gyrated to the beat blaring from the speakers in the main club area, Red slouched down in the comfortable leather sofa enjoying every minute of the private show. His eyes were tight from the Purp he and Chris had blown just before entering the club. Although he was damn near faded, Red was still on point. Being a true-to-heart stickup kid kept him on his toes because he couldn't afford to allow himself to slip.

Always gyrated between Red's legs and stared into his hazel eyes, which were bloodshot red from the weed. "Damn, you got some sexy ass eyes" she cooed into his ear as she felt him palm her naked ass.

"Yeah, just like Medusa, bitches get lost in 'em. So be warned." Red retorted as he smacked her smooth buttocks, making them quiver. Always closed her eyes sensuously, seductively biting her bottom lip, letting Red know that she was definitely into getting spanked. "Why you call yourself *Always*?" Red inquired while she continued to slow wind between his legs, her small hands resting on his knees.

The girl bent down and gently bit his earlobe before stating in a suggestive tone, "'Cause I'm *always* ready. I'm *always* willing. And—I'm *always* WET!" With that said, she turned around, bent over in Red's face and spread her bulbous ass cheeks to show him that she wasn't just talking.

Red straightened up and leaned in for a closer look. He saw the wetness glistening between her clean-shaven lips. Witnessing this, he bent the club rules and reached out to trace the crease of her soaked, puffy lips with his forefinger. He then rubbed his forefinger and thumb together, playing with the slick substance. "Daaaamn!" he muttered to himself.

Always turned back to face him and noticed he was still playing with her juices on his fingers. She took his hand and raised it to her lips and began sucking and licking his fingers. Her tongue ring played over his digits, making his dick tap his zipper, trying to escape the confines of his jeans. The stripper could feel the bulge getting larger by the second. So at this point she figured she had him right where she wanted him. She figured Red was rolling in dough because of the glistening jewels around his neck and because of the Hummer he was known to drive. She had seen Red many times in the club spending money as if it grew from the earth, and tonight he had spent a nice sum on her alone. Always figured any nigga who could order bottle after expensive bottle of Rosé like it was mere tap water *had* to be ballin'. Therefore, this night she decided to try to reel him in. She tried her hand. "Don't you want some company tonight?" she asked in her sexiest voice, still kissing his fingertips and gazing into those hazel eyes.

Red stared at Always for a minute, noticing the smoldering lust in her eyes. It was a look he had seen countless times before. The lust he saw was not for his dick, it was for his dollars. That look was *thirst*! Red was no square and he definitely wasn't a virgin to tricking, but he was also far from being a fool. He saw through Always' game as if it were glass. "Yeah, I want some company, ma," he stated, watching her eyes light up as if she had just won the lottery. "But not tonight, baby girl." Red then saw her expression change from that of elation to that of disappointment within a fraction of a second. He smiled to himself for toying with her, and then said, "Some other time, shorty. I promise." In addition, he intended to keep that promise. He grabbed her hand, placed it on his still throbbing dick, and allowed her to massage it, giving her a feel of what he was working with. "You know you bad, right?" He was enjoying the feel of her hand on his dick. "I'mma slide back thru later on in the week. Be ready for a nigga to get at you, aiight?"

The girl's face brightened up a little as she bent forward and whispered in his ear, "Always baby, always."

Red tipped her fifty more dollars on top of everything he had already given her throughout the night. The stripper smiled and took the money from between his fingers before sashaying off to retrieve her outfit from the other corner of the small room. Red sat his empty glass on the small table beside the sofa and stood, ready to leave. He took one last look at Always as she stepped back into her G-string. He kind of liked the girl and admired her thirst for dough. He had seen her a few times in the club hustling the hustlers and he respected her game. He knew everybody had to eat one way or another and he definitely couldn't knock the way she was getting hers. He thought hard for a minute before calling out to her, "Aye shorty, you wanna get some *real* money?"

Always' curiosity was piqued. She knew he wasn't talking about fucking because she had just tried him with that. Her mental cash register began cha-chinging. Those two magic words "real money" had her undivided attention. Red gave her his number and told her to get at him in a couple of days. "It'll definitely be worth your while," he'd told her. With that statement, he thought briefly about the money he and Chris had paid the twins a few days earlier before putting them on the highway to head back to their hometown of Columbia, South Carolina. He concluded that those few grand had been very well spent.

As Always watched the fine hustler exit the VIP area she kissed the tiny piece of paper in which his digits were written. She was already mentally spending the money she knew she would get from the nigga.

A few minutes after leaving VIP, Red sat at the bar next to Chris, his part-time lover and full-time crime partner. Chris was dressed in a short, form-fitting skirt that rose high up on her thick thighs as she sat on her barstool very ladylike, sipping on an apple martini. Her ample bosom was spilling out of her skimpy blouse and the niggas were eyeing her almost as much as they were the strippers. Chris's thick, pouty glossed lips were wrapped seductively around the slim straw as she looked up at Red with heavy eyelids. Her bedroom eyes were tinted with a shade of pink from the weed. Her long dreads were pulled back into a tight ponytail.

To Red, Chris was one of the realest bitches he'd ever met. Blessed with the beauty of a model and the brains and heart of a hustler, Christina Dawson was the epitome of the phrase "dangerous bitch." In fact, she was by far the most dangerous female Red had ever dealt with, and he had dealt with quite a few. Chris was the type of bitch who could murk a nigga one minute and then turn around and put her lip-gloss on the next without so much as a twitch.

Red saw Always coming out the VIP area and flashed a knowing smile at her, and she returned the gesture.

Chris saw the exchange. "I *know* you didn't fuck that bitch back there." She had her nose turned up in disgust.

"Hell nah, that was strictly bizness," Red retorted.

"When yo' dick fall off and yo' jaws start sinking in, we gonna see what kinda *bizness* your trickin' ass handled."

"Girl, ain't nobody fuck that bitch." Red laughed at Chris's rhetoric. Staring at Chris made him think back to the first time he had ever laid eyes on her . . .

Ironically, Club Pleasers was where they had first met, so to speak. *Twelve months earlier, Red had noticed the caramel beauty getting lap dance after lap dance from the baddest bitches in the club. Chris was tossing twenties like they were ones and Red took notice. That night the jack-boy in him had caused him to see past her beauty and made him look deep into her pockets. Red had just moved to Atlanta from Charlotte and was almost on his last leg. His dough was running out fast and stick-ups were few and far between. The only thing Red had left of value was his dead cousin J. T.'s Hummer and some jewelry which he absolutely refused to part with. He was thirsty as hell, like a vampire seeking blood. And Chris looked like the perfect mark.*

The way Chris had been rubbing the girls' asses and squeezing titties had led him to believe she was just some dyke who frequented the club often or either she was a dancer as well and was just paying homage. Either way, Red had decided that he had to have some of that dough she was spending. If she was contributing it that freely, Red figured it was plenty more where this had come from.

That night as the club wound down, Red followed Chris out to the parking lot and noticed she was driving a late model Range Rover with expensive looking rims. She had sat in the lot for a few minutes engaged in conversation on her cell before being joined by two of the dancers that had been all over her inside the club. "Three birds with one stone," Red thought as greed consumed his mind. He watched as the two dancers climbed into the Range with Chris, one in the front and the other in the back. As soon as Chris exited the lot, Red followed in the Hummer making sure to keep at least two cars between them at all times. He waited patiently for the Range to make a stop so he could make the girls run that paper! He already knew the driver was loaded with dough and he could just imagine how many tips the two dancers had received throughout the night. He wanted Chris's jewels also. He figured he could get a nice grip for all that ice.

Opportunity finally presented itself when Chris pulled up to a Ramada Inn hotel off Old National Road. Red fell back as he watched the Range and waited for it to park. Instead of stopping at the front desk, Chris pulled around back of the hotel and parked in front of room 118. Red parked the Hummer on the side of the hotel and got out with his pistol clutched tightly in his palm. Since it was so late the hotel was quiet and all of the rooms were dark. Red hid beside the ice machine and peeped around the corner and saw the girls enter room 118 giggling and stumbling. Two of them were hugging. "Damn, this is gonna be easier than I thought," Red thought to himself while smiling.

His plan now was to kick the door off its hinges and make the terrified girls come up off everything they had. He knew he would have to be in and out as quickly as possible because the noise of their door being damaged would wake a few guests. He also thought about the structure of the door and wondered if it would even bulge. As he contemplated this thought, he looked up from his hiding place and saw the answer to his problem being solved. One of the strippers had come out of the room with an ice pail and was headed in his direction. Red pressed his back against the side of the ice machine and waited for the girl to get closer. He could hear the click-clacking of her heels as she neared. When she was directly in front of the ice machine Red emerged from the darkness, startling her. She dropped the pail and let out a shrill shriek which Red quickly muffled as he placed his hand over her mouth and pressed the gun into her rib cage. "Bitch, you make another sound and I'll put a hole in yo' ass so big light'll be able to shine through it. Understand me?" Red whispered in a venomous tone. The girl nodded in agreement and began to walk back toward the room with Red guiding her by the elbow.

As they neared the room Red noticed the door had been propped open by the inside latch, apparently so the girl could re-enter without having to use the key. The only light visible inside the room was coming from the television. Red heard the shower running in the bathroom as he stood by the door listening for a second before making his move. He heard no movement so he figured the other two girls were showering together. "Caught these hoes slippin'," he thought to himself as he pushed the girl through the door and fell in step right behind her.

Suddenly, out of the corner of his eye he saw movement and before he knew what was happening, the barrel of a large caliber pistol was being pressed to his left temple and the lights came on, flooding the room with brightness. He wanted to fire, but the sudden incandescence of light had him momentarily blinded like a deer caught in headlights. When he was finally able to focus, Red couldn't believe his eyes!

Chris was standing there brandishing what seemed to be a Dessert Eagle .45, making it kiss his temple while the girl who had stayed in the room with Chris was easing from the restroom fully clothed with two chrome .380's aimed at him. She tossed one of the chrome pistols to the girl Red had just pushed through the door. There were now three barrels aimed at him. "What it is, shawty? Lemme get that there," Chris's syrupy voice commanded, in reference to Red's gun. Red thought for a minute, contemplating whether or not to fire on one of these bitches. Then he thought better against it because he knew he would not make it out of the room without catching a few hot ones himself. He slowly lowered his gun to his side and hung his head with shame at the realization of what he'd stepped into.

Chris reached out and took Red's Glock and stuffed it into the back pocket of her tight jeans. Then she commenced to pat him down for any further weapons. Satisfied he didn't have another gun on him, Chris started removing his jewelry. She snatched his ring off his finger, pulled off his bracelet and watch, then pulled his chain over his head. As Red felt his barrel-link white gold chain with his diamond encrusted medallion being removed from his neck he felt like a true mark! "Run dem pockets," Chris told Red, letting him know to empty his pockets. Red pulled out the two hundred dollars he had in his pocket and handed it over. "What else you got for us?" Chris asked. Red was at a loss for words. He couldn't believe the tables had been turned on him—by three bitches for that matter.

"Dat's it," he managed to say between tight lips while tossing the keys to the Hummer to the floor.

"Nigga, you drivin' a damn Hummer and you ain't got but $200 in yo' pockets?" Chris looked at her girls, then back at Red and commanded, "Fuck that. Nigga you got some mo' money. Strip!"

"What?" Red asked in disbelief.

"Nigga she ain't stutter. Strip!" the girl from the ice machine spoke up for the first time.

Red reluctantly began disrobing, but he left his boxers and socks on. "Nah nigga! Take all that shit off!" the girl from the restroom stated, seeming somewhat amused. Red took off the socks, then slowly pushed the boxers to his ankles and stepped out of them. The girl from the ice machine quickly began gathering Red's clothes from the floor. She also picked up the keys to the Hummer.

Red stood naked and embarrassed before the three women, while they seemed unfazed by his nudity. The girls started to leave the room one by one while keeping their guns trained on Red. The first girl stepped out the door with Red's belongings, followed by the girl from the restroom and lastly Chris. Just before Chris stepped out the room she looked Red up and down with inspecting eyes then smacked him on the ass with the barrel of her pistol and stated with a sultry smile, "Welcome to the 'A,' folk!" Red rubbed his stinging ass cheek, but didn't turn around as the girls left. Moments later, the door closed followed by the sound of the Range Rover cranking up and pulling off.

Two months later Red had bumped into Chris again, this time at Magic City with the same two strippers gyrating on her. First instinct had Red ready to blow all three of those bitches' wigs back. However, as he gave the situation more thought, he sat back and observed Chris and the dancers for a minute. After watching their interactions and wandering eyes, realization of what they were doing dawned on him. This was their game, their MO. Chris would sit around and make it rain all night with the same two girls who would scoop up the cash, and later Red found out that they would give it back to Chris at the end of the night. "Damn, these bitches had faked the whole scene, wanting a nigga to bite," Red thought as he continued to peep their game. They flossed all that dough hoping a thirsty ass jack-boy would run up and fall into their trap. Just as Red had done. This conniving bitch!

Red approached Chris at Magic City that night and she immediately went on the defensive when she recognized him. He sat down beside her and put his arm around her chair. She started to get up but he grabbed a handful of her dreads from the back and pulled her back down with enough force to let her know he wasn't playing with her but not so much as to be obvious and cause a scene. "Nah, don't get up on my account. Chill, let's rap." Chris eased back down in the seat and stared coldly into Red's eyes. "So what? You lookin' for some get-back? You feelin' some kinda way?" Chris asked. "You can let go of my hair too." She added as she calmly reached up, grabbed her glass and threw back the shot of Patron that was sitting in front of her.

"Gottdamn right I'm feelin' some kinda way. Where my shit at? I want my shit!" Red stated through gritted teeth while adding a little more force to his tug on her dreads. Chris's head jerked back slightly and a sharp pain shot down the back of her skull.

"I'mma tell you one mo' time to stop pullin' my fuckin' hair." She attempted to snatch away from his grasp but his grip was too strong. She settled into the seat and took a deep breath.

"Bruh, how you gonna come at me like you a innocent victim or some shit? Nigga, YOU tried to jack ME. You just got caught slippin. You know how this shit go. You gotta respect the game."

Although Red knew what she was telling him was the truth, his ego wouldn't allow him to accept it. "Bitch, like I said, I want my shit."

"Cool," Chris replied non-chalantly.

"Cool?" Red was skeptical because of her quick reply. "Aiight, let's go get that."

"That ain't no proble," she sipped her Carona. "As long as yo' broke ass can pay for it."

Red laughed at her response. Although he was pissed, he was also somewhat amused at Chris' bravado. It reminded him of himself. "Bitch, you know I ain't payin' you for my shit back."

Chris glanced over at Red. "I'on believe you tryna sit up here and act like you don't know how this shit work. You know damn well if you had been able to get MY shit that night it ain't no way in hell you would even entertain the thought of giving my shit back. Nigga, at least I'm giving you a chance to get yours."

Everything she was saying was hitting the nail on the head and Red couldn't deny it. He finally let her hair go and relaxed in his seat. He knew there was no way he'd get his jewelry back and decided to chalk it up as a loss and charge it to the game.

The waiter came around and Chris ordered them both a shot of Patron. Red was still in disbelief that he had gotten duped by this sexy ass scoundrel. They threw back the two shots and looked at one another and burst out laughing. They were on one accord and they both knew what Red was thinking. As bad as he wanted to punch her in her mouth, he had to admit that her and her girls's game was airtight.

"You know I had yo' ass that night, tho" Red stated as he sat his empty glass on the table.

"Yeah, that's why you ended up naked with no ride home." Chris laughed. For a moment and Red got heated all over again as he had a flashback of them making him strip.

Chris broke his thought pattern. "I can say this; I also found out that the gun you were carrying is not the only piece of steel you walk with." Chris stated as she gave him a flirtation grin.

"You ain't never lied, but that one is damn sure more dangerous." Red shot back. They spent a few minutes throwing slick comments back and forth as the chemistry between them began to heighten.

After a few more rounds, they began to see how they could benefit one another. Instead of beefing, they decided they could get more money if they were on the same team. The more Chris talked about the potential money they could get off niggas in the A, the more sense it made to him.

Needless to say, they decided to join forces and get money together. Being in the robbing game had both of them leery of the other and initially trust was damn near nonexistent. Chris proved her his loyalty to him one night a few weeks after their conversation when she'd pumped two hot ones into a mark who had gotten the ups on Red during a caper. Red became grateful and they wound up becoming tighter than a nun's pussy!

Business was booming, not to mention their criminal relationship was taken to another level and the sex between the two was off the Richter scale! Red had a real live "Ride or Collide." bitch in his corner with some snappin' sugar walls to match. What more could a nigga ask for?

"Let's go," Chris's voice snapped Red out of his thoughts and brought him back to the present.

"Yeah, let's bounce," Red replied. He set his drink on the bar and exited Club Pleasers with Chris at his side. Red felt totally relaxed as they stepped out into the night air. For Red, strip clubs had become his therapy when he was stressed. He had frequented every strip club in Atlanta at least once since moving there. He had also been to the hottest strip club in Chicago once just to see if it was really owned by Justice, the bitch he knew was responsible for his cousin J.T.'s death. Indeed Justice was definitely the owner. He had sat in the back of the club, incognito. He wanted to make sure that bitch suffered the same death she had made J.T. suffer, but he was just biding his time. He couldn't get over the fact that his first attempt to get at the bitch when he had first followed her to Chicago was interrupted by the Feds. He had been followed and was arrested on armed robbery charges. Although he had to spend a year in the county, he ended up beating the charges because J.T. and Cross, his cousins and co-defendants were both dead and the victims weren't cooperating.

Red and Chris stepped into the Hummer and were ready to pull out of Pleasers' parking lot when Chris told him to wait a minute. Red looked up from the steering wheel and saw an Indian-looking girl approaching the truck. He looked over at

Chris who was rolling a blunt and he asked, "Who is this?"

"Our toy for tonight. Open the door and let her in," Chris replied as she kissed Red on the lips.

Red's eyes widened with excitement. That is why he fucked with Chris, she knew when to get down to business and she knew when it was time to fuck around. And with this fine beauty that sauntered in the truck like a diva who owned the place, Red knew he was in for a fun-filled night. Red's dick got brick as he watched the Pocohontas-looking chick climb into the backseat. Chris reached across the seat and released his thickness, freeing it from the confines of his jeans. Red looked back and could see the Pocohontas chick licking her lips lustfully.

"If I didn't know any better, I'd think you wanted to trade places with my girl here." Red was cocky—he knew that they weren't going to be able to pull off before something popped up. Red quickly glanced outside and he was happy with the height of his truck off the ground. If the chick controlled his stick while he was driving the stick, they could be going places.

"You gonna give me a reason to come up there?" The chick said arrogantly. Without thinking, Red slipped his hand into his front right pocket, pulling out a Benjamin and flicked it back at her. He wanted to say something smart but Chris was stroking and applying just the right amount of pleasure to his manhood to keep him silent.

"That reason enough?" Red barely got out. He loved the way Chris was stroking him but at the moment, he felt that he'd produced a better use for the stripper chick's lips.

She rolled her eyes and twisted up her lips in a sarcastic

gesture. Red shook his head because he hated when broads did that shit. Nevertheless, the dancer picked up the bill, folded it and stuffed it in her bra. She and Chris opened their doors simultaneously and just like that, they traded places. Upon closer inspection of this chick, the blood continued to make his dick swell and caused it to dance to its own rhythm. As Red lustfully looked over the beauty that was now in front of him, his eyes caught the silver choker that rested on her neck and saw the letters T-A-S-T-E-E. "Tastee . . . that's what they call you?"

"Oooh, and he reads too." Tastee rolled her eyes. Red had enough of the attitude and the lip—it was time to put those mutha-fuckas to work. He gently reached across the seat and put his fingers through her hair—he got off on that shit and as he imagined pulling on it tightly while he was fucking her from the back. He guided her head to his lap and felt her soft moist lips on his tool, waxing it like a car and making his midsection squirm and dance to its own tune. Red's head laid back as Tastee went up and down, providing her own sauces for his meat. "Damn you good." He exhaled and tried to sit up straight.

"And you're Tastee—and juicy—just the way I like it."

Red put the truck into gear and looked over his shoulder at Chris who was smiling and still rolling the blunt. He smiled at her and pulled out of the parking lot with thoughts of what he was going to do to that ass clouding the front and the back of his mind.

***

"Fuck yeah!" Red shouted as sweat glistened on his body. He was naked save for some high top Nikes. Chris was

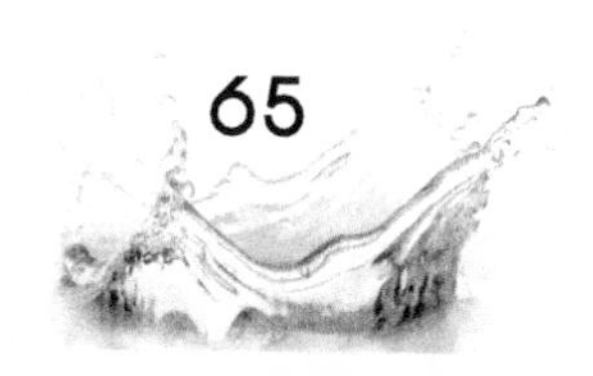

shouting—praising and cursing God in the same breath for the dick that continued to pulsate her insides and make her body come alive with fire. Chris was riding Red, cowgirl-style. She struggled to keep her rhythm in pace with Red's stroke game because truth be told, she'd never had dick like that before. Chris' powerful legs clamped around his waist as her body bounced like jelly up and down Red's taut body. Chris hadn't anticipated getting the ride of her life tonight but she knew it was in part to Red's excitement about the threesome they were having. Her eyes opened and she briefly enjoyed the view of Tastee's pussy as she masturbated on the recliner a few feet away, moving her fingers in and out of her soaked juice box with urgency. Tastee had already had a couple of rounds with them both and this finger flicking was her break. When Chris saw Tastee suck her own juices off her finger, this only encouraged her to nibble on Red's ear, which made him dance inside of her in a frenzy.

Just as Chris loved being watched as she was being fucked, Tastee was enjoying watching both Red's nutsack swing back and forth and the jiggling of Chris' titties as their bodies collided and became one. The red light flashing on the laptop for the viewers on a popular adult web cam site who were watching all three of them only seemed to entice Tastee more. Red had logged into his Black Friend finder account and set up the webcam as soon as they entered the apartment. Normally, he would have been the one observing live action on the site, but tonight he decided he would finally let the viewers watch him put in work!

"Take dis dick, bitch!" Red commanded as he thrust

upward. Chris held on tight as his dick pierced her uterus. She had another orgasm as the base of Red's dick rubbed her the right way. After Chris got off her ride, Tastee moved in position to get her slurp on and the excitement was too much for Red to handle as he nutted in Tastee's mouth. She swallowed his and Chris' juices like a champ and at that moment Red figured out the real reason she'd gotten the nickname, "Tastee".

Being spent from his third nut for the night, Red finally clicked off the camera, flopped his limp frame back onto the bed and drifted off slowly into a slumber.

CHAPTER EIGHT

"Who was it you sent to Bojangles?" Carlos asked as he looked into the mirror his nephew and personal barber, War, was holding up. His mother had named him Warren, yet Carlos had shortened it to War once he proved that he could not only run Carlos' barbershop/beauty salon *BobCutz* with the efficiency of a master chess player, but he wouldn't hesitate to lay his murder game down as well. War was often mistaken for Carlos as they were damn near identical at six feet and weighed 190 pounds. Both had the deep brown skin that ran in the family and both had sea-sickening waves that had the bitches spellbound and the niggas envious. They even sounded alike in person and on the phone, but they never said the same things due to the age difference and wisdom. Unlike Carlos, War kept two stripes in each of his eyebrows and his eyelashes were long and curly. In addition, War's lips were fuller.

"I sent Tia," War said as he took the mirror from his uncle's hand after Carlos gave the nod of approval.

"Tia wit the fat ass and small waist, from Detroit?" Preme was holding his crotch. "That bitch need'ta quit playin' wit' all dat ass and let a nigga beat that." He was resting his frame in one of the empty barber chairs even though he had no intentions of cutting his ridiculously long locs that were tied back into a big ponytail.

"I second dat," War laughed as he sprayed grape seed oil sheen on Carlos head, "She said she stoppin' to pick up her cousin, Rena too. They say that bitch can suck a bowlin' ball thru a straw."

"Yeah, but that bitch's legs stay spreadin' like cancer. You better strap up if you fuck dat bitch. I know for a fact she used to be on dat freak site *Back Passes* or some shit like dat," retorted one of the regulars who was getting his hair cut in the chair next to War's.

"*Back Pages*, muthafucka. Don't act like you'on know what dat shit is," another patron corrected as they all laughed.

"*Back Pages*? Hell, she already know what it is then. Now *that's* the bitch I wanna fuck. Ain't no datin' and all that ole shit, just straight to point fuckin'. I'mma text her real quick and make sure she still pickin' her up." War pulled out his phone and texted the message. Moments later, his phone vibrated and he flipped it to the side and read the response from Tia. "She said she just picked her up. They on they way back already."

"Aiight fellas, enough with the pussy talk, we need to get to some business in the back," Carlos insisted as he stood up and looked around his establishment. He inhaled the sweet fragrance from the sheen as he took in the orange walls decorated with blue, silver, and white pinstripes in honor of the city's NBA team. Toward the front of the shop where the salon area was located, some of the women were reading copies of *Ebony* magazine or some of the latest urban fiction or romance novels as they waited to get their hair dried under silver or white hair dryers. A few of the ladies had their heads in the blue basins as the stylists were getting ready to wash and rinse them. In the back where Carlos and his fam' were, men sat in comfortable white and blue faux leather barber chairs getting their hair cut and talking shit.

A few weeks after Carlos stepped out of the Charlotte-Mecklenburg County Jail on the bogus charges with the female federal agent two years earlier, War had called to tell him that he had finished barber school and got his license. Carlos had paid for his only nephew's school as a promise to his deceased brother that he would look out for him. Carlos also thought about old man Luther, the old man who used to cut his and his older brother's hair back in the day. Carlos had convinced him to come back to Charlotte from Atlanta to help his nephew run the new barber and beauty shop he was opening on W.T. Harris Boulevard.

BobCutz was Carlos' legitimate business and one of the easiest ways for him to launder his drug money. Most of the barbers and stylist either went to school with War or they once worked for and were trained by Luther, so Carlos felt confident in their barber and styling experience.

Carlos looked toward the receptionist area and watched as Luther's granddaughter operated the front desk with efficiency. He glanced at Luther sitting in his comfortable green reclining chair in the right corner of the shop. Carlos hated that chair because it fucked up the décor he was going for with the shop, but he kept his mouth shut because he wanted the old man to stay comfortable. In turn, Luther made sure War stayed on his P's and Q's and most importantly, kept the shop intact. Luther was the observant one. Just when you didn't think the gray haired, seedy-eyed man who had less wrinkles than men younger than his seventy-two years of age wasn't paying attention, that's when you realized he was looking right at your ass.

War had taken a brush and finished wiping off the loose hair from the apron that Carlos was still wearing. Carlos took the apron off and before he could instruct Preme and War to go with him to his office, Tia and Rena walked in. Tia carried two bags full of that Cajun-spiced chicken, southern biscuits and sides, while Rena carried two gallons of sweet tea.

Carlos realized that their business could wait until after they ate, so he motioned the ladies to follow him to the break room. He had a small lounge room in the back for the barbers and stylist to relax and take a break and where they could handle their personal business. He watched Tia walk past him, noticing how nice she filled out the pink Juicy Couture jump suit. The tight material highlighted her grade A sirloin ass that he wouldn't have minded having a piece of.

Rena was an insult to Tia. She was almost the same complexion as Amber Rose, same body type, but her hair was just a whisper longer. Normally, Carlos wasn't attracted to chicks with short hair, but Rena was turning him on a little. He caught himself staring at her ass in the tight jeans she was wearing.

"Los!" Tia raised her voice, breaking Carlos out of his daze.

"Yeah," Carlos half-answered while tearing his eyes away from Rena.

"I wanted to let you know they were talking about Ms.

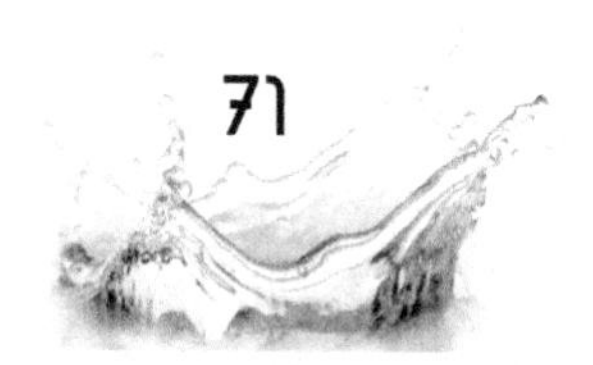

Evans on the news again." She was referring to Sapphire's mother. With Ms. Evans being the founder of a nonprofit organization that helped young ladies develop an interest in math and science and then helped send them to colleges nationwide, she became well known in the city and her sudden fatal illness was a shock. "You might wanna check on ole girl."

"Fuck!" Carlos said as he reached into his pocket and pulled out his iPhone. "Thanks for the heads up." Carlos saw War and Preme coming in his direction. "Y'all go ahead. I need to handle something real quick." Carlos turned around and headed toward his office. He spoke Sapphire's name into the small mic and the phone automatically dialed the number. On the second ring, Sapphire picked up.

"Hello."

Carlos could hear in her voice that she'd been crying. "Aye, what's going on?" Carlos questioned as he closed and locked the door to his office and sat behind his desk. "How is she?" he asked.

"The cancer has spread to her brain—the doctors say she may not make it to the end of the week." Sapphire sniffled. "The church is doing a prayer vigil and some of the ladies are putting together a bake sale so they can raise money to help pay for the hospital bills." Sapphire's voice was scratchy as she struggled to speak. "I don't want to bury my mama!" She burst into tears and her voice was trembling.

Carlos took the phone away from his ear and put her on speaker. He took out a key and unlocked the desk drawer where he kept some of his personal belongings. Taking out a blue bank book with the Bank of America logo on the bottom right corner, he looked at the amount in the book, which was just a few thousand shy of six figures. "How much y'all trying to raise?"

"No!" Sapphire stated and then cried some more. "No—I don't need no more of your money."

"But I wanna help." Carlos humbled himself, something he'd never done for a woman. "You know I got y'all. So I can either write you a check or I can send my people to the bake sale and make a donation." Carlos regained control of his senses and got firm. "Either way, I'm giving you this money—it's the least I can do." Carlos wrote a check for ten grand while he waited until Sapphire stopped crying. He made the check out to her and was determined to meet with her at the hospital and give her the money.

"Okay. But you know you don't have to," Sapphire said. She never did answer the question Carlos asked about how much she needed. "Justice will be here in a few hours and she's gonna help me with everything."

"Justice is coming today?" Carlos perked up in his seat with excitement. "I can come pick y'all up and—"

"That's all right," Sapphire cut him off. "You and I both know she still wanna kill your ass." Sapphire's words were sharp but true. "Just leave the check for me at the church. I'll be there to pick it up later."

"Aiight, baby girl. Stay strong." Carlos said as the call ended. He finished endorsing the check and then reached to the back of the drawer and found an envelope to place it in. He wrote Sapphire's name in big, blue letters and sealed the envelope and placed it in a black travel-size portfolio. He got up and unlocked the door and proceeded to walk out. He went to the break room to get Preme so they could leave. On their way out, Carlos smiled inwardly as they walked past Luther assisting one of the new barbers with a fade. *Old man's still got it*, he thought as he and Preme exited the shop and headed to his car.

***

"You need to get over that bitch," Preme told Carlos. They inconspicuously sat in Carlos' truck parked across the street from the church and watched Justice and Sapphire get into Sapphire's Audi A5 S coupe. Carlos almost let an admirable smile escape his lips as he saw Justice for the first time in over two years. She had lost a pound or two, but she was still as thick as he remembered. Her beauty was still intoxicating to him.

"I am over that bitch," Carlos lied through gritted teeth. Preme still had a vendetta against Justice because it was her brother's fault that he was walking with a cane.

"You ain't over that bitch because if you was, you wouldn't get mad if I slumped her ass right here."

Carlos saw Preme holding his cane as opposed to one of his automatics, but he knew Preme was serious.

"We out." Carlos put the truck in drive. "Let's go check this nigga's temperature." He changed the subject, pulled away from the church, and turned up Wacka Flacka's "Hard in the Paint" allowing the melody and lyrics to get him hyped. While listening to Waka, he briefly thought back a few months to when Waka had come to Charlotte to get his tour bus tricked out and some niggas had tried to stick him up on Independence Boulevard. He looked over at Preme and asked if he had heard about the incident.

"Yeah, I heard about it. I heard them niggas pulled up and

had ratchets on 'em."

"Did they draw?"

"Like Picasso." Preme laughed. "Them niggas was bussin' in broad daylight at Waka. Niggas out here thirsty. Can't be comin' round here flossin' all that ice an' shit like it's aiight. That's like dangling a piece of meat in front of a lion that ain't ate in two weeks. Niggas tried to get that up off him."

Carlos laughed, then changed CDs and bumped his favorite song by Rick Ross. By the time Rick Ross was halfway through "BMF," Carlos felt like he was Big Meech and Larry Hoover as he pulled up to Dave's partner, Lil' Joe's Trucking Company. A tow truck was just leaving the lot as they walked up to the door. They saw that Lil' Joe wasn't so big anymore as he'd lost a good fifty pounds from his six-foot-four frame and now looked like a respectable point guard as opposed to the college linebacker he resembled when he worked for Carlos. As far as Carlos was concerned, he and Joe had parted on good terms, but Dave's death may have changed that.

Dressed in a dingy one piece work uniform with the name JOE written in blue script across the right side of his chest, Carlos and Preme spotted him immediately.

"Fellas." Lil' Joe addressed both of them with the calmness of a grown man. A far cry from the hype young nigga they once knew. Lil' Joe had matured and changed a lot over the past two years, but Carlos and Preme knew he was still down for whatever. Carlos saw one of Lil' Joe's workers standing in the doorway of the garage that was attached to the front office.

"Let's go chop it up." Preme suggested more so than asked.

"Come on back." Lil' Joe stepped aside and encouraged the

men to step inside the garage. "Yo, Charlie, go ahead and go home man, I got it," Lil' Joe told his employee as he kept his eyes on Carlos and Preme as they crossed the threshold into his workspace. The smell of oil and metal assaulted Preme and Carlos noses.

"Damn nigga, you really tryna fool them crackas like you legit, huh." Preme said sarcastically as he hobbled around the garage, admiring the expensive tool sets and all of the gadgets that made the shop come alive.

"I heard Dave had a closed casket funeral and shit." Lil' Joe stated, while ignoring Preme and looking Carlos in the eye.

"You mean you didn't go?" Carlos questioned as he debated whether or not to reach for his heat and slump Lil' Joe right where he stood. He knew Dave and Joe were once inseparable and he figured Joe was feeling some kind of way about his death. He knew Joe didn't know for sure that they had murdered Dave, but Joe knew Carlos and his method of madness so it wasn't hard to put the pieces together.

"Nah." Lil' Joe swirled the toothpick in his mouth. "I ain't wanna see my man like that. I sent his people some money though." Lil' Joe looked around Carlos to see Preme admiring a brand new metal G-clamp. When he got Preme's attention, he asked him, "Did you?"

"Did I what, nigga?" Preme was clearly agitated from the direct question.

"Did you go to the funeral, nigga? Fuck you think I'm talkin' bout?"

"Fuck I look like goin to a rat's funeral?" Preme retorted as he turned his back to the two again and continued to look around the garage. At first, he thought Joe was asking if he had been the one who had killed his man.

Lil' Joe closed his eyes for a split second and shook his head.

Carlos sought to ease the tension for now and decided to cut the conversation short. "Look, I just wanted to see how you was copin'. How you was holdin' up an' shit. I see you handlin' that shit." He turned to Preme "C'mon Preme."

Carlos reached the door and he watched while Lil' Joe and Preme glared at one another as Preme eventually started limping away slowly. Carlos knew Preme and Joe never really liked one another and only tolerated each other for his sake. He watched as Preme kept looking over his shoulder to make sure he didn't have to body this nigga.

CHAPTER NINE

To'Wanda felt a slight breeze sneak through the slit of her crème halter top that amplified her breasts as she and Tan stepped foot into Mortimer's Café & Pub. They had decided to go out for a few drinks and watch the Bobcats play the Heat. Mortimer's had an upscale look with a huge white chandelier in the center of the pub and eclectic, modern dining accessories. With the Bobcats playing at home, she was astonished that the line wasn't out of the door as it normally was on a home night.

Originally, Tan had planned to stay home, but to appease her girl, she took her out. To'Wanda was a loyal Bobcats fan no matter how terrible the team played and it was too late to buy tickets with any decent seating to watch the game live at Time Warner Cable Arena. As far as Tan was concerned, if she couldn't get a seat in one of the suites, the tables or boxes, the game wasn't worth going to. She didn't buy the season passes that she normally would have because she wasn't happy with the team's performance and she decided that she did not like the owner after meeting him a year ago.

Tan saw her favorite bartender at the bar, but noticed that all of the spots at the bar were filled. Yet not all was lost because there were a couple of nice seats along the walls that would give them some sense of privacy.

"Thanks bae," To'Wanda whispered as she leaned closer to Tan. She glanced at her lover's light, cashmere top with a big, silver triangle pendant that danced across her breasts. The nippy weather had caused Tan's nipples to harden. To'Wanda took notice of the imprint and had thoughts of what she wanted to do to them once they returned home. Tan's appetite for sex was stronger than the average woman's, but To'Wanda's sex drive was off the Richter scale. She was a straight up, insatiable freak!

"Don't thank me yet." Tan still had a slight attitude as she looked at the flat screen TV and noticed that the Bobcats were being dunked on by LeBron James. A couple of boos and verbal assaults left the lips of the patrons as the home team sank further behind. "You just enjoy the game and the outing."

To'Wanda took that as her cue to back the fuck up. She quickly flashed a smile at the server that brought them a menu. "For the appetizer, we're having harvest salads and our entre will be the Cajun chicken Alfredo and two glasses of Moscato." To'Wanda ordered Tan's favorite, hoping she would lighten up a little. The server smiled at them, flashing all of her pearly whites as she notated the order and went to get their food.

Tan's mind had been on Loon and how he had the audacity to lie to her about the robbery that had taken place, but she couldn't quite figure out how she was gonna handle him just yet. She silently thought, *Ray Charles' mama was right, "scratch a liar, find a thief."* And she'd be dammed if she'd let some scheming, conniving, fat, fake Rick Ross-looking nigga beat her out of some money. Tan knew she needed to make an example out of his ass and set that shit right. Though it wasn't beneath her to go to the A and step her murder game up, she also knew she needed to tread lightly because she had other, more important fish to fry.

"Here's your food, ladies, and if you need anything else, just call on Joy." The sandy haired buxom beauty smiled as she lowered their trays containing their food. Tan checked the time on her Tiffany wristwatch, as she was amazed at how fast their orders had been prepared. She looked up and caught a glimmer in Joy's eyes that let her know that she got down with chicks. A bi-sexual chick could always see familiarity in other bi chicks. Even though she was fine in a Shakira-type of way, it was too bad for her that neither Tan nor To'Wanda were in the mood for another chick tonight.

When the smell of Cajun seasoning hit her nose, Tan's appetite doubled. As she lifted her fork to take a bite, she noticed a man who looked like a dark version of Vin Diesel walk into the entrance. His broad shoulders filled out the trendy sports coat he was wearing and his pecan tan complexion complimented the color of it.

"You see him, too?" To'Wanda asked as she rushed to wipe some Alfredo sauce from her lips. She licked her lips and wiped them off again as her eyes followed that sculpted frame with the low hair cut as he took a seat near the end of the bar.

Tan looked at To'Wanda and then back at the fine ass guy. She didn't want to admit it, but the Vin Diesel look-a-like had her clit tingling a little and her crotch area a little moist. It had been a while since she had seen a man who could make her stir like that.

While Tan and To'Wanda were lightweight lusting, the perky waitress came to them with two glasses of Chardonnay. "Ummm, we ordered Moscato," To'Wanda corrected.

"I know, but these are compliments of the guy in that corner over there." Joy indiscreetly pointed to a slim, mocha-colored guy with a bushy, curly Afro and rough but well-groomed facial fuzz. The man was slightly slouched in his seat as he lifted up his glass of wine as a gesture of a toast.

"I . . . want . . . to . . . get away," To'Wanda sang as Tan agreed that Lenny Kravitz was exactly who that fine man over her shoulders slightly resembled. "Oooh—Tan, what if we had the neo-soul brother *and* the football player."

Tan sighed and swiped a lock of curly black hair from her face, then promptly tucked it behind her ear. She raised her finger and pointed sharply. "No bitch, only one dick." She didn't mean to get mad, but she remembered what happened the last time more than one man at a time was in their home. Three men they didn't know rushed into their house. Monk, Cross, and D. C. had forced their way inside their home after Justice and Sapphire rang the doorbell. Monk had slapped her twice as he tackled her like a football player and tied her up.

"Aww, come on, it'll be fun." Tan wasn't surprised at how To'Wanda was so damn giddy over some dick. Like the thirsty bitch didn't get dicked down with a dildo almost every other day. But she knew her girl loved the real thing more than she did so she didn't mind To'Wanda getting happy at the possibility of getting her back blown out. It had been almost a year since Tan had some real dick herself, so she knew it was about that time.

"It'll be fun with one." Tan held firm. "We'll rent a room for the night." Tan smiled as To'Wanda nodded in agreement, as she understood Tan's desire for discretion.

Tan pulled out her phone and searched for the number for the Blake Hotel while the guy who looked like Vin Diesel made his way to the table. To'Wanda started getting excited because the nigga was definitely sexier up close. Tan even had to admit that she liked his swag as he made his way to the table. The dude nodded to the competition and they exchanged a mutual sign of respect.

"What's your name?" To'Wanda was being forward.

Before he could answer, Tan mumbled, "Walks like he got a big wee wee" She placed her phone back in her purse.

"Tan!" To'Wanda was shocked that she had made the comment so loudly as she playfully slapped her hand.

"You from New York?" the man spoke up in a raspy, deep voice.

"No," Tan said as she waved her hand to Joy. "Check please."

"My name is Marques," he said as he took his left hand from his pocket, discreetly showing off a rose-gold timepiece. Tan could tell from his mannerism that Marques was not a street nigga.

Tan stood up when Joy arrived with the check. Joy got a quick look at Marques and Tan could damn near smell her lust for the nigga standing before them. Tan took out two twenty dollar bills and instructed Joy to keep the tip. "I'll tell you what. Meet us at the Blake in thirty minutes," Tan said as she grabbed To'Wanda's hand and interlocked it with hers. "I'll be waiting for you in the lobby."

"Just like that?" Marques asked, flabbergasted that it was just that easy.

"Just like that," To'Wanda cooed.

Tan and To'Wanda walked away and Tan tilted her head to the man who had bought them the drinks. "Maybe next time."

***

When Tan saw Marques enter into the lobby, she looked around and thought about what Loon had said about being ushered through the hotel at gunpoint. The Blake was laid out almost identical to the Sheraton and she confirmed that the fat muthafucka was lying and she'd deal with him later.

To'Wanda was already in the room freshening up. Tan wanted to make sure that Marques was by himself and that this wasn't a set-up before they went up to the room. She knew fuckery came in all shapes, forms and fashions, and she didn't put anything past anybody.

"Nice to see you again," Marques said as he reached down to give Tan a hug and a kiss on the cheek. His Hearts and Daggers Ed Hardy fragrance smelled good and Tan could tell he had put more on between leaving the pub and coming to the hotel.

"Nice to see you, too." Tan paused as she quickly scanned the lobby before deciding to lead him to the elevator. They rode to the tenth floor. "Take off your jacket, please," Tan asked, and Marques complied. Tan searched the jacket and only found his metal business card plate bearing the insignia of his fraternity and a couple of Magnums. As Tan patted him down, she felt his well-sculpted chest, nice biceps, toned legs, and a healthy portion of dick.

"Your girl must be related to Obama," Marques joked as the elevator doors opened.

"She is." Tan smiled. "And I'm her Secret Service."

"I can't wait to get *serviced,*" he laughed.

"Patience is everything."

"No rush here, babe" he replied.

Tan and Marques took a few steps before they were in front of the room.

Marques smiled to himself as she took the card out of her pocket and slid it through the slot, opening the door. Inside, the smell of Bath and Bodyworks permeated the air as To'Wanda was laying on the king-sized bed in a white lace teddy.

"Why don't you take your clothes off and take a shower?" Tan suggested.

"You ladies sure know how to set it off."

"Of course we do." To'Wanda anxiously got up from the bed, walked to Marques, and loosened his tie. Tan undid the buttons on his shirt and threw the shirt behind him. To'Wanda undid the belt, unzipped his slacks, and let them fall to the ground. She reached for his dick, which began to stiffen in his loose fitting boxers. To'Wanda released it from its confines and complimented, "Nice."

With a strong jerk, To'Wanda tore off the boxers, leaving Marques standing in his knee-high socks. Tan grabbed his left side, To'Wanda grabbed the right, and they unrolled the socks from his feet. Marques opened the door and was pleased to find plush, crème colored towels. "We bring our own stuff," Tan pointed out as she and To'Wanda watched the way the man moved into the bathroom with a sophisticated swagger, not embarrassed by his nudity at all. As he stepped into the tub, Tan rushed to take her clothes off while To'Wanda stepped inside with him. Tan watched as To'Wanda and Marques kissed as if she were not in the room. Once Tan was naked, she went to the bed where she placed Marques' jacket and took out the condoms. She then walked back into the bathroom, placed the condoms on the marble basin, and stepped into the shower.

Marques was allowing To'Wanda to bathe him with a loofa that she'd lathered with liquid soap. Her right hand had a hold of his rigid penis and was slowly stroking it while she continued to clean his front side. Tan grabbed a bar of soap and a bath towel and started working his back, scrubbing and cleaning every nook and cranny while admiring his well-sculpted back. Marques moaned lightly as Tan reached between his legs to clean his balls and his ass before working her way to his legs and his feet. Marques moaned some more as To'Wanda got on her knees and started servicing him as if she were bobbing for apples. To 'Wanda reached behind her and turned the water off and when she stood up, Marques was making his way to his knees, licking and caressing her breasts and making a wet trail to her navel , then further south toward her well-trimmed pussy. Once he reached her vagina, he slowly eased a little of his tongue out, teasing and tickling. When he found her clit, he kissed and nibbled on it as it were a nipple. To'Wanda grabbed his head and buried him deeper into her crotch as she closed her eyes in ecstasy. After a few moments of frolicking in the shower, they moved to the bed.

To'Wanda lay on her back as Marques picked up where

he'd left off. While he tongue fucked To'Wanda, Tan lay down beside her and gave her a kiss, then started caressing her breast. Marques stopped pleasing To'Wanda with his tongue and started maneuvering his thick fingers through her soaked slit as he buried his head between Tan's parted thighs, giving her a sample of what To'Wanda had been getting. Tan relaxed a little as Marques' tongue dug deeper and ate with a hunger as if her pussy was going to be his last meal. Not to be left out of the triangle, To'Wanda assisted in pleasing Tan by grabbing both of her nipples; alternating between rubbing, squeezing and downright pulling them roughly the way she liked it, causing her to climax. Marques wasted no time lapping up her juices as he pulled Tan's midsection to his face. "Oh shit! Eat this pussy," Tan managed to mutter between trembling lips as her thighs quivered. Her second wave of orgasm was washing over her.

After taking Tan to cloud nine with his expert tongue, Marques went into the bathroom and retrieved the condoms. To'Wanda was on her knees lapping up Tan's juices when Marques returned to the bed. She was in the perfect position for him to penetrate her in her favorite position. After putting on the condom, Marques moved in behind To'Wanda and placed a hand on both ass cheeks to spread them apart so he could have total access to the pussy. He shimmied his hips in position so his dick was aimed directly at her opening. With one powerful thrust, he was inside her, stretching her walls beyond belief.

To'Wanda let out a deep sigh as she paused for a moment from eating her lover's juice box. Once her pussy was relaxed enough to accommodate Marques's full length and girth she moved in rhythm to his strokes and once again buried her face between Tan's parted thighs.

Marques stroked To'Wanda into oblivion as his throbbing dick continuously tapped her g-spot from the back.

Spent from so many orgams, Tan couldn't take the stimulation on her clit any longer. She moved away and positioned herself on her back; between To'Wanda's knees as her face was inches from her pussy. As she lay on her back, she raised her head slightly and licked To'Wanda's clit from beneath as Marques's dick brushed her lips and nose with every stroke. To'Wanda was screaming like a lunatic from the dual pleasure.

Marques pulled out of ToWanda briefly and forced his dick down Tan's throat at a downward angle. He alternated fucking To'Wanda's pussy and Tan's throat until he was about to explode. Tan was enjoying the taste of To'Wanda's juices on the condom each time he thrust his manhood down her willing throat. When he could no longer stand the ecstasy of it all, marques pulled out of To'wanda's tight pussy one final time and snatched off the rubber. He vigorously stroked himself until he erupted like a volcano, sending spurts of cum onto To'Wanda's ass and all over Tan's face which Tan wasted no time in lapping up.

After the last drop of semen oozed from his softening penis, Marques collapsed onto the bed beside the two women as if he had just been drained of life. The room was silent other than heavy breathing and To'Wanda's slight whimpers as she was still experiencing slight shock waves from the massive pounding she had just received.

All three lay on the bed motionless and spent until sleep consumed them. Minutes later, the only sound to be heard in the large suite was that of Marques's snoring.

CHAPTER TEN

God must have had a lot of favor and love for Ms. Evans because ever since she had passed, the City of Charlotte had been experiencing a heavy downpour of rain and chilling cold weather from the moment she took her last breath.

"You've got to eat something," Justice told Sapphire. The sympathy she had for her friend was beyond measure. She definitely related to what Sapphire was going through because she too had lost her mother to cancer some years ago. Sapphire had been staying with Justice at the Embassy Suites Hotel on S. Tryon Street since her mother's death. She just couldn't push herself to go home. Their family house would never be the same without her mother.

For the past two days, Sapphire had lay across the king-sized bed and refused to move, even for food. Although she knew her mother's death was imminent, she still didn't want to believe it had come to past. Reruns of Toni Braxton's reality show would make her smile weakly and emit a soft chuckle sporadically every time Tamar's dramatic ass said something stupid but most of the time her tears flowed like Niagara Falls. They say sleep is the cousin of death, so when she was not crying she was sleeping. She figured that a dream would be the closest she'd ever get to her mother again.

Sapphire stared at Justice with bloodshot eyes as she slowly sat up on the bed. For the past few days, Justice had done everything needed to arrange for Ms. Evan's funeral. From handling most of the business arrangements for the service, to contacting family and friends on Sapphire's behalf.

As it stood, the funeral was four hours away and Sapphire had not left the bed, not even for the viewing of the body the night before. Many thought she would not show up for the funeral. She was totally broken.

"Let's take a long, hot bath." Justice stood up and gently helped Sapphire off the bed. Justice went into the bathroom and turned on the water to just the right temperature. Then she took out the Dove bubble bath mix and poured it in the tub. As the bubbles started to form and the water rose, Justice continued to stir it with her hand so that there would be an ample amount of bubbles in the tub. She turned the water off, walked back into the room, and saw Sapphire, who was slowly making her way to the bathroom.

Once inside, Justice was at ease as Sapphire undressed herself, got into the tub, and relaxed for a few minutes before washing her body. Justice stood at the door to give her some privacy, but kept an eye on her to make sure that she didn't try anything stupid. Sapphire asked Justice if she could wash her back for her.

As she washed her girl's back Justice noticed the healed scars and dark areas where she once had multiple bruises from being beaten like a dog by Carlos's henchmen two years prior. Justice also washed her hair and in doing so, she felt pity in the

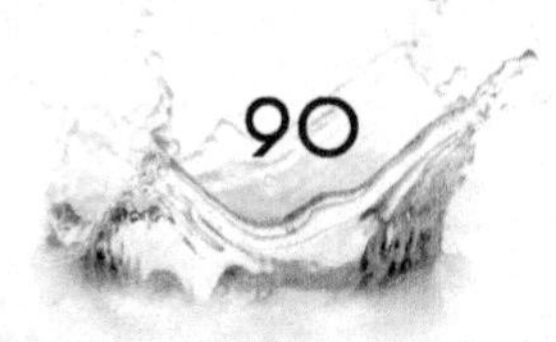

pit of her gut as she saw the permanent scar that ran from Sapphire's right temple all the way below her jaw line. If Sapphire's complexion were not so dark, you wouldn't have to look so hard to notice it. Justice had seen the scar many times before and each time it was like seeing it for the first time all over again. That scar told a story that Justice tried so hard to forget, but couldn't. She admired Sapphire for her strength and determination. She had fought for her life after that beating and had won against the odds. How someone could forgive the people who were responsible for such brutality was beyond Justice's comprehension, but Sapphire had forgiven and moved on.

Justice finished helping her girl bathe and get prepared so that she could be ready to bury her mother. After she bathed, Sapphire stood up and Justice handed her a towel in which Sapphire proceeded to dry her body.

After putting on her bra and panties, Sapphire put on the black blouse and skirt that Justice had laid out for her.

Justice jumped in and out of the shower after she was confident that Sapphire would continue at the pace she was going and she too got dressed and put on her black dress. When Justice looked at the clock, it was time to get to the church.

***

The rain was pouring and Justice had barely pulled the Audi into the parking space when a man rushed to open her door. "Oh hell no!" she cursed when she realized that man was Carlos. She recognized the smile under that umbrella anywhere and promptly locked the door. Instinctively, she reached for her purse but forgot that her gun was not in her possession. She wished she had it because she was not afraid to be the cause of a double funeral. Although Carlos had shown signs of remorse for his past actions, she still didn't fully trust the man and had no idea of his intent.

"Please . . . Y'all let's not do this," Sapphire started to beg. "I just wanna get this over with."

Justice saw the despair in Sapphire's eyes and she realized that she too wanted to get this over with so that she could get back home and take care of business. Justice sucked her teeth and let out a loud sigh before unlocking the doors. She opened her door hard, hitting Carlos on his knee. "Shit!" he cursed as he hopped in place on one leg for a moment.

Carlos adjusted his umbrella to shield Justice from the rain once she was to exit the car. "Good mornin'" He greeted and beamed those pearly whites that she had once fell so weak for. As Justice carefully climbed out of the car, she subtly noticed how good Carlos looked in his tailored suit and fedora. Once out of the car, Justice mumbled, "Make a bitch act up if you *want* to," as she looked him dead in the eyes. Her heels had her towering over Carlos by an inch or two. "I still won't hesitate to show my natural black ass . . . house of God or not. Keep that in mind." She knew Carlos was anxious as hell to try to talk to her, but she was still not ready to cross that bridge. Therefore, she tried to nip it in the bud.

"Look, ma."

"Justice, my name is Justice and whateva you gotta say to me can wait 'til after the funeral. Just let me and my girl go lay her mama to rest in peace." Justice snatched the umbrella from his hand, leaving Carlos with only the fedora to shield his head from the downpour. Justice rushed over to Sapphire's side and opened her door and Sapphire stepped under the umbrella. They quickly walked off so they could get to the front of the line and inside the church to start the processional.

"You need to forgive that man," Sapphire said weakly while they got to their place in front of the procession line.

"What?" Justice bit her tongue to keep from going off on her best friend at her mother's funeral. She couldn't believe the words coming out of Sapphire's mouth, and she still couldn't believe Sapphire didn't feel some kind of way for how Carlos's men had beaten the brakes off of her ass.

Just the sound of Carlos's voice took her back two years. Past scenes played in her mind like a movie. Briefly, she remembered the war that had gotten started that eventually caused the demise of innocent people. Carlos may not have pulled the trigger, but his anger and rage at the wrong niggas caused people to lose their lives over something that had nothing to do with them as far as Justice was concerned.

"I'm just saying," Sapphire said solemnly, "I have forgiven him and moved on and you need to do the same. After all, we are in church and my mama would have a fit if she could see how you're acting right now."

Justice wanted to rebut, but she knew Sapphire was right so she said nothing. Out the corner of her eye, she saw where Carlos and another man who looked almost identical to Carlos, along with Supreme were getting in line behind Sapphire's family and her mother's friends. As Justice stared at the younger man beside Carlos, she squinted. *I know that ain't Warren lookin' all grown an' shit.* The last time she had seen him he was running behind Carlos and his boys, begging to get into trouble.

Because of her charitable work in the community and how well known Mrs. Evans was, the church was packed beyond capacity. The doors were opened and Sapphire and Justice were ushered in first. They were led to the front of the church where the casket was. Once in front of the casket, the reality of her mother being gone washed over Sapphire like a riptide. She lost it! Justice tried her best to hold her up. Through the tears, Sapphire managed to look down inside the open casket and saw her mother's still face. Sapphire's emotions were so overwhelming; she could no longer contain the vomit that was coming up from her stomach. She threw up everywhere.

***

Justice and Sapphire stepped foot into the limo to go the burial ground where her mother would be buried. The family had opted to give Sapphire her space and the driver put up the privacy screen so Sapphire wouldn't be disturbed. She and Justice sat in silence for what seemed like an eternity before Sapphire finally spoke. She looked up at Justice and sniffled. "When I go, I wanna go in peace. I don't wanna have any regrets and I don't wanna hold any animosity. I wanna have a free heart . . . just like I know my mamma did. I'mma be all right because I know where she at. She up there rejoicing right now." Sapphire let a weak smile splay across her lips as she looked toward the roof of the car. She blew her nose into a handkerchief and then looked back over at Justice. "It took me a minute to forgive Carlos, but I did and I think you should, too."

Oh, here she goes with this forgiveness shit, Justice harped in her mind as she thought about how nice and friendly Sapphire and Carlos had been toward one another. It was as if she had forgotten all that he had done to her. Something just didn't seem to click with that shit. "I'll work on it," Justice nonchalantly replied as she looked out the limo window.

Just then, Sapphire's phone rang. She looked down and saw a number with a 305 area code. *Now is not the time*, she thought then pushed the ignore button and told Justice "Look at it this way." Sapphire sniffled a little. "You still wanna get Tan, right?"

Justice was astonished by how fast Sapphire wanted to talk about revenge when she was just talking about forgiveness. Nevertheless, Justice would rather talk about murdering Tan than thinking about Ms. Evans being minutes away from being stuffed in a hole forever. And if this meant getting her girl's mind off of it for a minute then she had no problem continuing the conversation. "Yeah, you know I want that bitch."

"Carlos told me that he still deals with Tan, even though she ain't his main supplier anymore."

Justice sat up. "Oh really?"

"We talk. Carlos tells me a lotta things. Just like a man to tell all his business. Sometimes, I think he tells me more than he realizes. A spiteful bitch would . . ." She cut her sentence short. "Neva mind. But anyway, I think he's still tryna convince me to forgive him, not believing that I already have."

Justice smiled as she realized that her ex-boyfriend might really be trying to make amends. If all else failed, he would at least be her best option to get to Tan. Therefore, she decided that it might be worth getting close to Carlos to get to her goal.

After a short ride to the burial site, the limousine stopped. Justice looked out of the window and saw the rain still falling and the tent set up in preparation for where the services were going to be. She looked at Sapphire, glad to see that she was more composed than at the church.

Their door opened and a hand reached in and Sapphire stepped outside. Justice followed and realized that her hand was in Carlos's. They walked to the burial site and for a moment Justice was still mad at Carlos for everything, but then she decided that maybe Carlos wasn't so bad . . . for now. Sapphire took her seat at the head of her mother's casket and Justice and Carlos sat next to her like a grieving couple.

This is wrong, Justice thought, *Carlos should be sitting next to Sapphire consoling her, not trying to console me.* Justice had put aside her own grieving for Ms. Evans to be there for her friend and she realized it was a nice gesture that someone had thought of her feelings.

The burial service was fast and short with the pastor reminding everyone that death was a necessary part of life and that they all would pass through that tunnel someday. Justice didn't want to think about her mortality, so she turned her thoughts to home and her business. She briefly wondered what was going on at Phire & Ice.

As Justice rose up to get her flower, she spotted a silver Jaguar creeping along the street. A light-skinned chick that greatly resembled an enemy was behind the wheel. "Can't be," Justice mumbled to herself.

"What was that?" Carlos inquired, as he looked in the direction that Justice's eyes were focused on.

"Oh, nothing. I just thought I saw a dead bitch driving."

The venom in her voice did not go unnoticed by Carlos. Justice stared as the car made an abrupt stop, then eventually crept off in the direction it was going in.

Justice and Sapphire watched the rest of the service continue, complete with the casket being lowered into the ground. Other mourners patted her and Justice on the back as they watched the dirt being thrown on the casket. "You ready to leave?" Carlos asked them.

"No," Sapphire said as she looked up. "I'mma stay until they throw the last speck of dirt on her grave."

Carlos walked away and Warren turned to walk off. Preme had already limped ahead. Justice watched Carlos and his goons walk away. She looked back in the direction where she thought she saw Tan's car and realized that she might be extending her stay in Charlotte.

CHAPTER ELEVEN

Tan and To'Wanda rode down Statesville Avenue after picking up some money from one of Tan's workers. She had a little over an hour to make it to the bank so she could deposit the money along with the receipts from the construction company so the money could be "washed and dried" over the next few days.

Her phone rang and she recognized the theme song from *Looney Toons* that she had assigned to Loon for his ringtone. To'Wanda busted out laughing. "You know you wrong."

"It's how I feel, baby." Tan paused to pick up the phone. She put Loon on speaker so To'Wanda could hold the phone while she talked and drove. "Speak."

"I know who did that shit at the hotel . . . and I'mma handle it," Loon boasted over the loud noise that sounded like a live band in the background. Tan and To'Wanda looked at one another and shook their heads.

"Where are you at?" Tan asked.

"Huh?"

"Where you at?" Tan repeated herself.

"I'm at the strip club gettin' some lunch," Loon shouted over the music, while watching the girl on stage make it clap.

"Why you call me and you can't hear? Hit me back when you leave."

"Aiight, 'cause you gonna wanna hear this."

To'Wanda gave Loon the tone and she handed Tan the phone as she put it back in her purse. "Dumb motherfucker's gonna make me kill his ass sooner than I anticipated," Tan spat as she struggled to see out of the window. Even with the windshield wipers on high speed, it still looked as though they had gone through a laser car wash instead of driving through a busy street. Everyone was driving at a slow pace and To'Wanda hadn't even wanted to come out of the house, but she compromised because Tan hadn't said anything when she went back to Marques alone for some more dick.

"Aye, you think this is the church where they were having the funeral for that bitch's mama?" Tan asked as she slowed and made a right to enter the church where the funeral procession was leaving. Tan drove all the way to the end and then put her blinkers on so she could follow the procession.

"I don't think so." To'Wanda looked outside, but of course, she couldn't really recognize anyone who looked like Sapphire. "You think Justice knows Sapphire's mother died?"

Tan looked at her as if she was stupid. "Why you think I asked if this was Sapphire's mama's funeral? You know it ain't because a bitch lookin' for Sapphire. I know that bitch every move. If I wanted her, I could've been gotten her ass. She ain't no threat. It's that bitch, Justice. I bet you that bitch here, too. I need to murk her right there in that church and they can continue the funeral service with an extra body." Tan's Spanish was getting thick and To'Wanda knew she was getting heated. There was no telling what she would do.

To'Wanda shook her head. She thought to herself if Tan was to do something stupid, there was no way in hell she was

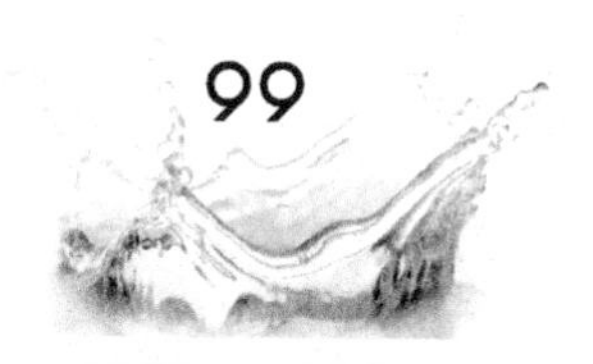

getting out in the rain to jump on the driver's side so she could play the get-a-way driver. Hell to the naw! She didn't sign up for that shit.

As the cars moved, Tan followed the procession to a burial ground just a few blocks away. They all drove up to the burial plot and when they pulled over and parked, Tan parked right behind them. To'Wanda looked at her as if she was crazy. "So if you see her, you gonna just kill her right here, just like that?"

"I should, shouldn't I?" Tan glared over at To'Wanda as if she had just made a wonderful suggestion. She knew murder wasn't To'Wanda's forte, and she really didn't want to show To'Wanda that beastly side of her, but if the opportunity presented itself she would definitely capitalize on it.

Tan pulled out of the parking space and drove along the street to get a closer look at the burial. She wanted to make sure she was at the right funeral.

"You serious right now? This is insane." To'Wanda had tried to reason with Tan as she continued to creep forward.

Tan looked at her and rolled her eyes. As the car crept along, Tan strained her eyes to try to get a good look but the rain was a distraction. All of a sudden, her eyes widened as she saw Carlos standing next to someone who looked like none other than her target. "Wow!" Tan laughed at the irony of the sight before her. *I knew that bitch would show her face.* "I told you she was here!" she excitedly stated as she turned to To'Wanda. To'Wanda sat up, looked past Tan, and spotted Justice as well. She immediately got nervous because she knew Tan's blood was boiling.

"Yo, you spazzin' right now," To'Wanda said as she sat

back in the seat and crossed her arms while rolling her eyes at Tan. She was getting upset because her job was to count money, help launder it, and when necessary assist with the delivery of work to Tan's minions. Being an accessory to a conspiracy to commit murder was not in her job description. To'Wanda may have been a hood chick and loved hood niggas and bitches, but she was a lover at heart. The last thing she wanted was for someone to get murked, even if they did cause her to be tied up and smacked around for a minute. Nevertheless, she knew Tan wanted to get Justice because she was more than certain that one day she would come after her for killing her brother.

Tan felt as if killing Monk was just a wound to Justice. Moreover, her father had always told her that there was nothing more dangerous than a wounded animal left alive. Tan came to an abrupt stop as she ran over a hump. "Damn, I didn't see that muthafuckin' speed bump. Shit!" Tan cursed, realizing that she had blown her cover and there was a good chance she had caught someone's attention.

"Fuck it!" Tan said. "If it was them, and I'm pretty sure it was, then they just got their lives saved." Tan continued to creep slowly and drive in the rain away from the burial service. She looked in the rearview mirror to see if anyone was pointing at her. Realizing her paranoia was getting the best of her, she started laughing. "Why the fuck am I trippin'? I can touch that bitch anytime I want, but I should've *been* took my ass to Chicago and got rid of that chinky-eyed bitch."

"You know you couldn't up and do that. It was too soon. Now enough time has passed that you won't be suspected," To'Wanda stated. Although she didn't want any part of the violence, she knew not to refute Tan.

Tan felt somewhat satisfied after leaving the cemetery. She knew it was time to handle her business with Justice because common sense was telling her that Justice would be coming for her eventually. From that point on, it would be a 'may the best bitch win' situation. Tan knew without a doubt, that bitch would be her.

Driving away from the cemetery Tan headed for I-485 South to head back to Ballentyne, questioning herself as to why Carlos had been there also.

CHAPTER TWELVE

"Man . . . I thought y'all muthafuckas forgot me!" Face yelled as he wheeled himself out of the old house on Pecan Avenue. His paraplegic state was a result of Monk catching him and Preme slipping a few years ago. His medium build now sat in a black leather wheelchair and he still was going to therapy to improve the use of his arms. His biceps were slightly bigger due to the excessive lifting of his own body weight day in and day out. The grotesque scar that stretched from his right temple to just below his chin seemed to decrease a little, but still set off the major characteristics of his face. Face now had a couple more scars like it on his upper torso near his left shoulder and a smaller one closer to his heart.

"Nah, nigga, we didn't forget you," Carlos said with a lot of regret because not one of his cars was handicap accessible. He got out of his Tahoe and met Face halfway as he rolled down the sidewalk. "Your aunt in there with you?"

"Yeah, she in there," Face said as he turned to the side. "Her bad ass sons drivin' a nigga crazy. I need to get out this bitch." Carlos pushed Face to the truck. Preme got out and limped to open the back door and then he got back in the front where he was riding. Once Face was situated, Carlos went back, folded his wheelchair, and put it in the back of the truck.

"You good, bruh?" Carlos asked Face as he closed the door

and got back in the driver's seat.

Face shook his head as he looked at Carlos in the rearview mirror. He wondered how Carlos felt knowing that his ruthless hitmen were no longer as mobile as they used to be. Face had noticed that he had been coming around a lot less frequently and was becoming a little distant. Face knew it wouldn't be long before he and Preme would be replaced by two younger niggas with full use of all their limbs.

When Carlos did come around, Face tried to enjoy the moment. Before pulling off, Face looked outside to see his six and eight-year-old cousins running out of the house and calling him by his government name. They were dressed alike in oversize black T-shirts with a minor league sports logo on them and some cut up black jeans. An older woman who could give Angela Bassett a run for her money ran out and grabbed each of the boys by the hand as she dragged both of them in.

"Daaaamn!" Preme said, sounding like Chris Tucker on *Friday*. "I swear to God if that wasn't yo' mamma's sister, I'd fuck the dog shit outta her ass."

Face pulled out a blue steel .45 and aimed it at the side of Preme's face. "Fuck the dog shit outta *this*, nigga," he offered.

"Nigga!" Preme turned and faced the barrel head on while looking at Face. "If you don't get that fuckin' pistol outta my face, I'mma come back there and beat your ass. Paralyzed or not, you know I'on play like dat."

"Why you always gotta make sex jokes when you come 'round a nigga? You know dat's fucked up."

"Both of y'all chill the fuck out!" Carlos stated from the driver's seat. Face lowered his pistol and still glared at Preme.

Carlos wanted to laugh but he knew Face was sensitive about being confined to a wheelchair, and no longer being able to get his dick hard. Carlos started the truck and drove off in the direction of one of his trap houses a few blocks down. "We got bizness to take care of and both of y'all niggas actin' like broads."

Carlos looked in the rearview mirror and saw that Face was still pissed and out of the corner of his eye, he noticed Preme silently staring out of the window. He was taking in the scenery of the houses that were old and deteriorating because the owners were too old to take care of them. Lawns needed to be cut and bushes needed to be trimmed. In addition, a couple of houses, including Face's aunt's house could stand a fresh coat of paint and some attention to fixing the roof. "These some old ass raggedy ass houses. They need to tear these shits down like they did in North Charlotte and take a few of them crab as niggas wit' 'em," Preme commented.

Carlos and Face ignored his statement. Carlos looked into the rearview mirror at Face. "You know we went to Sapphire mamma's funeral the other day." He paused, then added, "Justice was out there."

"Aww, don't tell me you tryna fuck wit' dat bitch?" Face got agitated as he used his arms to help him sit up. His mind flashed back to that day he caught hot lead from Justice's brother. "Man, fuck dat bitch."

"Yeah, fuck her and her dead brother. I'm glad Tan slumped that hoe ass nigga," Preme jumped in.

Carlos turned down the music and looked at both his partners with a scowl. "Hold up. Y'all niggas keep cryin' over

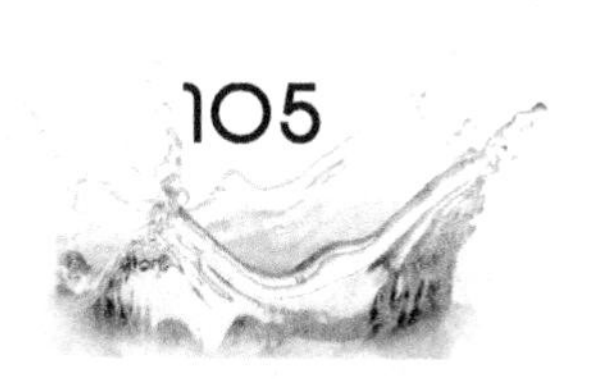

spilled milk and shit, but it's *y'all* fault he lived long enough to even squeeze a trigga at yo' ass. Don't act like y'all forgettin' about that fuck up at TGI Fridays. You had your opportunity then, but you missed and he capitalized on it. Shit happens. The nigga's dead! Let that shit go."

Preme sucked his teeth and mumbled, "Fuck him *and* his triflin' ass sister!"

"Anyway, like I was sayin'," Carlos addressed Face. "Justice was at the funeral and I tried to holla at her."

"Outta all these hoes out here that wanna give you some ass, you still wantin' to fuck wit' *that* bitch?" Face was genuinely disappointed. "Come on, bruh."

"Yeah nigga, I still don't trust that slimy hoe," Preme said as Carlos pulled the Tahoe into the driveway of a rundown house on LaSalle Street. Preme opened the door to get out. He looked back at Carlos. "Let Tan body that bitch, bruh."

"Nigga, that might be the smartest shit that ever came outta yo' slick ass mouth. I second dat," Face agreed.

"I think she came up to the gravesite to do that," Carlos said. "I saw her car and I think Justice saw her, too. I believe that crazy bitch woulda done it. That bitch 'bout worst than me when it come to that revenge shit."

"Yeah, but that bitch careless wit' her shit. Don't forget she was the one that sent a nigga up in TGI Fridays in the first place. But on the real doe, I think you really do need to let Tan handle Justice and you stay out of that shit."

Carlos sighed deeply before opening his door to get out. He didn't respond to what Face had said, but he'd heard him loud and clear. He had a decision to make because he knew it wouldn't be long before the two women started inquiring about one another. On one hand, he thought about his business relationship with Tan and how his decision would affect his paper. Although Tan was no longer his sole supplier, she was cheaper and more efficient than the nigga he was dealing with in Miami. Ever since Dave had gotten fucked up with those keys, Carlos had slowed down from copping from Florida.

Carlos also thought about Justice and how even after all that had transpired he still had feelings for her, and deep down, he didn't want anything to happen to her. As he helped Face out the truck and into his wheelchair he thought about what Face had just told him and realized there was no way he could just stay out of it because he was about to be dead smack in the middle of it.

CHAPTER THIRTEEN

Justice's desire to get revenge for the murder of her brother was growing minute-by-minute and hour by hour and she couldn't wait to deal with Tan. She knew she wasn't crazy when she thought she saw Tan roll by at Sapphire's mother's funeral. It had to be her…

Justice had tried to get Sapphire to hang out with her and leave Charlotte for a little while but she refused. Justice, trying to be understanding because she had lost her own mother when she was younger decided to give Sapphire some space and decided to clear her own head for a little while.

Concord Mills was the first exit outside of Charlotte on I-85 north. It wasn't as far as Greensboro or Raleigh or even a quick trip to the VA, but the trip would serve its purpose of getting a breath of fresh air and it was close enough in case she had to rush back to tend to Sapphire.

Justice hadn't even turned off the ignition good before she felt her phone vibrate. She pushed the button to accept the call.

"Justice are you sitting down?" Toni urged as Justice had opened the door and placed her foot on the pavement. She stepped back in and closed the door.

"Yeah, I'm in the car, what's up."

"Girl, you ain't gonna believe what these broads did today."

Justice was barely able to exhale before Toni continued,

"Precious beat up Fancy!"

"She what!" Justice shouted. She could feel her blood boil as she could picture Precious Amazonian ass picking on a stripper half her size. Justice reflected on the promises she'd made the young girl who was shaking her ass to pay for the expensive courses at Northwestern University. Being that the girl wanted to make something of herself and that this was a "temporary means" to an ultimate goal, Justice wanted to see the girl succeed. Justice had promised that she would do her best to keep Fancy out of conflict, and when the girl needed her most, she was hundreds of miles away.

"What the hell? How the hell did it happen?" Justice knew the answer to that question before she finished asking, but knowing Toni, she would get the answer anyway.

"One of the guys from the Chicago Bulls asked her for a lap dance in VIP and the guy was making it rain. Precious was jealous and she tried to move in on the dance and try to get some of the money. The guy told her nicely that he wasn't interested in her and Fancy laughed in her face. Precious couldn't take it and she backhanded Fancy so hard she fell down, then Precious pounced on her like a cat on a mouse and started nailing her."

"Are you serious?" Justice shouted as she banged her fist on the steering wheel. She pictured Precious' face and was tempted to hammer the wheel but she refrained in order not to look like a crazy ass black woman in the shopping mall's parking lot.

"Yes boss lady, and that's not the half of it." Toni continued. She quickly exhaled and continued with her soap opera, "Somebody posted a video on World Star Hip Hop of

Virgin giving two niggas head in the VIP."

"Da fuck?!" Justice was furious. The last place she wanted publicity for her club was on a website dedicated to posting random and sometimes explicit clippings that had gone viral. She had had it with Precious and Virgin's bullshit and she knew that when she got back to Chicago, she was going to have to get her hands dirty—but first, there was a more pressing matter to tend to. "Bitch, as soon as I get to Chicago, I'm cleaning house. I might start with your ass."

Justice wanted to kick Toni's ass so fucking bad. She had left a laundry list of objectives for the girl to accomplish and here she was getting more and more shit to clean. What the fuck was Toni doing being a manager if she couldn't manage any of these situations?

"Damn, I'm sorry. But what could I do?" She could hear Toni crying on the other end. Toni started wailing and speaking incoherently. All Justice got out of what Toni was saying was something about getting another chance and not wanting to be fired and some other shit that was trivial to her. Justice looked in the rearview mirror at her own reflection and she shook her head.

This is some bullshit, Justice thought to herself. She exhaled "I'mma kill them bitches." She said as she cracked the door open.

"What'd you say boss lady?" Toni was still sniffling. Justice could imagine Toni looking pathetic.

"Look, just do what you gotta do to keep the club open, I'll take care of Precious and Virgin when I get back." Justice commanded.

"Okay."

Justice ended the call. She opened the door, stepped out, and inhaled the fresh air. A fight and a fuckin' sex video—great! Precious and Virgin had successfully found Justice's last nerve and was working that lil' mutha-fucka to pieces.

"Aye Ma!" Some young man was shouting. Justice kept walking to the door because she hated being addressed in that manner and she wasn't about to give the young man the time of day. If he knew what was good for him at that moment, he would keep his distance.

"Baby girl!" Justice heard the voice again and then felt a tight grip on her arm pulling her back. Justice reached around to swing and almost hit War in the face.

"Fuck you touchin' me for?" Justice shouted, not caring whether or not she embarrassed him in front of his female friend, who surprisingly stepped to the side. "I will fuck you up out here."

"My bad, I saw you getting out of your car and noticed you left your lights on, I was trying to save you from having your car jumped." War defended. He wrapped his arms around the young lady who was with him who looked as if she couldn't have been a day out of high school.

Justice looked down the parking light and noticed that her lights were indeed still on. "I'm sorry." She said humbly. As she took a second look at War, she was mesmerized by how much he looked like Carlos. If she had not seen those cuts in his eyebrows, she would have sworn it was him.

"No problem." War said as they headed in the mall. "I think my uncle tryna get at you."

"Your uncle has my number." Justice lied. She didn't know what War may have known about her relationship with Carlos and she didn't feel like spilling her guts to a young man she barely knew either.

"Knowing him, he'll probably be using it real soon." War said as he peeped at her ass before him and the young lady strolled in the door. Justice watched as he kissed her on the cheek like a schoolboy in love with his first crush. She turned back to the parking lot to go turn her lights off. Once she accomplished that task, she made her way back to the mall without any more interruptions.

CHAPTER FOURTEEN

"*. . . I Had To Raise The Limit*!" Cash P's ringtone blared from Red's phone, jarring him out of his deep slumber. Red unwrapped his arms from around the body lying next to him. He rubbed his eyes while the ringtone continued to scream from the phone. After getting in a stretch, he sat up, grabbed the phone, and swiped the screen to answer it.

"Talk," Red commanded. He looked over at the nightstand noticing the bright red 5:45 illuminating on the digital clock, letting him know how early it was in the morning.

"Get up, cuzo, I need to holla at'cha." The high-pitched voice of his cousin, Kim called for his attention. "You still looking for that Justice bitch, right?"

"Hell yeah, you know I am, What's good?" Red replied with a hoarse voice. In addition, at that moment, he felt a set of soft lips on his dick, sucking him to an erection. He lifted up the sheets to see Always's head bobbing up and down. He shook his head with a grin.

"Yeah, that bitch came back to Charlotte for Ms. Evans' funeral," Kim went on as if she were carrying on a conversation in the middle of the afternoon. "I didn't even know she knew that lady like that. I woulda went to the funeral if I had remembered what time it was and shit, I loved Ms. Ev—"

"Is she still there now?" Red was trying to conduct business, but Always had gotten between his legs and started slurping on his balls, putting the right amount of pressure on them to make his toes curl and for him to start hissing.

"Yeah, they said she was hugged up on Ms. Evans' daughter and shit."

"Good looking Kim," Red responded. Always climbed on top of him, her wetness bubbling and slowly letting him enter her moist sugar walls, raw dawg. Red knew he should have put a condom on, but he was caught up in the moment and his dick was doing the thinking. Always was living up to her name; her pussy always stayed wet and ready. Her sugar walls were so tight and warm, Red came within a few strokes but that didn't stop him from rolling her onto her back and fucking her in the ass, missionary style. This was her favorite act and she came twice in succession as he stroked her tight hole and played with her clit ring.

***

"You gotta go," Red told Always as he rolled over. He had just busted another nut, this time in her asshole. His body was sweaty and he knew that he needed to jump in the shower to wash the smell of sex off him so he could go meet Chris.

"What you mean I gotta go?" Always questioned. Her skillful hands caressed his slowly deflating erection, trying to make it hard again so they could go another round. Her other hand played with the small curly hairs on his chest and around his nipples. "I wanna go again."

"Look, me and Chris got business to handle," Red said as he got out of the bed. He looked on the floor and found Always's lace panties and bra and tossed them to her. "You gotta go," he repeated with authority.

"Okay," Always reluctantly replied. "But what about my money you promised me from them last two licks?" Red had used Always in a few stick-ups over the past two months and had not paid her for the last two. Since Red was fucking her, she figured he thought she wouldn't ask for her share. But fuck that! Always was a paper chaser. The dick was good, no doubt, but it was not paying the bills.

"Fuck you talkin' 'bout? As many meals you done ate off me and as many nuts I done made your trick ass bust . . . bitch, you paid," Red said as if she were some random hood chick who was getting on his last nerve.

Red watched Always put on her bra and panties and search the room for the rest of her clothes. "I got somethin' for yo' ass." Always mumbled under of her breath.

"You say somethin'?" Red glared at her but she didn't repeat herself. She continued to gather her belongings while seething with anger.

Red knew she was heated but he couldn't have cared less. He had gotten two nuts off in her and had fun with her the previous night, but now it was time for her to go. All he could think about was what Kim had told him and he knew it was urgent for him to get to Charlotte and take care of that bitch before she could go back to Chicago. He guessed he would have a better chance of catching her off balance if she was out of Chicago. He wanted Justice so bad he could almost smell that bitch.

***

Red went through a couple a scenarios that ended with him busting two or three rounds in Justice's cranium and getting his revenge for her killing J. T. He was at Christina's apartment, waiting for her to get dressed. He thought about how she would go the fuck off if she knew he had fucked that bitch, Always without her being there, let alone without a condom. Over the past few months, they had tricked with Always a few times, but never one without the other until Red had broken the code the night before.

Christina stepped out of her bedroom dressed in an athletic jumpsuit, looking like she was ready to go play ball. He appreciated the fact that unlike most women, Christina knew how to get in and get the fuck out of the bathroom.

"You ready to go that fast?" Red asked as he picked up her already packed bag, ready to take it down to the car.

"Hell yeah," Christina confirmed, "you know a bitch like me don't take long."

Red cracked a smile, letting his dimples show. "Let's go murk that bitch and get back."

"Calm down, Denzel, this ain't Training Day. This shit gotta be done with precision," Christina said as she walked past him to get her cosmetic bag off the kitchen counter. "You think I'mma need some more outfits?"

"Depends on how long we stayin'."

"And how long might that be?" she asked while exiting the door.

"As long as it takes to watch that bitch take her last breath," Red replied with a venomous sneer. With that said, they were out the door.

CHAPTER FIFTEEN

"I'm just asking you to have lunch with me, no pressure," Carlos pleaded his case over the phone. Justice was in the mirror applying gloss to her lips. She knew that War had told his uncle that he had seen her at the mall and she had to admit, she wasn't surprised that he'd reached out so fast. The only way Carlos could have gotten her Chicago number would have been from Sapphire and she couldn't believe Sapphire had given it to him. Sapphire had just assumed everything was cool after the conversation at her mother's funeral. Funny how she couldn't get the girl out of the bed but Sapphire had enough time to try to play cupid with one of her old flames. Justice wished Sapphire were in the room so she could curse her out, but she was back in her own house now.

"Look!" Carlos was clearly agitated. The man was used to getting his way and didn't appreciate Justice rejecting his offer. "It's a spot on 28th and North Davidson called Amélie's. It's a French bakery and the food is off the chain. We'll be on neutral ground and it's a public place, so you ain't gotta feel secluded." He paused for effect, and then added, "So, what's good?"

Justice exhaled at the thought of her and Carlos sharing airspace again. True, she needed him so that she could rock Tan to sleep, but at the same time, she didn't want to fuck with him outside of that. On one hand, she didn't trust Carlos any further than she could see him. On the other, meeting at Amélie's was safe and probably the best situation for her to be in. She would be able to resist the temptation to kill his ass then.

"Okay, I'll go," Justice said reluctantly. She really didn't want to do it, but she figured she'd let him think he was getting back in, maybe even think he was getting some pussy. However, once she was to get the information she needed, it would be fuck Tan and fuck Carlos, too.

***

Justice looked in the rearview mirror and made sure her naturally curly hair was pressed to perfection. She looked around the crowded parking lot before she stepped out of the car and made her way up the stairs into Amélie's. Inside, she noticed the pleasant smell of pastries and soups, and sure enough, the place was packed even though it was four o'clock in the evening. She looked at all of the pastries and could not decide which one she should indulge in. The place looked like something straight out of a French magazine. Justice longed to go to Paris, but had not yet had the time. For now, this French deli was as close as she was going to get.

"See somethin' you want?" Carlos asked as he snuck up beside her. Justice took in the form-fitting Cavi shirt and the jeans that fit right about his waist and didn't fall off his ass. She was so glad he was dressed like a grown man now and not a thug. That shit was a definite turn off. He toted a leather laptop knapsack that made him fit right in with the other twenty-somethings who found luxury in the Internet café they were in. "I'mma recommend the Portabella and leek tartine and the salted caramel brownie." Carlos sounded more like a college-educated snob than a street nigga, and Justice was somewhat impressed.

"That sounds good, except I want the turkey and bacon sandwich and the strawberry cheese cake," Sapphire chimed in from behind, startling Carlos. She was sporting a gray button up jacket with brown slacks peeking underneath. She was looking vibrant and alive, an indication of how well she was dealing with her loss. "My mama loved this place."

After her conversation with Carlos earlier, Justice called Sapphire and told her to meet them there. Justice wanted to use her as a mediator, so to speak. Carlos turned in surprise when he heard her voice. Disappointment was evident in his features because he thought he and Justice were about to be alone.

Carlos smiled to himself at Justice's prowess as he placed their order while Sapphire showed Justice around. Justice took in the fact that every section of the restaurant was not only painted a different color, but was reminiscent of pre-World War II France. As they sat on the antique furniture, Justice observed the scenery and was completely taken away. She had passed this place a thousand times while riding through the North Davidson area, but had never stopped to come inside.

Carlos rejoined them and they began easing into light conversation before the food was brought out. Soon they were all reminiscing about the past and reacquainting themselves as if they were old friends. Not once did the conversation turn to the misunderstanding that had caused them all to part. It was true, what was understood did not need to be discussed.

Well into the conversation, Carlos took out his Dell laptop

and started showing Justice the layout for the house he was having built. Justice was impressed with his preference of modern eclectic selections of mahogany and sable pieces. If Justice didn't know any better, she'd think Carlos was showing signs of leaving the game behind and settling down for real. Moreover, she almost believed him, but years earlier when they had first met, Carlos had shown her a different layout of another beautiful house in Huntersville that she had fallen in love with when she thought she and Carlos would be a real couple. Nevertheless, it hadn't worked out and they ended up as only sex partners whose hearts stayed close to one another even after their split.

When the server brought their sandwiches to the table, Justice was staggered when she saw Carlos bow his head and say blessings. Justice bit into her Portabella and leek tartine and liked the way the flavors attacked her taste buds.

As they continued to talk, Justice thought she saw a woman who looked familiar sitting at a table in the corner conversing with a handsome man in a business suit and tie. Seemed like every time Justice looked up, the woman would glance in their direction, and then go back to talking to the man who was sitting at the table with her.

Justice dismissed it as paranoia as she, Sapphire, and Carlos continued to catch up on each other's lives while periodically taking a journey down memory lane. At times, she laughed so hard at past tales that she had to wipe tears from her eyes.

During the meal, she kept taking sneak peeks at Carlos and noticed he was still as handsome as ever. He even seemed to have a more calming aura about himself. She had to admit, if

Carlos was trying to win his way back into her good graces, he was starting to succeed. She had to keep reminding herself that she only needed him so she could get to Tan. However, Justice always had a soft spot in her heart for the man sitting across from her, and just like the cheese on the toasted open-faced baguette she was eating; she felt her reserve starting to melt.

CHAPTER SIXTEEN

Marques leaned forward and whispered something freaky in To'Wanda's ear and her boisterous laughter caused everyone in the back of Amélie's to gaze in her direction. She smiled and put her hand up to her mouth in embarrassment.

The bowl of legume soup on the table in front of her was almost empty and the only remnants left of the French baguette were the crumbs. To'Wanda was having a wonderful time with Marques, despite the unexpected visit of Justice, Sapphire, and Carlos. She knew that Justice and Sapphire didn't recognize her, but Carlos definitely did but chose not to say anything. While she was entertaining Marques and making plans for more dates and more dick, she had discreetly taken a couple of pictures of the three of them enjoying their mid-day break.

***

Look at what the cat drug in!!

Tan read the text To'Wanda had sent along with the pictures. Moments before receiving the message, she was about to dial Loon's number, but now that To'Wanda had confirmed that *that* bitch was out on the town, all hands were on deck. She wanted to body Justice so bad that she could envision herself shooting the bitch in the chest every time she blinked her eyes.

Tan picked up the phone and pressed TWO on her speed

dial.

"Hey baby," To'Wanda cooed like a schoolgirl who'd been up to something mischievous.

"Are they still at Amélie's?"

The pause between her question and To'Wanda's answer confirmed what she already knew. She had missed the bitch. "No, they all left 'bout an hour ago." Tan could tell To'Wanda was annoyed. "I tried callin' you and I sent you numerous texts. You didn't get them?"

A beeping sound rang in Tan's ear, indicating that yet another message was coming through. She put To'Wanda on speaker and checked the late message from her that read:

Are you sure Carlos is on OUR team?

"I got them. I hate this fuckin' phone. You sent the pictures an hour ago and I'm just now getting them!" She banged her fist on the table, pissed because of all days, her phone picked today to act retarded.

She thought about To'Wanda's inquisition for a minute and after looking at the pictures, she too began to silently question Carlos' loyalty. While sitting idly thinking about the rising dilemma she was facing, she thought back to the incident from two years prior that continued to make her blood boil. She was thinking about what had happened between her and Monk. She had sent him to tango with Satan and she was determined to make Justice join him.

"Tomorrow, I'm switching to Sprint because this shit is ridiculous," Tan told her girl and they ended the call.

Tan hung up the phone irritated and mad as hell. She wished she had listened to that little voice inside her head that told her to go with To'Wanda and Marques and she wouldn't have missed Justice.

The phone rang and when she heard Loon's ringtone, she got even more irritated. She picked up the phone with anticipation of giving Loon a good tongue-lashing, but she stopped short of that when she heard what sounded like a female's voice on the other end.

"This Tan?" the woman was bold enough to speak her name with authority as if she was the creator and Tan were the clay.

"Depends on who this is and what you want. Matter of fact, bye bitch." Tan looked at the phone and then shook her head because her first thought was that one of Loon's tricks had the audacity to dial her number. That fat bastard was becoming a bigger problem than he was worth and whoever this woman was had sealed the deal.

Tan was about to hang up the phone when she heard the woman scream, "Wait! I need to talk to you."

Tan huffed, and then rubbed her temples. "Look, I ain't fuckin Loon. Don't want Loon. And couldn't care less about who he fuckin', so—"

The woman cut her off. "Nah, it ain't 'bout nuttin' like dat, folk. I just wanted to let you know that nigga Red and some stick-up bitch is on they way to Charlotte from Atlanta."

At the mention of Red's name Tan suddenly developed an interest in the mystery woman on the other line because Loon had not too long ago revealed that Red had been the one who had jacked him and Jo-Jo. Tan believed Loon could have long ago handled the situation, but she knew he was too soft to confront Red. She thought, *it always takes a bitch to do a man's job*!

Tan knew that whomever the girl was she was speaking to was more than likely either a stripper or a prostitute of some sort because that fat muthafucka was always paying for some ass. Tan was getting even more heated by the fact that Loon had put some bitch in their business. In her eyes, Loon was already a corpse that refused to lie in the casket.

"And why *you* tellin' me this and not Loon?"

"Because I told Loon I wanted to be the one to tell you," the girl stated with confidence. Tan thought maybe the bitch wanted money for her information and if that was the case, she concluded that Loon would definitely be the one to pay her ass.

As an afterthought, Tan questioned, "How you know he on his way up here anyway?"

"Just know that I'm *always* on top of my shit—always!" The girl bragged as she hung up the phone.

Tan remembered how Red had trailed Justice to Chicago two years ago and she knew that if he was coming to Charlotte, he was coming for Justice. She also knew that if he was the one who had robbed Loon like he'd told her a while back, he may as well had put his hand directly in her pocket.

"This is going to be easier than I thought," Tan said aloud as she altered the plan in her mind. She remembered that Carlos had mentioned to her before that it was actually J. T., Cross, and this same nigga, *Red,* who had robbed his stash spot. Tan threw the phone on the bed and had to laugh aloud at how fuckin' small the world was and how everything seemed to be coming back around, full circle.

Red didn't know it, but his plans to come back to Charlotte

to seek revenge on Justice had just moved him up a couple of notches on Tan's shit list.

CHAPTER SEVENTEEN

Justice almost could not believe that she had agreed so easily to go with Carlos to Northlake Mall to see the latest Madea movie. She was even somewhat taken aback from the fact that he had been the one to suggest that movie, as it was one she could see herself watching with Sapphire or Toni on a girl's night out type of deal. When Justice thought about it, it had been awhile since she had seen a movie in the theater because she had one helluva bootleg man in Chicago who had every movie on DVD before it hit the theaters.

Justice got out of the car and walked to the front of the theater when she saw him walking up. He was wearing a skullcap, a black form-fitting shirt with black jeans and Prada sneakers.

He look the way he did when I first met him, Justice thought to herself as she walked closer to him. When she got closer to him, she appreciated the tantalizing scent of his Creed cologne.

"Lookin' good, babe." Carlos said while checking her out with inspecting eyes.

"Likewise." Justice complimented back while giving him a friendly hug.

When they got to the ticket booth, Carlos paid for their

tickets and they walked inside the lobby of the theater. After stopping at the concession stand for a large bucket of popcorn and some soft drinks, they entered the room where the movie was showing. As they entered, they noticed that the seating was light for the show they were viewing. They chose a spot in the back of the theater. They could see a few other couples sprinkled around the theater and groups of women who were having a girl's night out thing going on.

"Soooo, yo man don't mind you coming out with me?" Carlos asked as he dug into the bucket of popcorn.

"I haven't had a "man" since—" Justice didn't want to admit that J.T. was her last *man* nor did she want to relive the situation that surrounded it. Just the thought of it made her want to call "Earl."

"It's okay if the last time was wit' me." Carlos joked. Justice smiled to herself as she took a sip of her fruit juice drink. "Why we didn't do shit like this back in the day? I'm talkin' bout actually datin' and shit." Carlos added.

Justice looked at him. *Where is the* real *Carlos and who is this imposter sitting next to me?* She looked at his side profile again and she knew that she was sitting next to the real thing. She just couldn't believe that she was seeing *this* side of him—who knew? "I didn't know that this was a date."

"I called you, I asked you out, we sittin' up in the movies.... Sapphire ain't around; it's just the two of us—sounds like a date to me."

"Point well taken."

"We gonna grab somethin' to eat and a drink after this wack ass movie" Carlos laughed.

"Wack? You the one who suggested it." Justice laughed.

"I know y'all chicks like shit like this, that's why I did it".

The movie came on and within five minutes, the couple who had gotten cozy on the right side of the theater distracted her.

"I guess they couldn't wait to get home." Carlos leaned in and whispered in her ear, wishing it were the two of them who were getting it in.

"Guess not." She addressed as she continued to watch the movie. The plotline started to interest her so she kept her mind focused on that. After a few minutes, one of the movie attendants came down the aisle and the happy couple calmed their nerves.

"So what else didn't we do back in the day?" Carlos asked. Justice knew that he wasn't feeling the movie as much as she was.

"Join the Mile High Club." Justice joked and covered it with a smile. "No, I'm just playing, we done a lot together, but some simple things like eating at a park, going on a joyride, going to church . . ."

"Whoa!" Carlos said loud enough to draw the attention of everyone in the theater. Justice laughed at him and everyone else had turned back around. "I didn't know you went to church."

"I go sometimes." Justice told the truth. She meant to add only for weddings, funerals, Easter and Christmas service but he did not need to know all of that. After conversing further during the movie, Justice began to warm up to Carlos a little. However, an image of Monk kept flashing through her head and she knew that indirectly, Carlos was responsible for his demise. As they watched the rest of the movie, Justice pondered whether she could completely forgive and forget, but one thing she did know, Carlos was softening her heart one iota at a time—something she never thought would happen again.

***

Carlos was feeling good after he had spent time with Justice. She seemed to have forgiven him, or at least she acted as if she had. He figured he had already won Sapphire over, and with her help, he would win Justice over and everything would be as it was a few years ago with Justice by his side and him still on top of the game.

It was the day after him and Justice had gone to the movies when Carlos was driving down North Davidson heading toward downtown, he saw a Charlotte-Mecklenburg police car get behind him. He looked at the speedometer to make sure he wasn't speeding. In doing so, he saw the picture of his deceased lieutenant, Ali's daughter on his dash, smiling with her missing tooth and her big pigtails. Damn, he missed his brother from another mother. He made a mental note to stop by and check on his goddaughter soon. He heard his phone beeping with a ringtone he designated for business. As he reached for it, he accidentally dropped it between the seats. He didn't retrieve it since the police were behind him.

After getting into the downtown area, the patrol car turned off on 5th Street and he reached beneath the seat for his cell, swerving a little before finally feeling it. He picked it up and saw the missed call was from Tan. Before he could return the call, he received a text from her with a coded message letting him know that she wanted to meet with him immediately.

Carlos sucked his teeth, took a deep breath, and decided he would wait a few minutes until he was away from the downtown area before he responded. The last thing he needed was to see another Charlotte-Mecklenburg police car and be pulled over for texting while driving.

***

Carlos chose to meet Tan at Freedom Park in East Charlotte. Even though Carlos had lived in Charlotte all his life, he was still in awe at how Charlotte was so visibly divided by class. West Boulevard, his old stomping ground was all 'hood'. As soon as West Boulevard turned into East Boulevard, only separated by one intersection, you ventured into Charlotte's upper middle-class. Many of the houses were Renaissance style surrounded by large trees that kept the neighborhood shaded. Carlos took in the scene as he drove through the Dilworth neighborhood headed to the park.

Ten minutes later Carlos entered the park near the tennis courts, parked and walked down to an empty bench. The weather was a little warm this day and people were definitely taking advantage of the sunshine. He had been seated for only a few short minutes before he saw Tan approaching. As usual, she looked stunning, dressed in an off-white sleeveless sundress and casual pumps. Tan walked as if she owned the entire park. Before she could even sit down Carlos sensed animosity. Even though he could not see her cold eyes behind the tint on her Gucci sunglasses, he knew she was glaring at him.

"When were you gonna tell me that bitch is in town?" Tan spewed with much venom. She didn't even give him a chance to answer the question. "You know how I feel about the bitch and I feel like you tryin' me."

"Fuck you talkin' 'bout? Ain't nobody tryin' your crazy ass." Through gritted teeth, Carlos boldly gave her back as much venom as she had spewed. "That girl ain't thinkin' about yo' paranoid ass." His brows were knitted in anger. He sarcastically added, "Lemme find out ole girl got yo' gangsta ass shook." He was toying with her emotions as he sat all the way back, arms stretched out along the back of the bench. "It's been two years since that shit went down. If she wanted to move on you, I think she would've done it by now." He was trying to see where her head was at.

Tan's head whipped so hard in his direction that her sunglasses almost flew off. "Yeah, I see you got jokes. You know I'on fear shit." Her face was turning red.

She looked at him with disdain. "Do I have to question what team you on?"

"Nah, gangsta. You know you ain't gotta question that." He looked at her with seriousness and added, "you know what team I roll wit'. If y'all still beefin' you know I got you." Carlos stood up as he looked around to see whether some of her "friends" were in the vicinity. He knew not to put it past this bitch to have him murked right there in the park full of kids. "If I hear anything, I'll get at you."

She nodded, seemingly halfway appeased. With that said, he turned his back and walked to his Tahoe. He didn't know if Tan actually believed him or not, because she showed no telling expression. If she did not believe him, he knew he would have a problem on his hands. Disloyalty meant instant death with the Mendozas. He decided he would have to tread on thin ice with this matter.

***

After leaving Tan, Carlos went to his barbershop. When he got to the back he saw Lil' Joe sitting in War's chair getting a shape up. He was dressed in his street clothes--oversized T-shirt, jeans, and black low-cut Timbs. He looked like the old Joe Carlos was used to seeing.

"Aye 'Los, lemme holla at you for a minute when I finish getting this shape up."

Carlos just nodded his head. Last thing he wanted was to deal with some bullshit. He figured Joe had probably heard some more shit about him and Preme slumping Dave. Fucking with Tan earlier and now about to deal with Joe's shit had him contemplating whether it was really time for him to get out of the game and just focus on going legit. BobCutz was making a profit, and that was without the drug money. He had opportunities to expand and open another location in the Charlotte area and he was entertaining the thought of some of War's ex-classmates that wanted to franchise. Or he could pull a Justice and open a strip club, but Charlotte already had enough of those and he didn't want to be dealing with random hoes day in and day out.

Carlos walked into his office and took a seat behind his desk. He took out his Dell laptop and pulled up an episode of *The Wire* from iTunes. Watching the show reminded him of his current situation and he knew he had a choice to make. He felt like Stringer Bell when he was faced with that life-changing decision of whether or not to remain loyal to his fam'. While the show played in the background, he picked up the phone and called Justice.

"Carlos?"

Hearing her voice made him smile. "Yeah, it's me. What's good, ma?"

"I told you my name ain't ma . . . but I'm glad you called. I was just tellin' Sapphire how much fun it was talkin' and trippin' with you. It's been a long time."

Carlos imagined Justice on the other end of the phone smiling that beautiful smile. "I wish I was over there with you."

"Yeah right," Justice replied like she used to when he used to try and sweet talk her. "You probably got some bitch with you right now while you're tryna sweet talk me."

"Trust me, if some bitch was wit' me, I wouldn't be on the phone with you." Carlos laughed as he relaxed in the chair. He saw Luther walking past his office, headed to the break room. "Look, I just wanted to let you know to be careful."

"Lemme guess . . . yo' Mexican bitch asked about me, huh?" Justice always called Tan Mexican even though she knew she was Dominican. It was a form of disrespecting her nationality.

"Just be careful."

Justice laughed sarcastically. "I wish yo' bitch *would* try me."

"Why you keep sayin' *my* bi—" Before he could finish his question, Justice hung up.When he looked up, he saw Lil' Joe getting ready to knock on the door. Carlos didn't say anything, but waved his hand to motion Lil' Joe to come inside. Lil' Joe entered and shut the door behind him.

"What it do, bruh?" Carlos said as he stood, looking up at

the taller man. He quickly scanned him to see if Lil' Joe had any weapons and if he needed to stay close to his desk where his pistol was hidden.

"I'mma get to the point. I'm ready to get back down," Lil' Joe stated as he walked to the desk. "Don't get it twisted, I love working on cars and I like having my own garage and shit, but it ain't the same since I been away from the game. It's like a nigga just workin' to pay bills and shit."

Carlos thought about Lil' Joe's situation for a second. Lil' Joe having his own legit business would come in handy should he need him. And Lil' Joe did know how to run a trap. A part of Carlos wished things had not gone down with Dave the way they had because he missed the David and Goliath team that kept the Westside of Charlotte from becoming a headache. Then again, with Preme limping and Face in a wheelchair and Ali gone, he needed a young gunner. Truth be told, Lil' Joe was nowhere near as ruthless as Preme or Face with the ratchets, but Carlos looked at the young man and saw that he was hungry.

"You finally gettin' tired of eatin'crumbs, and ready for some real bread again, huh?" Carlos asked, not sure of Lil' Joe's intentions.

"No doubt, a nigga miss that shit." Lil' Joe said as he reached out for a pound.

Carlos hesitated for a minute because he knew that pound would seal the deal. He thought maybe Joe was trying to get close enough to find out the truth about his man, Dave. He also knew he had to make Lil' Joe show him he was serious about getting put back on the team. He finally reached out and pounded his once protégé's outreached fist. Carlos dismissed him and told him he would be in touch shortly.

Once Lil' Joe left the office, Carlos sat at the computer and pulled up some pictures he and Justice had taken a couple of years ago at various clubs and on dates at spots like Crave and Kabuto's. He even found a few intimate pictures of the two of them being mischievous with the camera before, during, and after sex. After all that had gone down, he had never gotten rid of these mementos.

Damn I miss her, he thought as his dick began to stiffen at a picture of her silhouette on top of the bed they once shared. He thought about his betrayal to Tan by telling Justice that she was looking for her. He also thought about the money he would lose and the inevitable war he would have to endure with the Mendoza family if he betrayed Tan and didn't assist her in harming Justice. Tan hadn't asked for his help yet, but he knew it was indeed coming. He sat back in his chair and huffed. "Damn, a rock and a fuckin' hard spot. What da hell is a nigga to do?"

CHAPTER EIGHTEEN

Chris looked at all of the construction taking place on North Tryon near the new Wal-Mart. She glanced over at Red and noticed that he had become frustrated. He hated traffic just as much as she did and the drivers in these slow moving cars were not doing anything but being nosey and wasting valuable time. As she looked at Red on the passenger side, she knew he was up to something, but she couldn't figure out what it was just yet.

"How the hand feel?" Chris asked out of concern. Red looked at her, sucked his teeth and exhaled. She wanted to smack Red because she hated that shit and he knew it, but she knew his anger was his way of expressing that his hand was still sore.

Before Red and Chris left Atlanta, they had a change of plans because they had gotten word that some clown ass nigga from Patterson, New Jersey was in town flaunting his street wealth. It was one thing for a nigga to come to the ATL and get quiet money, but when you came and flaunted that shit in a nigga's face, it was an insult. To put the icing on the cake, the nigga didn't even like niggas from down south. He even talked mad shit about how green and how soft they were. This infuriated Red. This nigga had moved himself to the top of

Red's hit list and he decided to touch that nigga before they hit the road. Initially, Chris had objected. She wanted to get to Charlotte, handle their business, and get the hell back to Atlanta because she had heard the police in the Queen City didn't fuck around.

"We gonna touch this nigga and hop straight on 85. In and out, babe," Red had said, trying to convince Chris.

Satisfied that they would be in and out in a matter of minutes, Chris finally agreed.

They donned ski masks and promptly kicked the back door in and stormed the nigga's trap house like the SWAT team. He was not there, but two of his flunkies were. Once Red demanded the money and dope, they promptly told the two robbers to kiss their asses.

Red hauled off and smashed the older of the two in the jaw with a right hook. As soon as his fist made contact with the man's face Red felt the bone in his hand crack. Seeing the older man get his jaw broken, the younger guy led Chris to a small stash of cocaine and seven stacks. Holding his throbbing hand Red announced, "Y'all niggas lucky we ain't got time to tear this muthafucka up." He looked down at the man on the floor holding his jaw. "Nigga, think about me when you sippin' soup for the next few weeks, bitch!"

Red and Chris exited the same way they entered, swiftly out the back door. They were surprised they didn't hear any gunshots as they ran toward their getaway car. They hadn't wasted time searching the house for guns and were certain the two guys had them stashed close by. They dropped off the six ounces to Chris's cousin before they hit the highway.

"We should've stayed on I-85 like the GPS said instead of driving all the way down here like this. This is outta da way," Chris complained.

"I need to stop by one of J.T.'s old spots. I gotta check on something."

Chris rolled her eyes. "Nigga, you couldda did this shit on your own time. This a fuckin' waste of time. We here to catch a body or two and that's it," Chris stated as casually as if she were talking about going shopping. She was frustrated, hungry, and a little tired from the three-hour drive from Atlanta. In addition, she was still psyched about the robbery of that stash house they had committed hours earlier. Red's unnecessary stops had her ready to reach across the seat and slap the shit out of him.

"Yo, this some important shit. I gotta stop by there to see if something's still there. It was some ratchets and shit. I got locked up before I could go get that shit. I couldn't come back when I got out because I know them crackas was watchin' a nigga."

"Whatever nigga! What make you think that shit still there? It's been two fuckin' years." Chris was agitated with Red and his miscellaneous antics. Her mind was made up. She was not stopping. She looked down at the GPS and asked, "Where you say Kim live again?"

"In them apartments near the Verizon Amphitheatre—you can't miss 'em." He didn't argue.

Chris continued to drive until she reached the intersection of North Tryon and Pavilion Boulevard where she turned right. And just as Red said, she noticed the apartments about a block down the street from the amphitheatre. Chris turned into the gated complex and went to the intercom where she searched for Kim Turner's name. When she called the number to let Kim know that they were present, Kim told them which gate to go in and how to find her apartment. Chris followed the directions and soon Red and Chris were walking up three flights of stairs to Kim's apartment.

Red and Chris knew they had reached Kim's apartment because they could hear Young Jeezy's remix of "Hustle Hard" shaking the ground from her residence. Red looked at Chris and laughed while instinctively mouthing off the words to the chorus. Chris shook her head. "Ghetto as hell!" she mumbled. She rolled her eyes and marched into Kim's apartment. The cheap ass furniture and fixtures were very different from what she was comfortable with. As the song ended, Kim came out of the bedroom.

"Heeey!" Kim ran up to Chris and greeted her like they were long lost sisters, even though they had never seen each other before that moment. Kim looked up at Red. "What up, punk?" She gave him a hug also.

"What up, bitch!"

"Bitch? Nigga, you know what? Neva' mind." She was a firecracker for a five foot two, one hundred-ten pound chick. She looked comfortable in her baggy off brand jeans, extra long T-shirt, and pink and white low-cut Nike shoes. Then she pushed him away before giving him a hug. "You lucky I love you, nigga," she said as she took two sets of keys out of her pocket. "These keys work the locks on the bedroom and the front door."

Red reached for the keys. "Cool." He walked to the bedroom and opened the door to find the room fully furnished with neutral colored bedding, lamps and furniture. Ready to relax, he started to reach for the remote to turn on the television, but remembered he needed to handle something. He got up from the bed and walked to the common living room area. "Yo Chris, I'mma get yo' bags and bring 'em up 'cause I gotta go handle some bizness."

Chris dug into her pocket, took out the car keys, and tossed them to him while she and Kim went on with their conversation as if he were some random nigga walking up to them at the club. He couldn't believe how Kim and Chris were really hitting it off. Usually, women were not so girly-girl with one another upon first meeting, especially not Chris.

He retrieved the bags from the car and took them upstairs. He grabbed a box cutter out of his bag and headed out the door.

***

Red drove back down North Tryon and turned onto Mallard Creek to a second set of condo apartments near UNC-Charlotte. He parked, exited the car and made the flight up the stairs to J. T's old condo. Luck had it that it was empty. He looked toward the sky and thanked God. He picked the lock and entered the unit. It looked like someone had just recently moved out. He hadn't been to the condo since he followed Justice to Chicago, opting to leave everything in case he needed to come back to it at a later time.

Red looked up and couldn't believe the bullet hole near the ceiling fan was still there. He could remember the day Cross was playing with his pistol and it went off. It brought a feeling of dread over him as he reminisced about his cousin. As he stared at that hole, he remembered that Carlos was the reason for Cross's demise.

"I'mma slump that faggot ass nigga, too. Two birds wit' one stone, my nigga," Red vowed, as if he were talking to Cross. "I put that on everythang."

Red made his way to J.T.'s old bedroom and panicked because he noticed the carpet had been replaced. He walked over to the closet and knelt down to the spot where the loose floorboards should have been. He took out the box cutter and cut a chunk out of the carpet. Once the carpet was up, he tapped on the floorboard and noticed it was still loose. He used a key to pry it up. Inside was one of J.T's safes. Elated, Red reached in his pocket and took out the small piece of paper in which he had written the combination. As he opened it, he found some of the most treasured ratchets he and J.T. had owned. He found his old Desert Eagle and one of J.T.'s Tec-9's. "I'mma toss this on that bitch's grave," he muttered.

Before Red stepped out of the condo, he glanced back up at that small hole in the ceiling and he had a vision of how Carlos and his boy pulled up and murdered Cross execution style. He shook his head as he closed the door behind him. Now he wanted that nigga just as bad as he wanted Justice.

***

"I'm up in here all the time." Kim bragged as she and Chris stepped into BobCutz. "Deb always make sure my shit tight."

Chris nodded her head. She liked Kim and felt a closer friendship with her than she had thought she would. Probably because Chris and Kim were a lot alike. They both liked money.

Kim wasted no time in pointing niggas out as they walked towards the back of the shop. "That second nigga right there—" She pointed to the young man in an orange barber jacket with baggy blue jeans, "That's War. His uncle, Carlos, owns the place. And them niggas look just alike, too, you'll see," Kim rambled.

Chris made a mental note of War's features for future reference.

"And that old man sittin' on dat ugly ass green chair is Luther, he runs the place. The man sitting next to him with the long locks is Supreme—he always in here. He talk a lotta shit, but he perfectly harmless," Kim said with confidence. She just didn't know how ruthless 'Preme really was. "And the nigga in the wheelchair that look like he could be Chucky's daddy is Scarface."

Chris shook her head at Kim's description of Face. However, she had to admit, those facial features and that scar definitely put him in the running to play "Who's the Father" on *The Maury Povich Show.*

"What up, Kim?" Carlos asked as he walked up behind them. He had just entered the shop. He and Kim hugged and then Carlos stepped back and admired her for a minute. Then he looked over at the fine stranger standing beside her.

"Hey Carlos. I didn't see you come in." Kim spoke. She saw him scoping out Chris so she made an impromptu introduction, "this my friend Jasmine. She just moved here from Alabama." Chris was impressed at how quickly Kim had changed her name and came up with a lie about who she was and what she was doing with her. Kim had definitely won some brownie points with her for that. Carlos extended his hand to shake Chris' and she obliged.

"You gettin' that 'do' did today?" Carlos asked, not really caring because he was still checking out Chris's thick thighs in the short skirt she was wearing.

"Nah, not today. I just wanted to bring Jasmine by to check out the place so she can make an appointment to get her locks twisted." Kim lied.

"Oh okay, that's what's up. I'll holla at 'cha." Carlos said, and then added. "Nice to meet you Jasmine. Hope I see more of you." The flirtatiousness in his voice was hard to miss.

Chris smirked. "Oh, I'm sure you will." she replied.

After the brief exchange, Carlos walked off and headed towards his office while Face rolled his wheelchair to the back after him. Chris did a double take between Carlos and War and noticed that Kim was on point when it came to describing their looks. She had taken in everyone in the shop from the young receptionist at the front to the baller who had just graced her with his presence. From what Red and Kim had already told her about Carlos she knew he wasn't gonna be an easy mark, but she figured with the proper planning, she and Red could pull it off and probably end up with some paper as well.

CHAPTER NINETEEN

Normally, Tan would have had one of her workers serve Loon, but she decided that she would meet Loon herself this time. She had visited Club Nikki's, a popular strip club off Little Rock Road. There, she befriended a dancer that called herself Honey because of her moist-looking D-cups and cinnamon colored ass that had niggas licking their lips every time she graced the stage. Her curly, blonde-streaked hair had her looking exotic.

Tan had put a couple of hundred dollars on a pre-paid debit card and sent Honey to check into a hotel on Sugar Creek and she began to put her plan into action.

Honey was the type of chick that was down for whatever and thirsty as hell for dough. Besides, she was no stranger to getting involved in some grimy shit! In fact, the grimier the better. No one expected a chick that looked like Lisa Raye in the face, but had a body like the porn star Pinky, to be up to anything scandalous other than fucking for a buck.

Once at the room, they stepped out of the rental and Tan popped the trunk. She grabbed two large suitcases and handed Honey a traveling bag and a suitcase of her own to carry. She followed Honey into the hotel room and immediately went to work. Honey went into the bathroom to change into her outfit and Tan focused on taking down the hotel's stale white curtains and putting up a mesh purple set she had gotten at Wal-Mart. She pulled the sheets off the King-sized bed and put on a foam mattress pad and white fitted mattress sheet that she had gotten from Bed Bath & Beyond. Then she put on a purple and crème sheet set that she had also gotten from Wal-Mart. After fixing the bed, she took the light bulbs out and replaced the white lights with blue ones. Once she finished, Tan sat on the bed, picked up the remote, and set the channel to BET. When she looked up, she saw Honey walking out of the bathroom in a French maid outfit.

"How a bitch look?" Honey asked as she modeled her outfit for Tan. Tan licked her lips, but remembered that this outfit was for Loon, not for her.

"You good, babe," Tan said, letting the stripper know she was pleased. At that moment, the *Loony Tunes* ringtone blared and she put her finger up to her lips to tell Honey to be quiet. "Where you at?" she spoke.

"I'm getting off the Sugar Creek exit now. I should be there in a few minutes; traffic fucked up."

"Cool," Tan said as she gave him the dial tone. Meanwhile, Honey was cleaning up the room, setting up the air fresheners, and creating the perfect ambience for Loon. "Remember what I told you. Follow the script, boo boo."

"No doubt."

Tan got up and gave Honey a hug, squeezing her ass a little. She shook her head, knowing that she would never be able to grab a piece of that again. She exited the room.

***

Loon knocked on the door and Honey opened it. Loon stared at the girl, momentarily dazed. Honey licked her lips and curled her fingers, enticing Loon to follow her inside. "Welcome to the Sex Room," she cooed. Honey stepped aside and watched as Loon waddled in and took off his jacket. His rank smell offended her, but like a true actor, she kept the charade going, pretending she didn't notice. "Why don't you take a shower and loosen up while I finish cleaning up?"

"A shower? Fuck I'mma take a shower for." Loon laughed as he walked around the room, checking shit out.

"Tan told me *to take care of you.* But if you in a hurry . . ." She let her words trail off.

"Business first, shawty. Money over bitches all day," Loon lied.

Honey smirked. "Tan havin' your work put in the trunk right now."

Loon peeked out of the window and saw a man taking out the bag of money and placing the familiar looking duffel bag full of yayo in its place. Loon smiled at the thought of how much profit he was gonna make off the twenty keys. At ease that everything was going smoothly and that Tan had set him up with a sexy ass bonus as well, he wasted no time taking off his clothes. He was anxious as hell and silently thanking Tan for setting this shit up.

Once Loon was in the shower, Honey stepped to the window and gave the signal for Tan to come to the room. Tan was back in the room in less than two minutes. Seeing that Loon was still in the shower, she had changed into a khaki-colored trench coat. Underneath, she was rocking a purple leather Teddy that matched the décor of the room. Her gloves and her boots gave her the ultimate dominatrix look. She looked at the chilled bucket of chanpagne on the counter next to the nightstand and smiled at Honey. "Thanks, babe." Tan took out three one hundred dollar bills and placed them in Honey's garter.

Tan had opened her trench and smiled when Loon stepped out of the bathroom with an extra large towel wrapped around his waist.

"Surprise!" Tan yelled excitedly as she dropped her trench coat, revealing her dominatrix outfit to Loon.

"I'll be got-damned!" Loon responded in shock. "I heard your ass was a freak, but I didn't think it was true." Loon was shocked beyond belief at the fact that he was about to fuck Tan's fine ass.

"Well" Tan played coy even though she was repulsed by the comment. "Let's just say money makes me cum and you've been makin' a bitch plenty of that. So I just thought I'd show my appreciation."

"That's what I'm talking about." Loon dropped his towel, showing off his thumb-sized erection peeking through the hair and fat. Tan and Honey tried not to laugh.

"Babe, won't you give us a minute." Tan told Honey and watched as she stepped into the bathroom. "Let's get on the bed," Tan said seductively as she crawled on one side and Loon fell on the other side. She handed Loon a glass and she took one and poured both of them some of the chilled champagne. "To gettin' money . . . and gettin' bad bitches." She nodded toward the bathroom where Honey had gone. "And many more to come," she added. They toasted and both of them downed their first glass. Tan refilled both glasses and she sipped hers slowly while she watched Loon down his like a glass of water. Repulsed, Tan refilled Loon's glass while putting hers down. As Loon downed his third glass, Tan started playing with his dick, wanting to laugh at how firm the tiny dick got in her hand. As she stroked, she realized that the head peeked past her hand just slightly and that Loon was leaking pre-cum. Fortunately, her hands didn't have to touch it as she was still wearing her gloves.

"Damn, girl. Yeah, stroke that big muthaucka," Loon moaned as Tan continued to stroke him with one hand and reached under the pillow and pulled out three small syringes filled with rat poison and battery acid with the other. She switched hands and lowered her face to his dick as if she were going to give him a blowjob. "I'mma get you ready for my girl."

"Hell yeah, suck this shit," Loon commanded, not believing his luck. He couldn't wait to get back to the ATL and brag about this shit to his niggas. He had his eyes closed in ecstasy, so he didn't see when she grabbed the syringes. However, he felt the sting as she jabbed him in his ass with all three needles simultaneously and pressed the caps, releasing the poison. Tan jumped up from the bed and watched as Loon's eyes widened in disbelief. He didn't know what was happening to him as he felt his blood begin to warm in his veins. The acid was already eating away at his arteries.

"You mutha-fuckin' bitch!" He foamed at the mouth while attempting to get up and reach for Tan, but his movements were slow as his circulation weakened. Loon rolled off the side of the bed and went into convulsions as the deadly combination sent him into immediate cardiac arrest.

Tan watched as he took his last exasperated breath. "I told you in the beginning, fat muthafucka . . . fuck with my money and you'd have to leave the country or leave this world. You had a choice to take a journey or take a gurney! Guess you chose the gurney, bitch!"

Just then, Honey came out the bathroom and saw Loon's body lying on the floor with his eyes rolled into the back of his head and foam oozing out the side of his mouth. She let out a shrill scream that was quickly muffled by Tan's hand.

"Bitch, be the fuck quiet!" Tan snapped. "You just as much a part of this shit as I am."

Honey's eyes were wide in disbelief as Tan's hand slowly eased from her mouth. Honey was slowly shaking her head from side to side as if in shock. She mumbled, "You didn't say nothing about killin' nobody. I thought we was robbin' him."

Tan looked her square in the eyes and calmly replied, "We did rob him . . . for his life." She knew she couldn't let Honey leave the room after witnessing this.

Honey was still in shock as Tan walked behind her and coughed into her hand once, spitting out her signature razor. She reached around and promptly sliced Honey's throat with the precision of a surgeon just the way she had done Monk.

***

Satisfied that her crew had cleaned the hotel room in record time and properly disposed of Loon's and Honey's bodies and Loon's car, Tan called it a night and decided to go home.

When she walked in her house, she saw To'Wanda sitting on the couch reading a novel. She leaned over her and kissed her on the lips.

"How was your day?" To'Wanda asked, picking up a bookmark to hold her place.

"I feel so much better, like a huge weight has been lifted off my shoulders." Tan exhaled as she thought of Loon's last moments and was convinced that she had made the right decision. "And in two days, I'mma be able to sleep like a fuckin' baby."

"I just want you to be careful," To'Wanda said cautiously.

Tan looked at her like she was crazy. "What? *Me be careful?* Chile please!"

"I'm serious."

"That bitch a lightweight just like her brother was."

To'Wanda exhaled, as she knew that arguing with Tan would be useless. She saw how happy Tan was when she walked in the house and decided not to mess up the mood. She knew that Tan wanted nothing else in the world than to be rid of Justice, and the sooner that happened, the happier they both would be.

CHAPTER TWENTY

When Lil' Joe walked into BobCutz to meet with Carlos. His uniform was dirty from helping with a few tows that he had made in the area and he was tired as hell. He made his way to the back where the fellas were sitting down. He walked past Preme's chair, observed that he still hadn't cut the locs, but he was just hogging another seat and Lil' Joe shook his head. He noticed Preme grilling him and squinting his eyes real low.

Lil' Joe kept it moving because he wanted to catch Carlos in his office so he could handle his business and be out. Truthfully, even though he had asked Carlos to put him on, he only trusted Carlos as far as he could see him.

Lil' Joe knocked on the door and didn't get an answer. He looked at his watch and noticed that he was on time so he decided to knock again. He turned around when he heard Face rolling past him and then Preme hobbled by as he opened the door without knocking and saw that Carlos was on the phone. "You still a bitch nigga," Preme hissed as he walked past Lil' Joe and took a seat across from Carlos at his desk. Lil' Joe walked in behind Preme.

"Fuck you say, nigga?" Joe wanted Preme to repeat himself. He walked in and took the next available seat across from

Carlos's desk. "I don't like you and I don't trust you. That's what the fuck I said, nigga. Straighten it."

"Fuck you, clown," Lil' Joe said in a voice no higher than a murmur as he leaned forward in the seat. Lil Joe knew Preme never really liked him. Moreover, it all stemmed from a no good ass bitch who they were both fucking back in the day. Sabrina, the bitch who had initially gotten the war started between them and Monk when she had told Carlos that she had seen Cross at the park with Monk and D.C. Throughout the years, that animosity just seemed to grow like the snowball effect. Preme had been more than happy once Lil' Joe had called himself getting out of the game. Now that he was back on the team, Preme was salty because his paper was growing like grass.

"Don't let the third leg fool ya, nigga. I'll still wipe this floor wit' yo' ass." Preme kept the beef going.

Lil' Joe got up and stood over Preme, looking down on him. He wanted to punch the nigga in his grill, but instead, he kicked Preme's cane across the room. Not satisfied, Lil' Joe picked Preme up from his seat and tried to body slam him on Carlos's desk, but Face was holding on to Preme's leg. Carlos reached over his desk to break the two of them up.

"Both of y'all chill the fuck out!" Carlos bellowed, not caring if the customers in the lobby could hear him. He'd gotten between Preme and Lil' Joe, pushing both of them to opposite ends of the room. War had entered the room and quickly rushed to hold Lil' Joe back while Carlos maintained a grip on Preme. "Just chill the fuck out."

Carlos was frustrated because Lil' Joe, Preme, and Face weren't the same obedient niggas he knew two years ago, and

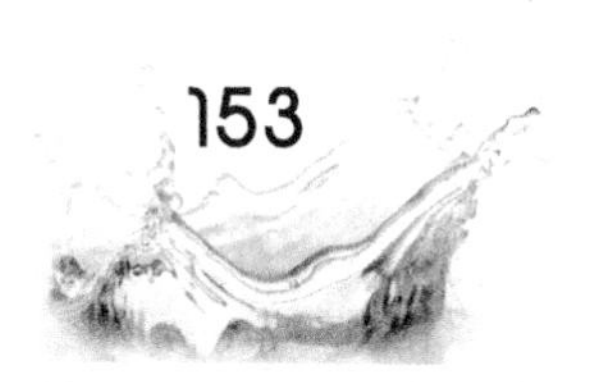

even though he knew he couldn't make the three of them like one another, he hated to see his old crew fall apart. He needed all three of them to be cohesive and bond like glue in order for his team to coexist.

Preme laughed after Carlos loosened up his grip. He reached in his pocket and tossed something to Lil' Joe. Lil' Joe caught it and looked down at it. It was a .45 caliber bullet. "The next one ain't comin' outta my hand, nigga. Trust that," Preme taunted.

Carlos sent Preme out the office with War and closed the door. Preme was still talking loud in the hallway. "I'mma end up sendin' that nigga to hell just like his partna."

"Yo, shut the fuck up!" Carlos yelled, realizing that Preme had just confirmed Lil' Joe's suspicion. He looked at Joe and tried to read any expression indicating that he was listening to what Preme was saying. Joe acted like he hadn't heard him because his expression hadn't changed and Carlos was hoping that was the case. Joe was sarcastically smirking while looking at the bullet Preme had tossed him.

"I brought y'all niggas back together 'cause I thought we could go back to gettin' money like we used to. But if y'all wanna go to war with each other, do that shit in the streets and not in my muthafuckin' office. Stupid ass niggas."

Lil' Joe reached in both of his pockets, slammed two knot-fulls of money on the desk, and reached in his waist for the paper bag full of money he'd stuffed in his pants. "Here go yo' muthafuckin' money, nigga. Y'all niggas ain't shit." He nodded his head slowly with fire in his eyes.

Seeing the look in Lil' Joe's eyes, Carlos knew without a doubt that he had heard Preme's statement. Now it was no secret that they had been the ones that had bodied Dave. Lil' Joe slammed the bag on the desk as well. He took a step back and glared at Carlos. "Yeah, I'll see you," Lil' Joe said sarcastically while still nodding his head and biting his bottom lip in anger. He calmly walked out of the office and out into the hall where War stood in front of Preme, blocking him from Lil' Joe. Lil' Joe tossed the bullet back at Preme and stated, "I'll see you in the streets, nigga." He exited the barbershop.

"Aye Unc," War spoke up from the hallway. "You want me to let this nigga go?" He was referring to Preme. War knew if Carlos said yes, Preme was going to slump Lil Joe immediately. Carlos thought about it for a moment, then told War, "Nah, let him calm down for a minute. Preme, you need anger management, nigga," Carlos joked. "But straight up, you know that nigga already feelin' some kinda way about Dave. Now, he *know* we did that shit. Keep an eye out for that nigga. I doubt if he'd test a nigga's gangsta, but don't put nothin' past that nigga right now."

"Fuck dat nigga! You need to let me eliminate that problem so a nigga ain't even gotta worry about it," Preme stated as he limped back into the office.

"Nah, we gotta chill wit' the bodies. That nigga, Chief Monroe on his game right now because the crackas from *First 48* down here filming. They ain't slippin' right now. Shit is tighter than mosquito pussy."

They all nodded in agreement. It was true, ever since the hit TV show *First 48* had been filming in Charlotte; homicide detectives had been solving murders in record time. They all agreed they would chill with the violence unless they felt it was absolutely necessary.

CHAPTER TWENTY-ONE

I can't believe you talked me into coming to Chicago with your ass," Sapphire said as she put her carry-on bag in the overhead compartment and sat next to Justice. "And you got me in the back of the plane. You are wrong for that."

Justice looked up from the Nook she had just purchased. She was reading *Shiesty 3 by T.N. Baker*. "Girl, stop complainin'. I had to kidnap yo' ass to take you to Greensboro just so you could get outta town for a little while." Justice pushed her hair back and took a deep breath. "You wasn't complainin' when we was at Four Seasons Mall spending up Carlos's money or when we went to the Maxwell and Jill Scott concert."

Sapphire smiled as she looked down at her Red Bottom boots, courtesy of the two stacks Carlos had laced her with earlier. If one didn't know any better they would have thought that Sapphire was Carlos's bitch. Sapphire looked at the black business-style blouse and slacks Justice had on, courtesy of the trip as well.

"So you really are startin' to feel Carlos again?" Sapphire asked.

Before Justice could answer, the flight attendants were doing a song and dance on how to put on the seat belt and how to conduct oneself in the event of an emergency. A few of the passengers were seen pulling out their smart phones so they could put the routine on YouTube.

After the routine, everyone clapped and Sapphire noted, "Lemme find out we stepped on *Soul Plane.*"

"You would think we did." Justice looked up momentarily. If Sapphire hadn't been the chick talking her ear off, she would've regretted not bringing her headphones to tune out the distraction. She hated to be talked to during flights.

"But back to what I was saying. Things gettin' serious with you and Carlos again?"

"We'll see," Justice said, looking up from her electronic book again. "It's not like I let the nigga fuck—we just talked a few times and I hung out with him one more time after Amélie's. When he gave me the money, it wasn't like I asked for it. If that nigga think he gonna get some because he was financing that cheap ass trip to Greensboro to get shit I could've got in Charlotte or better yet, Chicago, then he got a long way to go."

Those were the words she told Sapphire but in reality, her and Carlos hung out more than just one time after they all had dinner. In fact, they saw each other four times while she was in Charlotte. The first three times were movies, dinner, and deep conversation, getting to know one another again. It was the fourth date when Carlos made his move. Justice almost fell weak, and as much as she wanted to give in, she stuck to her guns and it didn't happen. She had forgiven him for the most part and was actually starting to lose her reserve but deep down inside, she could not help but to reflect on how his anger had caused so much turmoil in her life. And for that very reason, she felt as though she was at a crossroad and didn't know which path to follow.

"Aw, go easy on the brother," Sapphire teased. She wished she had brought a book to read and was frustrated that she couldn't see the words on the Nook from where she was sitting. "You done forgave yet?"

Justice nodded her head. Sapphire's persistence and Carlos's remorse had paid off. She had forgiven Carlos but she could never foget. However, nothing would change the fact that Monk was still in the ground. And somebody was answering for that.

***

Given the drama that had taken place not too long ago, Justice almost didn't take Sapphire to the club; but since Sapphire had never been there before, Justice figured she could take the risk.

"Oh shit, this is nice!" Sapphire shouted when she saw the Phire & Ice insignia on the building. A prideful tear almost escaped her eyes. Although she had heard about the club and had seen countless pictures, Sapphire was still in awe. "I still can't believe you did this."

Without having to be told, she knew that she was the *Phire* and that Justice was the *Ice*.

"I had to do something with that money I got from J.T." Justice confirmed as she took out her key and proceeded to open the door. "We earned that money and I needed a legal hustle, so this is what it is."

"Sistah, I ain't mad." Sapphire followed her in and proceeded to walk down the hallway. "I know you don't have this long hallway for the niggas to come through. What happens if a fight or fire breaks out or shit get outta control?"

"Girl, this *the back* of the club." Justice looked at Sapphire as if she were crazy. Then it dawned on her that her girl hadn't been in a strip club before. "Let's go to my office, I need to change and you can take your nosey ass and snoop around a lil' bit," Justice teased.

Justice led Sapphire to the office and allowed her to marvel at the décor. Justice reached into her closet and grabbed a bag containing more casual wear and some sneakers and rushed into her private bathroom and did a quick change. When she came out, she was wearing sneakers and some tight-fitting Robin jeans that showed off her curves.

"Girl, look at you." Sapphire admired Justice's figure as she walked out of the bathroom ready to meet and greet with the patrons and the staff. "I ain't seen you in jeans in so long, I ain't think you owned a pair."

"I wear jeans all the time, what the hell you talkin' 'bout? Anyway, wait 'til you see these bitches on the floor. I'on know where these hoes be buyin' these bodies from but you 'bouta see some unreal shit." Justice said as they left her office. She made sure the door was locked and they walked down the hallway that led to the main club area. Justice could tell that Sapphire was shocked to see just as many women in the lounge area as there were men.

"Damn, it's a lotta dykes in here." Sapphire turned her nose up.

"Nah, these bitches come in here because they know this where the ballin' niggas at. Half of 'em ain't payin' these dancers no attention. They peepin' these niggas, tryna see who got the deepest pockets. It's all game babe, and I most def can't knock their hustle."

Sapphire watched as a thick dark-skinned chick wrapped her ass cheeks around a pole comfortably. Sapphire knew she had a nice ass as well, but there was no way in hell her ass cheeks could wrap around a damn pole.

"Hey girl," a young dude who looked like he couldn't have been out of high school addressed Sapphire. "Why don't you get on stage and shake sumpthin'?"

Sapphire laughed and shook her head. "Nah bruh, I don't work here. I'm with my girl, Justice." She stated as she pointed at her girl.

"Aww damn," the young man pouted. "I wanted to see what that fat ass look like outside them clothes. He took out a stack of ones and threw a few in the air towards Justice and Sapphire.

"No this nigga didn't." Sapphire stated with much attitude.

Justice felt totally diserespected! This was her establishment and no one was going to treat her like an employee in her own shit. "You wanna see somethin'? How about you see my foot up yo' ass. Matter fact, see the door nigga." She turned towards her security guy and motioned for him to come over. As security approached, the young man started pleading with Justice not to have him put out.

She ordered the security, "Twin, put that nigga out or make him pay to stay."

Twin turned his six-four, three hundred pound frame towards the table of young niggas and asked Justice, "which one?"

"That lil disrespectful ass nigga in the Gucci." Justice pointed at the young man who had thrown the money at her. Then she and Sapphire walked off.

"Got'cha." Twin replied, and then motioned with his finger for the young man to come to him. Once he was in earshot Twin told him "I'on know what you did but you just pissed the boss lady off." He paused, then continued, "Now, she want me to put yo' lil ass out but I'mma let you stay."

"Preciate that big dog" The young man replied and turned to go back to his table.

Twin put a hand on his shoulder. "But it's gonna cost you. Run them pockets nigga."

The young man sighed ,"damn, y'all some real hustlas up in this bitch" he reached into his pocket and dug out some money and gave it to Twin.

"That's what's up." Twin grinned, and then added, "Next time recognize the bitches from the boss. Now y'all lil niggas enjoy y'all's night. And don't make me have'ta come the fuck back over here." Twin glared at them then made his exit. Twin caught up with Justice and Sapphire and handed Justice all but fifty dollars of the money he had taken from the young man.

"Good look, Twin. And make sure them niggas don't get outta line."

"No doubt." He replied, and then walked off.

Once Twin was gone, Justice handed the money to Sapphire. "That lil nigga said he wanted to see you. Guess he paid to see you walk away, huh?"

"Chile, I ain't arguin' with that." Sapphire laughed and stuffed the bills in the back pocket of her jeans.

As Justice and Sapphire walked past the dressing room, Virgin and Precious were leaving the room ready to perform. Justice rolled her eyes and Sapphire noticed the tension between her girl and the two chicks. Virgin pretended to be cleaning her nails as she walked into Sapphire on purpose, damn-near knocking her into the wall.

"I know that ain't a new bitch you got comin' in here on a weekday." Precious was loud and ghetto as she addressed Justice.

"Yeah, this bitch couldda said excuse me too." Virgin looked Sapphire up and down and then shoved her into the wall. "Don't she know who *really* got the say-so in this bitch? This my spot!"

Sapphire regained her footing and without hesitation, she backhanded Virgin with her left hand. Then she followed up with a fist to the same cheek. Sapphire pulled Virgin by her weave, pulling some of it out and started banging her head against the wall. "Bitch, you must not know who I am!" Sapphire yelled as she delivered an uppercut, landing on Virgin's grill. Virgin spit up some blood on her white laced Teddy. "*My* name on the fuckin' marquee, bitch. *You* better recognize!" Sapphire's anger and sudden violent temper shocked Justice for a moment. Justice knew Sapphire had it in her, but she was just astounded to see it come out of her so easily.

Sapphire had set it off and all of the anger that had been built up in Justice for those two bitches came rushing to the surface. Justice turned to a stunned Precious while Sapphire continued to go to work on Virgin. Justice started throwing upper cuts and hooks, boxing Precious as if she were Laila Ali. In between dodging Precious's windmill-like swings, Justice connected with combinations just the way Monk had taught her. For each time Precious called her a bitch, Justice delivered a fist to her jaw. Justice and Sapphire felt arms pulling them off of their victims as a small crowd gathered in the hallway.

"Get these bitches outta here!" Justice ordered her security team as she shook off the miscellaneous hands that were holding her back.

"Oh, no bitch, it ain't over," Precious spewed while spitting blood from her mouth, while a loose tooth hung on by a thread. Then it fell out. "Oh, hell no, bitch!" She bent down to pick it up. "I know all about how you killed that nigga you was fuckin' and that's how you opened this place." Precious struggled to get free from the security team and continued to run off at the mouth.

Virgin chimed in, "Yeah, bitch, we know all about that shit. You and that bitch gonna get y'alls, believe that." She struggled to free herself from security. "Fuck that! Lemme go. I gotta get my shit outta the dressin' room."

Just then, Toni walked up with her hand to her mouth in shock. "Toni, get them bitches shit and toss it out wit' they asses," Justice instructed.

Justice stood there breathing heavily with her arms crossed over her chest, shaking her head as her security team escorted the two troublemakers out of the club. She knew she was gonna have to fix her problems with the two of them once and for all. After checking on Sapphire to make sure she was okay, she looked at the dispersing crowd and saw one of the local known jack-boys in the back. Just that quickly, her devious mind began formulating a plan.

CHAPTER TWENTY-TWO

Red dipped back in the front seat of the car and watched everyone come in and out of BobCutz. He had hoped he would catch Carlos slipping because he knew that this day was his day to come to the shop. Red wanted so bad to get another shot at that man—he felt the last job that J T, Cross, and he did was incomplete—Carlos was still breathing. His plan was to follow Carlos to his house and he and Chris would murk him and take him for everything he had. He remembered how the plan went without a hitch last time; so good that Monk and D. C. took the fall for that shit.

After he got Carlos out of the way, he would continue his search for Justice. Kim was good for keeping up with what a nigga was doing, but when it was time for her to find a bitch, she was proving to be just as useless as a wet postage stamp. He watched as some of Kim's friends were going in and out of the shop in preparation for the upcoming night. The Bobcats were playing the Lakers at home and Wale and Rick Ross were performing that same night at Club Lux. Needless to say all the groupies were making sure they were looking their best for a baller or a sucker for sponsorship.

"You see that Mercury Cougar?" Chris had tapped Red on the shoulder, jarring him out of his daze and causing him to focus on the mission at hand. "That belongs to Preme; he drives that up here every day." Red looked in the direction Chris was pointing and took note of the car. "And the black Taurus, that's Carlos's nephew, War's car. Carlos and that nigga look alike except War got a few cuts in his eyebrows and bigger lips. Now his other boy, Joe, something . . . whatever the fuck his name is, he got two cars. The orange Pontiac he drives when he's here on business and the blue F-150 he drives when he's just getting his hair cut. But he ain't been up here in a minute. Kim said he fell out with them niggas."

Red looked at Chris as she shook the platinum blonde, bob-style cut wig hiding her locs. The wig was a different look for Chris and almost made her look like Faith Evans when she first came out on the arms of B. I. G.

Red needed to be one hundred percent sure about everything. As bad as he wanted to catch Carlos, he wasn't looking to fuck up. If he had to, he would abandon the plan, and just get that nigga another day.

While sitting in the car it had begun to rain a little. Then the rain began to pour for a few minutes, making the visibility undesirable. Red started to turn on the windshield wipers but decided against it, figuring that it would give his position away if he didn't get out the car.

"Anyway, the white Chevy Tahoe is Carlos's and no one drives it but him."

Red smiled. This was news he wanted to hear. "You ready?" He asked.

"No doubt . . . but hold that thought. I gotta go to the bathroom. Be back in a minute."

Before Red could object, Chris had already hopped out and

slammed the door. The light rain had let up again and the sun was once again peeking through the clouds. Red watched the Tahoe like a hawk and then noticed movement from the shop. He saw Carlos exit the building and place a travel bag in the back seat of the Tahoe. Red picked up his phone and started calling Chris.

"Yo, the nigga gettin' in the car."

"Okay cool, I'm coming outta da deli in a minute." Red turned on the ignition and was relieved to see Chris running out of the building. He watched as the Tahoe made a left turn out of the shopping center, and once Chris was inside, they followed the Tahoe out onto W.T. Harris Boulevard.

CHAPTER TWENTY-TWO

Justice hated that she and Sapphire had to beat some bitches down during her first trip to Chi-town but they had to set an example. To celebrate, Justice had taken her to see the Chicago Bulls play at a home game and she treated Sapphire like royalty.

After seeing Sapphire off to the airport, Justice met her father Tyson at the Buckingham Fountain. She hadn't seen him in a few weeks and she was missing him. She also hadn't been to the Fountain since she was a little girl before she and Monk moved to Charlotte. She appreciated the view of Lake Michigan and the weather was perfect for them to walk around and enjoy the view.

Tyson arrived and she greeted him with a hug and a kiss on his gruffy cheek. "Hey old man."

"Hey baby girl. You been dissin' me lately. What's goin on with you? Everything ok?"

"Yeah everything's good. And NO I haven't been dissin' you. I been busy workin'. And you been outta town so don't even try it." Justice replied as she took his hand and they began walking. How you been?" she asked.

"I'm good. Blood pressure been a lil' higher than usual lately but all in all I'm good."

"I told you about that pork and all that red meat," she looked

at him. "Why men so bullheaded and stubborn?"

Tyson laughed because she always got on him about his eating habits. "You already know I ain't leavin' my pork chops alone."

Justice just shook her head because she knew she was fighting a losing battle as usual. He was stuck in his ways and there was no changing that. She decided to change the subject. "Sapphire just left."

"I know. I hate I missed her. How she holdin' up?" He asked.

Justice thought back to how Sapphire was throwing blows a few days earlier and she replied "Oh, trust she is doing *very* well."

"That's good. It helps that she's got a friend like you who can relate to her situation. Someone who has also been through it" Tyson replied.

"Do you ever think about her? My mama?" Justice asked. At the mention of Justice's mother, they both felt a sense of dread wash over them for a moment. "Every waking hour. I also think about Monk and your brother, Joaquin. I still can't get over the fact that they were both murdered on the same day and no one has been charged with their deaths." He shook his head.

Just hearing J.T.'s name being mentioned caused Justice to feel queasy.

"Let's not talk about them right now. Let's just enjoy this father-daughter outing on this beautiful day." She did not want to think about her dead brothers at the time.

They walked to *Bobtail Ice Cream and Coffee* and got two scoops of their favorite homemade strawberry ice cream.

Walking through the park with her father had her feeling like a little kid again and it brought calmness to her soul.

Justice and her father spent the next few hours walking and talking, catching up on what they had been missing out on in each other's lives over the past few weeks before Tyson announced that he had to leave. "I'll see you soon, babe. Call me when you get home." Her father instructed.

"I will. Love you daddy."

"Love you too baby." Tyson responded with a genuine smile as he walked towards his car.

Justice was not yet ready to leave so she returned to her car and got her Nook so she could finish reading the book she had started on the plane. She found a nice quiet spot near a large oak tree in the park they had passed earlier and she sat down with her reading material and her ice cream. As soon as she pulled the book up and found her bookmark, her phone rang and she picked up immediately, seeing that Toni was calling from her office. She had hoped that after having to beat a bitch, there wouldn't be any more fuckery at the club.

"Hey Toni," Justice said excitedly, hoping to set the tone for the conversation.

"Bitch, where have you been?" Toni shouted into the phone. Justice peeled the phone away from her ear and looked at the screen again to verify that she was talking to Toni. "I've been tryna get in touch with you for the past few hours." Toni added.

"What's up?" Justice asked with a little venom in her voice.

"Giiiirl, I don't know if you heard or not, but Virgin, Precious, and Sincere got killed last night."

"WHAT?!!" Justice screamed. She looked around and

noticed a few patrons in the park were staring in her direction. She composed herself and continued to listen to Toni for details.

"Yeah. Word on the street is they agreed to meet up with some guys who was looking for some kind of orgy and they tried to set the niggas up to get robbed."

"Get the fuck outta here!" Justice didn't care whether or not she was disturbing anyone in the park.

"Yeah, fucked me up too when I heard it."

Justice stood up and grabbed her Nook. "When you hear this?"

"Earlier. That's why a bitch been blowin' yo' phone up."

"Damn girl." Justice sighed.

"I know, right." Toni stated, and then added, "I hate to sound so cold-hearted, but I'm glad them bitches gone."

"Me too," Justice let it slip. She didn't miss those bitches one bit, and she could picture her life at Phire & Ice being a whole lot easier.

"Well, you gonna like one of the new girls I got. She bad as hell!"

Justice could tell from the tone of her voice, something more was going on and decided to call her on it. "Toni, what I tell you about messin' with the dancers."

"No Justice, I got it under control. I saw this one before in Atlanta when I went on vacation last year, and we been talking through e-mail and on the phone for a while."

"Aiight." Justice exhaled. "I'm tellin' you now, I don't want no shit. You know how you be flirtin', and you know how bitches quick to get in they feelings."

"It ain't gonna be no shit, I promise."

"Well, you get back to watchin' the club, and lemme know if you hear some more details about what happened with them girls.

"Aiight." Toni sighed. "Man, karma's a bitch, huh?"

"Yup. I'm just glad to be on her team."

"Huh?" Toni asked.

"Never mind. I'll holla at'cha later."

Justice hung up the phone and a smile crept across her face. She loved it when a good plan came together! When her idea to get Travis, the local stick up kid to go along with her idea of robbing an old dope boy, she wasn't sure if she could depend on the young man to handle the job. As it turned out, Travis had become very resourceful.

Justice had told Travis about a dope boy she knew that was a regular at the club who had it like running water. Instinctively, his thirsty ass antennas went up. She told him where the dude rested his head and where he reportedly kept the money and drugs hidden. When asked how she knew so much about the nigga, Justice told him that she had fucked him a time or two, and he had gotten comfortable enough to let his stash spot be located. He had gotten drunk one night and tried to impress Justice by going to a wall safe and extracting racks upon racks of dough, reiterating the fact that was Boss! Justice played along with him and acted nonchalantly about the money in the safe. However, her sheisty ass was doing somersaults as she schemed and plotted.

Hearing about all of the potential money he would get from this nigga, Travis already began spending it in his head. All

Justice said she wanted out of the deal was five grand. She knew throwing an exact amount at him would make him think she knew exactly what she was talking about. Justice also told him that the dude was just like most tricks that frequented the club: He was a sucker for a bad bitch. And what better bitches to use for the job other than the two baddest that had once worked at the club. "You already know I don't like them bitches, but Precious and Virgin would be perfect for that," she had told him. "The only thing about it, you gotta promise you don't mention my name, especially to them two."

"Ah, Justice, you already know how I carry it. You done heard about my pedigree. I ain't made it out here in this game this long by runnin' my mouth," he assured her. "Them bitches ain't gonna know shit other than they goin' to get some dough wit' me. When I tell 'em I'mma throw 'em a few grand, they ain't gonna ask no questions anyway."

Justice told Travis everything he needed to know about getting into the dope dealer's spot. What she failed to mention was the fact that he had security cameras and three ruthless niggas who busted nuts by squeezing triggers. No one had ever been able to touch this nigga, and the last ones that had tried to jack him ended up found floating in Lake Michigan. Justice was hoping that Travis didn't know the dude, because if he did, there would be no way in hell he'd try to pull this off. From the conversation, she gathered that Travis did not know him.

Later, justice would find out that Travis had convinced Precious and Virgin to go along with him and his part-time girl, Sincere, to pull off the caper. Once the three girls had gained entry to the guy's spot by enticing him, Travis burst through the door brandishing two pistols and yelling demands. What Travis didn't know was that one nigga was hiding in the bedroom and two more were in the basement watching the scene unfold on the security monitors. Before Travis could get into the living room good, he was met with a hail of bullets from the guy in the bedroom. Moments later, the two men who had emerged from the basement also executed the three girls. The element of surprise! All four died right there in the dude's living room, but were dragged into the garage and loaded into two SUVs. Kids who were playing hide and seek found the bodies the next day in an empty field.

She still had NO idea how those two bitches had known so much about her. However, now it didn't even matter! Justice licked her lips and nodded her head as she began feeling a sense of rejuvenation knowing that her secret was now safe. She also knew now that her biggest concern was Tan.

CHAPTER TWENTY-FOUR

Red turned down the volume on the system and proceeded to get his mind right. It was time to get into murder mode. He was trailing Carlos's Tahoe on I-85.

"Time to put this nigga on ice," Red said as he saw the Tahoe get off Exit 52 heading into Huntersville. He sped past a slow-moving car and went from being three cars behind them to just one.

"Relax, babe," Chris said as she started straightening out her wig in the rearview mirror and readjusting her glasses. "All we gotta do is follow this nigga to his spot and we in like Flynn."

Red nodded his head and pictured himself putting two hot ones in Carlos's chest. His mind was on murder as he drove west on Poplar Tent Road and made a left at the Huntersville-Concord Road light. The blue Saturn in front of them made a turn at the Skybrook Golf Club, leaving only asphalt between themselves and the Tahoe.

As they were directly behind the Tahoe, they continued to trail at a car length's distance. Chris took out the Glock in the glove compartment and popped in the clip.

"I want this nigga to see my face." Red said. All he could see was Cross lying in the back of that blood-splattered taxi two years ago. He wanted his revenge for that shit.

"Fuck that. We need to surprise this nigga," Chris told him. "We gonna stick to the plan. Follow the nigga to his house, get the loot, then bust him in his ass and be out." Chris's mind was moreso on money than murder, but she knew death for Carlos was inevitable today.

Red exhaled. He knew the time was coming soon for him to put an end to Carlos's life, and he was more than ready to get it poppin'. He continued to follow the Tahoe until they were in a secluded subdivision. He could see the waters of Lake Norman behind some of the houses.

Red watched the Tahoe make a turn down a long stretch of dirt road, which led to a house that sat on the lake. He gave the Tahoe a three-minute window before slowly creeping down the dirt road behind it. Once Red almost reached the end of the road they watched Carlos exit the Tahoe and enter the house.

"Damn, this shit too easy." Red laughed. He and Chris simultaneously exited the car and quickly walked toward the house in which Carlos had entered.

Once they reached the house, Red and Chris both crept around to the back. The house sat alone near the woods that surrounded the large lake, which was perfect for robbing this nigga and leaving him leaking. No neighbors to hear the gunshots.

Red eased his way up to the back door and listened for movement. He didn't hear anything, so he looked at Chris and gave the signal that he would kick the door in on the count of two. He rose one finger in the air, and as soon as he rose the second, the back door flew open and all Red could see was a flash of light. Then he felt the thud that hit him square in the chest, knocking him off the back porch. Red landed on his back in the damp grass. He heard a second shot that was not quite as loud, and heard a shrill scream that came from a voice he recognized as Chris's.

Red's chest was leaking blood like a faucet as he tried his best to roll over and crawl toward the pistol he had dropped. His limbs would barely move and his vision was becoming blurry.

Chris was on her knees trying to crawl to the side of the house, but the gunshot she'd taken to the side was too unbearable for her to stand it. She heard another shot and felt her limbs go numb as she fell face first in the grass. This bullet pierced her spine, instantly causing paralysis. The pain was gone, but her limbs were immobile. The wig had fallen from her head and her locs were now visible. Out of the corner of her eye, Chris saw someone walking toward her. As the person neared, she noticed he was carrying a wooden cane and had a slight limp. Preme recognized the girl from the barbershop just before he raised his pistol and let off two more shots that entered her head, ending her life.

Red was still lying in the grass, struggling to breathe as blood poured from his chest where the shotgun had blasted him. His vision was still blurry, but he was coherent enough to know that Chris was undoubtedly dead from the gunshots he'd just heard.

Preme walked over to Red and bent down to whisper in his ear. "Fuck nigga, you think my man didn't peep y'all followin' him?" He laughed. "We been doin' this shit for years. We *stay* on point, bitch." Just then, Preme felt a hand on his shoulder telling him to move aside.

Once Preme was out of the way, Red looked at the man who was now standing before him. Once Red saw the lines in the man's eyebrows, he realized he had been following the wrong man the entire time.

War raised the shotgun and let it rip! The slug entered Red's throat and exited out the back of his neck. He died instantly!

Good thing Preme was home when War had called and said he was being followed. If not, War would've had to handle this situation on his own. Preme limped back inside his home followed by War and made a phone call. Now it was time for the bodies to be disposed of.

CHAPTER TWENTY-FIVE

The young women walking past Carlos looked like they had just come off the catwalk as opposed to being flight attendants for his trip. He watched as their long hair danced off their shoulders and flew as if a gust of wind had blown by as opposed to them dragging their rolling suitcases to catch their next flight at the United terminal at Chicago O'Hare International Airport. Had their skirts been a little bit shorter, those jiggling cheeks could have played peek-a-boo.

The phone vibrated in Carlos's pocket. He pulled it out to see that Preme was calling him. "What it do?"

"We gotta problem, bruh."

"What kinda problem?" Carlos wanted to know.

"This shit crazy as hell." Preme sighed. "That nigga Red from back in da day . . ."

"Red?" Carlos cut him off. "Red who? Not the nigga who robbed my spot a couple years ago?"

"Yeah, *that* nigga."

"You seen that nigga?" Carlos fumed.

"That's what I called to tell you. Him and that bitch who just started comin' to the shop wit' Kim followed War in yo' truck."

"The cute bitch wit' the dreads?" Carlos was confused.

"Yeah, but she ain't that cute no more. They followed War, and War called me while they was behind him. I told him to come up to my spot on the lake just to see if they would follow him here. They did, and they got what they was lookin' fo'," Preme reported.

"You think they was on some robbin' shit or what?" Carlos asked as he walked out the airport and stood on the curb.

"I'on know. But they both had ratchets and didn't get a chance to squeeze."

"Where they at now?" He wanted to know what happened to the bodies.

"I called ole boy an' nem already. They on the way to clean this shit up," Preme reported.

Carlos rubbed his temples and let a deep sigh escape his lips. "Aiight, tell 'em I'll pay him when I get back."

"Get back? From where?"

"I just landed in ChiTown."

Preme let out a sarcastic grunt. "Wow . . . damn, bruh. Lemme find out that bitch got you like that."

"Nah, I just need to check some shit out. Tan pressin' a nigga for info I ain't got. I need to get that."

"Yeah, aiight, *info,*" Preme stated sarcastically, and then added, "You know they prolly thought nephew was you."

"Yeah, I just thought about that," Carlos replied. "Hit me after they clean that shit up."

"Aiight, bruh. One."

"One." Carlos ended the call. After he hung up he thought about what Preme had just told him and it confused the hell out of him. What was Kim's friend doing with that nigga, Red? He went through scenario after scenario and couldn't put the pieces together.

He realized that whatever their intentions were, they failed miserably and it had cost them. Carlos dismissed that situation and decided that he'd deal with it once he returned from Chicago.

***

Carlos pulled up to Justice's block. He picked up the phone and scrolled down to find Sapphire's number. As soon as he came across it, he pressed the TALK button. Sapphire answered within one ring. Carlos told her his location and asked whether or not she was sure Justice was home.

"Yeah, I'm sure," Sapphire told him. "I just got off the phone with her. If I didn't know better, I'd think you kinda shook."

"Nah, never that," Carlos reassured her, "I just wanna make sure she ain't got company an' shit. You know a nigga up here wit' no pistol."

"Boy, you don't need no gun. You'll be aiight. Where you at now?"

"I'm pullin' up now. GPS had a nigga lost for thirty minutes."

Carlos got out of the rental car and listened to Sapphire tease him about being scared to surprise Justice, while he grabbed a dozen roses from the passenger's seat. He grabbed the Godiva dark chocolate truffles gift box and exited the car.

He walked confidently to her condo and rang the doorbell.

After waiting for a few seconds, Justice came to the door wearing a silk pink bathrobe with matching slippers. She cracked the door and was shocked as hell to see Carlos standing there holding flowers. She immediately slammed the door and left him standing there.

"What the fuck?" Carlos muttered. He knew she would be caught off guard, but he didn't expect this kind of reaction. He rang the bell again and heard Justice holler from somewhere inside the condo. "Wait a minute!"

Carlos stood there for about five minutes, looking stupid as hell while Justice moved about inside. A few more minutes passed before Justice finally opened the door for him.

"What the hell you doing here?" Justice asked, looking at him with a slight smirk.

"Nice to see you, too." Carlos handed Justice the card and the candies.

"Sapphire gave you my address?" Justice asked as she folded her arms across her breasts.

"Nah, I Googled your important ass," he replied sarcastically. "You know she did. How else a nigga gonna get it?" Carlos said with a smile.

Justice pulled out the card from the bouquet and read it aloud: "Mistakes are human, but forgiveness is epic."

Justice smiled at the irony of the words. She put the card back in the placeholder, took the dozen roses with one hand and Carlos's hand with the other, and led him inside her home.

Carlos stepped inside and was impressed with the simple, yet modern-style of her home. The pearl colored sofa set looked soft as cotton balls and when he sat down, he liked how easily his frame sank in, almost like quicksand. He looked at the black oriental style lamp with its ancient animated frame. He was about to reach for the remote for the television when he heard Justice grunt.

"You want somethin' to drink?" Justice asked.

"Yeah, what you got?"

"Tea" she replied while pouring him a cup. She brought it to him and he took it from her hand.

Carlos took a sip, "thanks."

Justice sat on the love seat. She reached for the remote and turned *Basketball Wives* off. She watched as he swallowed the tea in the next sip as if he had not drunk anything all day. After taking a sip of tea herself, she sat back on the sofa and stared at him. Justice had taken a slight liking to him, but she wasn't quite sure she wanted him in her house at the moment.

"So what brings you here?" Justice got to the point.

Carlos looked at her in shock because he hadn't expected her to be so blunt with him. "I came to see you—maybe find out what your plans were."

"You should've called first." Justice played the tough girl role. Even though a small part of her was happy to see him, she didn't want Carlos to get the impression that he could just come to her house whenever-the-fuck-he-felt-like-it. He had to earn that and Justice was determined to make sure that he did just that.

"You want me to leave?" Carlos was clearly agitated. He didn't know what kind of game Justice was playing but he was two seconds from saying fuck it and going on about his business. There were plenty of bitches in Chicago who would love him to wine and dine them and then keep him up all night long. His problem was that he wanted to do those things with Justice.

"Want you to leave?" She repeated his words, "Hell, I didn't ask you to come."

"You funny," Carlos got up and straightened his clothes. "I come here and you got a nasty attitude and shit. I thought I'd surprise you with some flowers, and some chocolates—maybe take you on a walk or to dinner or somewhere. Anything to get you out of the house and to spend some time with you."

Carlos looked at Justice and he could see that she was in thought about what he said. After not getting a response, he turned to walk out of the door. As he turned the knob, he felt Justice pulling his arm back. "Wait—don't leave." She stopped him.

"Why shouldn't I?" Carlos was sharp with her. He could see that Justice could tell that she'd pissed him off. "You play them high school games with them clown niggas you used to dealing with." Carlos opened the door and stepped out.

Carlos walked to his rental, heated that he had flown all the way from Charlotte to try to spend some time with Justice and to see where their relationship could go and her response was some bullshit. He sat in the car fuming. As far as Carlos was concerned, she could shove the candy and the flowers in her ass.

Tap-tap-tap! Carlos could hear someone tapping on the passenger side window. He unlocked the door when he saw Justice standing outside. Justice opened the door and got in. He looked at her and then he looked away.

"I'm just trying to figure this shit out okay!" Justice

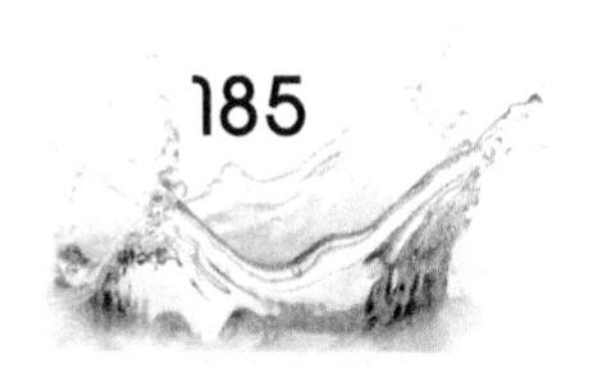

defended herself.

"What is it to figure out?"

"You went from loving me to being my fuck buddy—to trying to kill me behind some shit I had nothing to do with—now you love me again." Justice said as she put the seatbelt on. Carlos turned on the ignition and he pulled away from her condominium. "I told you that I had nothing to do with them running up in your spot—didn't even know who was involved in it and you ignored me like I was some random, basic bitch.

Carlos shook his head and acknowledged the truth. He remembered ignoring her calls and messages. "You ran with Cross and I warned Monk not to try me—what did you expect?"

"I expected you to believe me and trust that I'd *never* let Monk cross you. I did not know Cross was running with Red and J.T. I pieced together the puzzle after the fact and that was after y'all tried to kill Monk at TGI Fridays. Hell, I didn't even know that Sapphire was fuckin' Cross until after she told me that's why he was at her house the day yall killed him."

Carlos felt guilty because this was the first time he was hearing the truth. He didn't even know that Sapphire and Cross was fucking, but that made since for him to have left her house like that. That made him feel extra bad for how Ali later reported that Sapphire had been handled.

"T.G.I. Fridays." Carlos sighed. "That wasn't even my call," he looked over at Justice and admitted "Tan ordered the hit on Monk and D.C."

Confused, Justice locked heated eyes with Carlos to see if he was lying about what he had just revealed. The look in his eyes told her that he was telling the truth. "Grimey ass bitch."

she mumbled under her breath as she turned back toward the window and stared out as if in a daze. That revelation had just added fuel to the fire and Justice's blood was starting to boil.

Carlos hated to admit it, but this conversation had to happen if he expected to move forward with Justice. Just as he had to trust her, he knew that Justice needed to believe that she could trust him and that he wouldn't snap off on her like that again.

"So where does this leave us?" Carlos got straight to the point. He hadn't realized it, but he was just a couple of blocks from U.S. Celluar Stadium. The crowd was getting thick from all of the Cubs fans exiting the stadium from a pre-season game.

"If we gonna be together, we need to be together—if not, then we'd probably do better to go our separate ways. Because this time around I ain't tryna just be a booty call" Carlos joked, then turned to face her. He took her hand in his, "I wanna be with you."

He looked in Justice's eyes and he knew she was trying to decipher whether or not he was telling the truth.

"You wanna be with me—you gonna have to prove it."

"And how am I gonna do that?"

"Help me find Tan."

Carlos exhaled slowly. "Come on, Justice."

"Naw fuck that," Justice didn't back down. "I knew that bitch asked about me when I was in Charlotte and you think I forgot about that shit because I never brought it up again. I got news for you—I'm gonna get that bitch one way or another so you can choose. Either be with me when I bury that bitch or watch that shit from the sideline. Because trust, it's gonna happen."

Carlos thought long and hard before responding. His jaws had tightened. He took a deep breath and let out an exasperated sigh before reluctantly responding "aiight, I'll help you."

For the next few minutes, there was awkward silence. An old school Musiq Soulchild cut about love was playing in the background as Carlos had begun to approach her condo again. Carlos hadn't realized that he'd driven in a circle. Once he pulled up to her spot, Justice jumped out of the car. He turned off the ignition, got out of the car, and caught up with her. "I'm serious, I'm on Team Justice. I'll do what I gotta do to help you out."

Justice turned to face him. She searched his eyes once more for the truth.

Justice pulled out her keys and opened the door. Carlos tried to follow her in but she held her hand out, keeping him at an arm's length distance. "Not tonight."

Carlos wanted to curse—he'd wanted to at least come in and see where things would lead, hoping things would lead to her bed. And he definitely wasn't expecting to hear "no" for an answer. Instead, Carlos kept his composure and played off the brush off. "I respect that."

"Cool." Justice replied. "Thank you."

Carlos watched as she walked in and closed the door, leaving him standing outside looking like a lil' boy who had just lost his puppy. He felt his phone vibrate with a text and as he walked away to look at it, he saw that it was from the devil herself.

"Did you find that bitch yet?"

Carlos shook his head. If it wasn't one thing, it was another and his lesson for the day was that women were the most difficult creatures to please. As he began to conjure up a response, he knew that before it was all over with that neither Tan nor Justice would ever be completely satisfied with him.

CHAPTER TWENTY-SIX

Justice had barely gotten out of the shower when she heard her phone ring. Recognizing Sapphire's ringtone, she quickly rushed to the phone because she had a few words she needed that chick to hear. Sapphire had a lot of damn nerve giving Carlos her address and she needed to know that shit wasn't cool.

"Bitch!" Justice answered the phone—not mincing words about how she felt about the girl at the moment. She heard Sapphire laughing uncontrollably in the background and that only seemed to make her madder. Justice quickly re-wrapped the plush towel around her body and put the phone on speaker as she walked back to her bed and put on the clothes that she'd laid out earlier. "That shit wasn't cool and just so you know, I don't appreciate that shit."

"Girl, I'm sorry." Sapphire played with her.

"No you're not—don't ever do that shit again."

Sapphire continued laughing, "Just, I'd thought you'd be cool with Carlos beating down your door and begging for forgiveness."

"Well, he did just that if that's what you called to find out."

"How did it go?"

"We talked." Justice stated, not going into detail as she put on her matching panties and bra, then slipped into the slacks

she'd had pressed a week earlier.

"Okay. I was calling to make sure he got there okay."

"Yeah, with yo' help, he got here just fine." Sarcasm was thick.

"Good, now look, I also called to ask you what I should wear for his Biker's party next week. Because you know a bitch like me don't do bike parties. I'll ride with Joe every once in a while but I'on do them ratchet ass parties. Them chicks be looking a hot mess and the nigga's be thirsty as hell."

Talking about bikes made Justice think about Monk and that candy chameleon Suzuki Hayubussa 1300 he had purchased months before he was killed. He'd taken her joyriding on it one time and she also used to like riding on the back of Carlos' bike as well.

"Just wear something comfortable, yet classy and you'll be alright."

"Damn, you a lotta help." Sapphire said.

Justice was about to say something slick when she heard her doorbell ring. "Lemme see who this is at the door." Justice put her top on and rushed to the door. Upon seeing Carlos standing there, she opened it and let him in. "Let me call you back." She told Sapphire.

"No problem."

Justice looked Carlos over and she was happier to see him today. "I hope I ain't interruptin'." Carlos said while peeping inside to see if she had company.

"Nah, I was just talking to Sapphire."

"I hope you ain't blast her for giving me your info."

"No but I should have."

"Going somewhere?"

"I'm going to the club to meet with some of the new dancers who will be performing this weekend. And then I have a meeting with the management for the artist that's coming in a few weeks."

"Who's coming?"

"I can't announce that yet, but look, after the meeting, we can hang out somewhere okay?"

"Cool—lemme come to the club with you. I wanna finally see what the infamous Phire & Ice look like."

Justice thought about his request for a minute. "Follow me. But once the meeting starts, I won't be able to see you until afterward."

Once Carlos stepped out of the apartment, Justice locked up and then headed to her car. Upon pulling around the front, she found Carlos' rental and honked her horn for him to follow her.

***

Both meetings went well and Justice was happy with the idea of a major artist hosting a party at her club. The last time she had hosted an artist it was Jaime Foxx. The event was bananas and everyone from the strippers, to the servers were happy with their tips.

Carlos drove her to the John Hancock Observatory. She didn't think he knew the place had even existed.

"They say this thing goes a thousand feet in the air." Carlos said.

"Yeah, it does." Justice looked at Carlos and noticed that he kept a straight face. "Lemme find out you scared."

"Hell no I ain't scared of heights," Carlos responded as if

that were the craziest thing in the world. "I got frequent flyer miles, remember?"

"Aiight." Justice wasn't convinced. They stepped on the elevator with a few other people and the ride up seemed to take forever. The music that was playing in the background was annoying, and Carlos gripped her hand tighter than usual. When they got off the elevator, they enjoyed the view of Lake Michigan and they overheard someone saying they could see the location where Illinois, Indiana, Michigan and Wisconsin met.

After listening to the tour guide and the recordings at the observatory, Justice and Carlos grabbed a bite to eat at one of the hot dog stands. They continued playing and flirting like little kids, teasing and lightly caressing one another. Every so often, Carlos would sneak a kiss on her cheeks or a peck on the lips. Slowly easing his way in.

They rode the red Double Decker buses as they toured the attractions around the city. Although Justice was a native and had seen all of this a thousand times before, she was enjoying seeing it with Carlos. Carlos got to see the Sears Tower, the U.S. Cellular Stadium again—they were even taken to some of the historical sections of downtown Chicago; heard old mob stories and rode past Harpo Studios, where they filmed the now defunct *Oprah Winfrey Show.*

After their ride, Justice talked Carlos into taking her to The Chicago Chop House. The last time she was there was to commemorate the one year anniversary of Phire & Ice with Toni and Twin.

"This is nice," Carlos interrupted her thoughts as they took a

seat.

"Yeah, I wish I'd come to this place more often but it's so many great places to eat in Chicago."

Carlos opened the menu and he smiled when he saw the offering. "I think I'm going to try this lamb lollipop joint—they serve this at Crave."

The waiter came and took their order, which Carlos completed with potato pancakes, turtle cheesecake with Sauvignon Blanc white wine. As Justice listened to Carlos order, she realized that she never had a man who treated her the way Carlos treated her. She became impressed with the way Carlos wooed her and tried to win her heart. She was trying to remember the last time she was wined and dined—guys usually did half the work and expected to get the ass as if it were that easy.

After dinner, Justice took Carlos to meet her father. This was Carlos's first time meeting the man and upon first glance he thought he was seeing Monk in reincarnation. "Wow," was all he could say as he stared at the older man in disbelief.

"I know, right," Justice said as she read Carlos's silent thought.

The three of them had a glass of wine as they talked well into the night. Justice never mentioned to Tyson that Carlos was the one who his son had been beefing with just before his death. After a few hours of conversing and getting to know one another Carlos and Tyson found a mutual respect for one another and Justice was pleased that they had hit it off so well.

***

Justice and Carlos didn't make it past the living room before

things heated up. Carlos's long sleeve button up and his A-line T-shirt were off his chiseled body before they'd gotten to the couch. Justice sucked on his nipples while she reached into his pants to grasp his hardening dick. As she reached up to kiss him, Carlos had unbuttoned her green button up top to reveal the top half of a black lace bra and panty set. Carlos effortlessly unhooked the latch with one hand and freed her breasts from bondage. It was his turn to play with her nipples and when he bit the tip, Justice moaned in ecstasy.

Carlos moved back a little, so Justice could unhook his jeans, and in the meantime, he kicked his Gucci sneakers off. As Carlos crawled out of his pants, Justice was reacquainted with the dick she used to be so obsessed with. Carlos continued to suck on each of her breasts, flicking his tongue in circles, spelling out their names with his tongue, and the occasional bite that seemed to make Justice moan even louder. He continued to lick and go low and slowly pull her skirt down. Justice reached up to undo the hooks at the top of her knee-high boots. And without missing a beat, Carlos slid them off of her feet.

Justice felt Carlos's tongue find her clit. She looked down, enjoying watching Carlos wine and dine on her moistening pussy as if he were having his last supper. The way Carlos paid attention to her body and continued moving his tongue and lips to play with all parts of her pussy was making Justice squirm. Her body was so heated and Carlos was playing with her clit with just the right amount of pressure to make her feel as if she needed to pee. As he sucked her clit with fervor, she tried vigorously to push his head away because she could no longer hold back the liquid aching to escape her vagina. All of a sudden, her body became electrified, and she screamed as she squirted for the first time in her life! She had heard tales of women ejaculating, but had never had a man make her experience this sensation until now.

"Oooooooh-shit!" Justice continued to moan as she could feel her toes curl. Carlos lifted his head up and she could see her wetness dripping from his goatee. Then he raised her legs up, pushing back as far as he could and proceeded to toss Justice's salad, tickling and teasing her asshole. That excited her in a way she never thought possible. "Fuck!"

Justice wished they had more room so she could suck his dick—make him feel the way he was making her feel at that moment. As he continued to alternate between eating her pussy and eating her ass, she wondered where he had learned that trick from because it was definitely causing her to have orgasm, after orgasm, after orgasm. Her body continued to shiver as he continued to make her soaked. Carlos persistently licked at her love as he slowly stroked his throbbing erection.

Justice exhaled and screamed, and when she couldn't stand it any longer she now was ready for the dick. She brought him up for air. She wanted to stand, but she couldn't because her legs felt like rubber. Carlos sat beside her and she was determined to climb on top of him and ride that thick, thug dick in a way that it had never been ridden before.

Justice was able to get up and sit in Carlos's lap. She gyrated on his dick while she kissed his lips and sucked on his neck. The last thing she wanted to do was interrupt their flow, but she was determined to make Carlos put on a rubber. She asked if he had any and watched as he reached for his jeans.

After rolling the condom down his rigid penis, he sat back down and Justice climbed back on top. She moved her hips up and Carlos looked her in the eyes as he slipped inside. They paused for a minute, so Justice could get used to Carlos's thickness. It had been a minute since she had let a nigga break down her sugar walls, and Carlos was reveling in how tight she was. After the initial shock, they wore the couch into the ground, rocking it against the wall with each thrusting of their hips.

Carlos lifted Justice up and she wrapped her arms around his neck as he carried her to her bedroom so they could have more room to play.

***

"So what's the real deal with you and Tan?" Justice asked once Carlos had awakened from his sex-induced sleep. It was the first time either of them had climaxed at the same time, and the first time they went to sleep shortly afterwards.

Carlos looked at Justice, gritted at her, and stood up, exposing his backside. He pulled up his pants and walked to her bathroom. After he finished doing his business, he came back into the room and searched for his T-shirt. He looked at Justice and shook his head. "You *would* fuck up a good night by asking about that broad."

"You act like you didn't think this was coming." Justice got out of bed and rushed to put on her robe. "I wanna know what's up with that bitch because we got unfinished business."

"But, do you gotta finish it right now?"

"Better time than any." Justice responded. Carlos got out of the bed and looked out of the window. A large part of him wanted to return to the bed and get in another round, but

thinking about murder and Tan made it hard for him to keep his dick hard. After staring at the skyline, he walked back to the bed and reached out to Justice.

"If you wanna murk that bitch, it's simple," Carlos said as he nuzzled on her neck. "Make her come to you."

"Make her come to me?" Justice pulled back, trying to focus on the issue at hand, and not be consumed by the tingling sensation Carlos was causing by kissing on her neck.

"Yeah." Carlos looked her in the eyes. "Make her follow you. And you do her on your terms, not because you think she's chasin' you. You know that bitch'll travel all over the world to find you. Bring her to Chicago. In fact, I can put the word out that you will be at Phire & Ice on a certain date. Tan will try to come in incognegro to blend in with the crowd. She'll come in, she'll see you, and take the first shot. Once you see her, you're on your own turf and you just shoot the bitch and be done with it. You'll even get to claim self-defense."

"This sounds *too* easy."

"That's because it *is* easy." Carlos continued. "Don't you have a major artist comin' to the club soon?"

"Yeah, Kanye's comin' thru." It was the first time Justice had revealed who she had gotten to come to her club. "But I ain't tryna fuck up my money. I'd rather handle it after Kanye comes to the club. I need that business."

"What's more important to you, Tan or Kanye? That bitch murked Monk in cold blood."

At the mention of Monk's name, Justice immediately became overwhelmed with grief and anger. Carlos peeped her demeanor and continued to lay out his idea. "Your excuse for your actions will be that she came after you after an argument about a man or some shit like that. You let it go. And after a few days she brings the drama to your club. You kill the bitch in your club and everyone will see she came at you first. Then everything you say will stick because you'll get to play the victim."

Justice smiled a little. In her mind, she could see painting Tan as some psycho-stalker bitch, which wouldn't have been too far from the truth.

"So lure her to the club?" Justice repeated.

"It's just that simple," Carlos repeated, as he slowly slipped Justice's robe off. His thickness had returned to the middle of his waist. He snuck a finger down and could feel Justice getting wet. He slipped his pants off and began to grind on Justice. He really wanted to feel her wetness engulf his dick without the barrier of a condom hindering it, but out of respect, he put on another rubber as Justice turned around and allowed Carlos to pick her up and slid her down on his dick. The familiar carnal lust had returned and he moved her up and down his shaft while he reached down to her nipple and placed it in his mouth. As he moved her to the bed, he made a few quick thrusts before he got on top of her and gave her everything he had, thrusting deeply while massaging her clit making a vow to continue bringing her to ecstasy.

CHAPTER TWENTY-SEVEN

Tan waited patiently in her Benz for Carlos to come out of the gate at the Charlotte Douglass Airport. She looked at the nine and the silencer sitting in the passenger's seat next to her. As she looked at the gate, the thought crossed her mind to murk Carlos upon arrival if he was trying to play her. The problem was there weren't too many people in Charlotte that had a silver-color S-Class Benz, and one trip to the DMV would've put her on the suspects list easily. *But killin' his ass may not get me close to* that *bitch,* Tan reasoned.

And there was nothing more important to Tan than seeing that bitch bleed in the worse way.

Tan unscrewed the silencer and placed it in the side panel and the nine back in her purse. She decided she would listen to what this nigga had to say. She looked up and saw Carlos walking toward her with a huge, black overnight bag over his shoulder. Tan popped the trunk for him to put the bag in and unlocked the door for him to get in.

Carlos took a seat inside the Benz. "Is that Justice you've got tucked away in that bag for me?" Tan joked to see the reaction she'd get from him.

Carlos laughed. "You funny. I actually chopped her up and I got one of my boys sending you a piece of her every week until you get all of that bitch."

Tan rolled her eyes and sped off. His attempt at dry humor pissed her off more than it amused her. When Tan looked out of the side view mirror, she saw the security guard following behind her in one of their trucks. She slowed down so she wouldn't get a ticket. Carlos looked out the side mirror and saw the guard make the circle at the gate. He leaned into Tan's space like he was going to kiss her and whispered, "These muthafuckas hate seeing Black or Hispanic people flaunting the success they'll never have." He readjusted himself in his seat.

"So what's the bitch been up to?" Tan said as she pulled out of the airport and got on Billy Graham Parkway, heading toward I-85.

"Justice ain't doing too bad." Carlos admitted.

Tan's face got red with envy. How dare this nigga sitting next to me gloat about that bitch?

"She got a strip joint named Phire & Ice," Carlos continued. "If you wanted to get in and out of Chicago undetected, the best thing for you to do is to hit her up at the club. She's planning a big party for Kanye in the next few weeks. He doin' a home concert and she just landed the contract for them to have an after party."

A smile crept across Tan's lips. "So what do I do, just walk in there and shoot her ass?" She was being sarcastic because Carlos had not divulged any details.

"No." Carlos was firm and deliberate. "You don't walk in at all. What you do is create a diversion in the club and her ass'll come runnin' out with everybody else." He paused, and then continued. "When she comes out the front door, you peel her wig back with that chrome and that silencer you got tucked away in your purse, and disappear in the crowd and no one will ever notice that you were there."

Tan nodded her head to indicate that she understood. "The place is always packed to capacity. Get two niggas in there to stage a fight and let another nigga pull out some firecrackers and light them bitches up."

"Firecrackers?"

"Yeah, 'cause it ain't no way in hell somebody gettin' in there with a gun. The firecrackers will make it seem like a nigga shootin'. You know what happens when niggas hear gunshots inside a club."

"Muthafuckas run out." Tan was now getting the idea.

"Some of the ladies will be in heels and folks will be running all over each other. After you dead the bitch, all you gotta do is start running and screaming with everybody else. Nobody would ever suspect that you were part of the melee."

"I like that," Tan said. "And I can see myself pulling that off," she said with excitement. She daydreamed again about Justice running out the front of her club and her being right there, getting two shots off in her face. She looked at Carlos and hated that his ass was so fuckin' fine, but she knew that within a year, she'd probably end up having to snuff his ass, too.

Twenty minutes later, Tan pulled up to BobCutz to drop Carlos off. "You got the pictures of the club I sent, didn't you?" Carlos asked as he opened the door. During his visit, Carlos had indiscreetly taken as many pictures from inside the club as possible and he texted them to her phone. Carlos even went back to the club without Justice on the incognito tip just to see what type of strippers Justice was working with, and to get more pictures for Tan.

"Of course. All I'm waitin' on now is the time and the opportunity." Tan popped the trunk opened and Carlos got out and grabbed his bag. She waited until Carlos got to the door and reached under her seat, grabbed her purse, and placed it in the passenger seat. She smiled to herself at how well Carlos thought he knew her by making that comment about the pistol and silencer she had.

CHAPTER TWENTY-EIGHT

It was finally bike party day, Carlos pulled into BobCutz parking lot on his brandy-wine colored 2011 Harley Davidson Street Glide, and the envious onlookers at the bike party were seething that he had one of the hottest bikes on the streets. Young Chris's, "Racks on Racks" blasted from the bike's stereo system. Carlos took off his matching colored helmet and the savoring smell of cooked chicken, beef and pork assaulted his nose and challenged him to take care of his senses.

"This you?" Preme asked as he walked up to him licking his fingers with a plate full of ribs smothered in barbeque sauce. He hadn't seen this bike before. Preme was a bike fanatic and he spent a good portion of his dough buying old bikes and restoring them. Since he couldn't ride them no more, he flipped the bikes instead, earning himself a small, legal hustle that kept him under Uncle Sam's radar.

"Yeah bruh, I just picked this up the day after I got back from the Chi."

"Ain't you hot in that muthafucka?" Preme asked in reference to the red crosswing jacket that Carlos was wearing.

"Naw, I breathe."

Carlos grabbed a plastic plate from the table that was set up in front of BobCutz. As the line moved forward and baked beans, potato salad, butter rolls and of course, the beer soaked chicken wings filled the air, he got him a bite before he and

Preme met Face back at his bike. He looked at the propane-fueled grills and saw that War and Luther were running the grills as if they ran the shop . . . with efficiency. Carlos knew that War could burn in the kitchen and on the grill just like his father.

"Yo' nephew took that cookin' after yo' brother very well." Preme said after he took a bite out of his ribs. His words were barely intelligible, but Carlos understood that he was saying what he had just thought.

They saw a green Chopper pull up with a tall dude driving and a thick chick on the back. Preme licked his lips because the ass poking out on that bike was hard to miss. When the driver of the bike stepped off, Preme's grin turned to disgust as he realized it was Lil' Joe.

"Fuck niggas always tryna shine an' shit." Preme mumbled loud enough for Carlos and Face to hear him.

Carlos just shook his head. He and Joe had talked briefly after the confrontation in his office and Joe seemed to be cool after he had calmed down a little, but the beef with him and Preme was never-ending.

When Sapphire took off the helmet, revealing long, flowing hair that caught lightly in the wind, Preme leaned back, "damn—fuck boy done came up didn't he?"

"Yeah," Face dragged the word out as if it were a sentence, "I remember the days when all Lil' Joe could get was whatever leftovers Dave left him with."

Preme and Carlos chuckled because they knew the statement was true. Back in the day, Lil' Joe was so big and ugly, he had to pay a chick to touch his dick. What a difference

two years, a weight loss plan and some confidence made. Sapphire was a definite step up from any broad that had pity-fucked Joe in the past.

"Sup 'Los," Lil' Joe greeted Carlos with a pound and a manly one-armed hug, bumping shoulders. He saw Preme and Face but did not acknowledge them. He saw War looking at him and Joe tilted his head. "Whatup War! Uncle Luke!!!" Lil' Joe bellowed over the music.

"Dis nigga don't see us?" Preme asked Face.

Lil' Joe stepped to Preme and got in his face, "Yeah I see yo' hoe ass. We outside now nigga! Leap like you got some frog in ya." Lil' Joe taunted Preme. Preme hopped up from his seat and stumbled back a few inches because Joe had caught him off guard.

"No!" Sapphire quickly jumped between Lil' Joe and Preme and pushed Lil' Joe. "Y'all don't need to be fighting out here."

"Fuck is y'all's problem?" Carlos said as he once again found himself in the middle of his soilders.

"You know what it is. I ain't forgot about that nigga tryin' me like that in yo' office." Lil' Joe was salty. He had moved Sapphire behind him and on the strength of her; he resisted the urge to drop Preme. "Look, 'Los I only came here for three reasons: one, because 'Phire asked me to. Two, we got business and I was gonna dip in, dip out. And three . . . you already know niggas ain't turnin' down no free food."

"Well, you should've stayed yo' ass home if them the only reasons you here." Face interjected.

Lil' Joe scrunched his face up and shook his head. "One of these days I'mma deal with yo' lil cripple ass. Trust that!"

Face pulled a large pistol from his waist and laid it on his lap. “I’ll be waiting.”

“Come get some food man,” Carlos encouraged Lil’ Joe to follow him. His face was beet red and he was beyond pissed with all of them.

“’Phire,” Face yelled to Sapphire. “I can upgrade you baby!”

Preme and Face started chuckling but Sapphire didn’t find it funny. In fact, it pissed her the fuck off but she held her composure. Her thoughts were so jaded and dark at the moment that it took everything in her being for her to keep a straight face. *In due time, nigga. In due time*, she thought. As Carlos, Lil’ Joe and Sapphire made their way through the line, Carlos spoke his piece. “I didn’t think the two of you would get together so fast.” He was referring to Joe and Sapphire’s newly blossoming relationship.

“Well, it didn’t just happen.” Lil’ Joe explained. “You the one that told me years ago that if I like a chick, I should let her know how I felt and when I saw Sapphire again at the shop, I let her know how I felt.” Lil’ Joe hugged Sapphire and kissed her on the forehead.

Carlos nodded in approval. He always thought that once Lil’ Joe cleaned himself up, he’d be a good catch for any bitch he wanted. He was shocked that the chick had been Sapphire though.

“How you holding up?” Carlos asked Sapphire as she was loading her plate.

“Every day is a struggle, but every day I get better and better.” Sapphire spoke with confidence. “It’s funny, I find

myself doing things that my mama used to do, like reading my Bible for a few minutes every night, giving a few dollars to the homeless, talking to young ladies about knuckle heads and encouraging them not to drop out of school and for the ones who did I'm tryna encourage them to go back."

"Ms. Evans would be proud." Carlos responded.

"I'm working on this knuckle head now," Sapphire said as she playfully tickled Lil' Joe on his side, he almost dropped his plate from laughing so hard.

"Don't work on him too hard," Carlos warned.

"I won't," Sapphire winked at Carlos as she walked with Lil' Joe to socialize with some of the other bikers. Carlos liked watching Lil' Joe and Sapphire mingle with the others and Sapphire genuinely seemed to have found a man that made her happy. For her sake, Carlos hoped Lil' Joe didn't do anything to make him have to slump him like he did Dave.

Carlos walked back to the where Preme and Face were still eating and talking shit.

"Carlos, I'm tellin' you . . . get what you gonna get outta that nigga now, because I'mma body that muthafucka. He ain't gonna make it past the summer dawg." Preme declared.

Carlos exhaled and took a bite out of his chicken wing, he responded. "You can't kill that nigga now because he getting shit in order on the Westside for me. And right now, I don't trust too many niggas and I at least know Lil' Joe."

"You got War—you don't need that nigga." Preme pressed.

"I got other plans for that nigga and for you too—and nothing's gonna work if you kill that nigga like you been threatening."

Preme shook his head. Carlos could see that Preme was disappointed in him but at that moment in time, Carlos didn't care. He needed for Preme, Lil Joe, Face and the rest of his niggas to get along and get money.

CHAPTER TWENTY-NINE

Justice turned on her computer and logged into her Skype account. She hardly ever used the thing except to log in and to check on Toni every now and then when she needed to make sure Phire & Ice didn't burn to the ground in her absence. Justice saw Sapphire sitting in front of her computer screen. She was shocked seeing that Sapphire had cut her hair short and made it curly.

"When did you do that?" Justice was excited.

"A day or so ago. I went to BobCutz to hang out with Carlos and the crew and after seeing this one woman with the style, I decided I'd try it and I like it." Justice's heart warmed up after seeing her friend light up. She decided that she was feeling the Skype thing and she'd have to use it more often. "Carlos looked like he was glowin' and shit. Did you finally gave him some?"

"I need to be asking if *you* been gettin' some." Justice chuckled. She tried to shift the weight because she knew she couldn't hide the truth from Sapphire for long. She always seemed to know when Justice had gotten some good dick.

"Yeah, I finally put the end to this dick drought I was in." Sapphire looked around as if she was trying to see if he was still in the room.

"Girl! Don't tell me you got me on camera while the nigga still in the room?"

"Well, he's not in the living room . . . but he is knocked out in the bed." Sapphire laughed. "Thank God he doesn't snore."

"Details, damn it." Justice was excited and genuinely happy that Sapphire had found someone who'd made her happy. It had been two years since Sapphire had messed around with Cross, and shortly after one of their freak-sessions, he was murdered execution style.

"Let's just say everything about Lil' Joe isn't little. He's lost all the weight and he's definitely cut and built in the right places."

Justice shook her head. "You bold as shit." Justice reached for the glass of wine she had been nursing earlier and took a sip. "What if he walks in there while you're talking to me?"

"Then maybe you'll get treated to a freak show." Sapphire laughed and Justice smiled. "Naw, I'll have to turn it off. I don't want no peeping Tom jacking their dick while watching me and Joe bone, and trust me, Joe knows how to bone."

"Well, if Joe makes you happy, then you need to know that I'll support y'all. Do you see it going past the sex?"

"Right now, no." Justice was startled that Sapphire was being frank. Usually, every time she got a piece of dick, L-O-V-E came along with it. "But we'll see. I like the fact that he has a legitimate hustle with the tow truck and he shared with me that he's entertaining the thought of going to Johnson C. Smith and getting his bachelors. Now that he's a little older and more mature and has some life experience under his belt, maybe college would be a good thing for him. I'm even thinking about going to UNC-Charlotte and taking a few classes even though I don't know what I'd major in."

Justice had considered college herself once, but she, Monk, and D. C. were making too much money for her to commit to it long term. *Maybe college would be good for her friend,* Justice thought. She might get a chance to see life beyond Charlotte.

"Lemme go check on Joe real quick . . . stay on the line."

"Cool."

Justice minimized her screen and pulled up a game of Spider Solitaire. She'd never played this game before and didn't even know she had it on her computer until she saw Carlos playing it. She began clicking on cards that were matching. She still hadn't beaten the game but it amused her and was a great time passer.

"Justice, you still there?" Sapphire asked.

"Yeah girl, I'm here. I'm playing this game Carlos showed me how to play when he was here." Justice switched screens and went back to the cam. "He still sleep?"

"Yeah girl, punanny put his ass out."Sapphire joked and then changed her tone.

"But I wanna tell you something." She paused and then looked away. "I didn't think I'd be able to get it in with Joe when I first met him. In fact, it was Carlos's idea that we go out for a night on the town when I got back from Chicago. We went to a few places and mostly, just sat down and talked. We went to that biker party that Carlos had at the shop a week ago too. Joe has made me feel something that I haven't been able to feel with a man—comfortable."

"What you mean by that? I thought Cross made you *comfortable*," Justice stated sarcastically.

"Cross was just somebody I got it in with from time to time.

Don't get me wrong, I was devastated when he was killed. But now that I'm older, I realize things with Cross wasn't getting anywhere close to serious as I see things possibly growing with Joe—at least the potential is there. The reason I said Joe makes me comfortable is because there was a night that happened some years ago that changed my life and had an impact on how I viewed men."

Justice was about to take a sip of her wine, but decided she needed to hear what Sapphire was saying while she was sober.

"I done did some shit that'll shock the shit outta you right now and might cause a tornado of confusion. Seriously, you have no fuckin' clue as to how devious my mind can be at times." Sapphire found herself getting emotional and had to pause and check herself for a minute before she revealed too much. She took a deep breath and continued. "I'mma tell you about this one episode though. When we were high school, I decided to meet up with this guy I barely knew in a hotel room. I knew I was gonna screw him, but I wanted to chill with him and try to get my grown woman on first. We drank and smoked—I'd never even tried weed up until that point, but unbeknownst to me at the time, the weed was laced with cocaine."

"Wow, are you serious?"

"Yeah, and that's not all that happened. I started feeling funny. I remembered what fast ass Joanne an' 'nem used to tell me what getting high felt like and my high didn't match theirs. I told him how I was feeling and he admitted to lacing the weed with cocaine. I was scared—*so scared.* And to think I was gonna give that nigga some."

"Who was it?" Justice asked. She thought she knew all the niggas Sapphire was talking to when they were in school.

"He didn't go to school with us." Sapphire told her. "But anyway, I demanded that he take me home and the nigga went ballistic on me. He demanded I give him some pussy and he threatened to just take it if I didn't go along with the program. He started walking around the room screaming and shouting about how I was gonna give him some and how I was gonna do all kinds of shit. I regretted not telling anyone where I was because I realized that this nigga was a lunatic.

"When I got up from the chair I'd been sitting in and tried to make it to the door he grabbed me. He threw me onto one of the twin beds and started choking me while trying to pull off my jeans!

"He squeezed my neck and I felt like I was fading in and out of consciousness. I tried to reach for my purse, but I ended up knocking the alarm clock over. When I was able to get it the second time, I snapped because I remembered what my stepdaddy Ty used to do to me."

Justice shook her head. She remembered how Sapphire's stepfather used to rape her and how her mother ended up killing him when she found out. A sympathetic jury subsequently acquitted her mother. It was then when her mother started the non-profit program she was so known for. Justice always figured that Ty was part of the reason why she used to accept lower standards and a lower class of men, but as Justice sat intrigued by the tale, she knew that Sapphire was about to reveal something deeper.

"I rushed to get my pocketknife out of the purse as I

scratched him. He was foaming at the mouth and had this dazed and confused look on his face. He didn't realized that I had flicked open the switchblade until it was too late. He was still choking me and I jabbed him. I continued to stick him just as hard as he was choking me. At some point, I passed out.

"When I woke up, I couldn't remember what happened until I looked at the blood on my hands. I followed the trail of blood from the bed to the bathroom, where I found him lying face up with his eyes open. I threw up in the toilet next to him.

"I panicked and I was scared Justice. I was so freakin' scared girl because I didn't wanna spend the rest of my life in jail because this nigga attacked me.

"I took a towel and wiped my prints from everything. I made sure I got the door, the table, the television, I didn't miss a spot. As I cleaned, I was now glad that no one knew I was at the hotel."

Justice stared at the computer in disbelief. She couldn't believe that Sapphire had it in her to kill someone—even in self-defense. "So did they find the man?"

"They found him two days later and to this day, no one knows it was me."

"Wow." That was the only word that Justice was able to get out of her mouth. She was in utter shock and disbelief! Her mind reverted to that time period and she began to try to remember if she heard anything about that back then but she couldn't recall the incident.

"But I'll tell you this, when I got out of the coma from that incident with Carlos an' nem' and began my therapy sessions, I'd learn to forgive everyone, even him. I used to think about that dude every time I smelled weed."

"That's why you was so pressed every time Monk and D. C. would smoke around you."

Sapphire nodded in the affirmative. "But now weed doesn't bother me. If you noticed, the last time Carlos blazed up around us, it didn't bother me."

"Yeah."

"That's why I was so into making sure you had inner peace and had forgiven Carlos. I know what inner peace feels like and I want you to know, too. I've forgiven him, Preme, Face—I even forgave my attacker from that night at the hotel, although it's too late for him. I would tell you to forgive Tan too, but-"

"I understand—I get it now." Justice really did. She'd forgiven Carlos and was even interested in seeing where things could go with them from that moment onward. She relayed this to Sapphire and Sapphire beamed. But there was no way in hell she was going to forgive Tan for what she did to Monk.

"Well, I hear Joe moving in the bedroom. I may need to go suck his dick so I can get my mind off what I just told you." Sapphire smiled wickedly then she turned around and looked in the direction of her bedroom. "Yeah, that's him. Lemme let you go."

"You be careful, okay?" Justice was still concerned. At least she didn't have to worry about Sapphire being able to take care of herself. After listening to that story, she was convinced that Sapphire would be just fine.

"All right, see you later."

Before Sapphire logged off, Justice was able to see the sculpted man walk down the hallway. She still couldn't believe that Lil' Joe had lost all that weight. Before she could see more, Justice logged off her Skype account to give Sapphire some privacy and to digest what Sapphire had just told her. She reached for the wine glass, but got up and went to the kitchen because she realized she was going to need the whole bottle instead.

CHAPTER THIRTY

Tan walked into their bedroom and admired her sleeping beauty. She hadn't seen her in a few days since she had been following up on Carlos's leads about where Justice was located in Chicago.

Tan had revealed her plan to her father earlier, who had not only given her his blessing but offered assistance, which Tan declined. For her, the murder was personal and even though it would've been easy for her to send her father's goons to slump Justice, she felt that this situation needed to be handled alone.

Tan was confident that she was ready to handle Justice—she'd laid low enough and done thorough research and now she was ready to make her move.

Tan sat on the edge of her bed and placed To'Wanda's newly pedicure feet in her hands, slowly kneading them, causing To'Wanda to come out of her slumber. "Wake up, sleepy head."

To'Wanda slowly awoke; she almost didn't recognize the woman making her feel calm and sedated. Gone were Tan's long, curly locks that she had come to admire. In its place was a short mane, dyed chocolate brown with platinum blonde streaks—almost the same styling Monica had for her *Still Standing* album cover.

"Wow, babe . . . I like it." To'Wanda said. Groggy, she sat

up and ran her fingers through Tan's short mane. "So that time's near, huh?"

Tan nodded silently to answer her question. "Well, you do what you have to do." To'Wanda sighed.

Tan moved closer to the bed and sat next to To'Wanda. "You know I'm comin' back, right?" Tan assured her with a smile. To'Wanda shook her head. "That bitch will pay for what she did to us. That I guarantee, but the only way to make sure she get it is if I go myself and give her the bizness. I wanna see the look on her face when I confirm the fact that I was indeed the one who slumped Monk."

"I just want you to be careful," To'Wanda said as a lone tear fell from her eye. Tan reached over to the dresser and pulled open the drawer. Inside, she felt for the cloth-like envelope that had To'Wanda's name on it. "I got this for you three days ago." Tan put the envelope in her hand. "Open it."

To'Wanda opened it and she shrieked when she realized she was holding two tickets to fly first class to Paris, France. The departure date had been set for three days in the future. "Oh my gosh! Tan!" A tear fell from To'Wanda's eye.

"See baby." Tan cuddled To'Wanda in her arms. To'Wanda's face was buried in her breast as Tan started playing with To'Wanda's hair. "I'mma be gone for two days. When I come back, me and you . . . we you goin' to see the world," Tan promised. "Paris is just the beginning."

To'Wanda sat up and looked Tan in her eyes. "But what if you don't come back? What if somethin' happens?"

"Take Marques, I'm sure he'll enjoy the trip," Tan joked. However, she was confident that Marques would not be

accompanying To'Wanda. Tan told her about the suite near the heart of Paris that they would be staying in. She had gone online and viewed the layout of the suite, and instantly fell in love with it. "But I promise you, Marques will not be making that trip with you." Tan brought To'Wanda's face to hers and they shared a passionate kiss. "You'll be making that trip with me," Tan whispered.

Tan slipped in between the sheets with To'Wanda and pulled To'Wanda's nightgown over her frame. After Tan got undressed, she began to use her tongue and her fingers to work To'Wanda's body into a frenzy. She dedicated herself to making sure that no one, man or woman could please her girl the way she could. As she watched To'Wanda gasp from pleasure after achieving her first two orgasms, she enjoyed the look of pleasure in her sultry eyes. She knew that after she left Justice dead and stinking, she'd have something pleasant and sweet to come home to.

CHAPTER THIRTY-ONE

It was rare for Carlos to lounge around BobCutz without doing business, but today he decided to show his face and just hangout for a while. Carlos took a seat in one of the barber chairs at the back of the shop. He and the fellas there had been shooting the shit and telling war stories for a while when he heard a loud voice calling his name.

"Carlos! Carlos!" Sabrina walked in talking loud and ghetto. Everyone in the shop cut his or her eyes toward her. "Carlos!" she yelled again.

"Fuck wrong wit'choo?" Preme limped to her and strongly grabbed her arm. "This a place of business." He was preaching something that he hadn't practiced when he and Lil' Joe had almost gone to blows in Carlos' office and again at the bike party.

"Well, I need to speak to Carlos." Sabrina issued the demand.

Carlos rose up and walked to the lobby. He saw Face roll his eyes and he knew that seeing Sabrina made him salty. *He gotta get over that shit,* Carlos thought to himself. "'Brina, what's up?"

"I need to talk to you," Sabrina said with much attitude.

"Like you ain't got my number."

Sabrina rolled her neck and spoke to him as if she were his woman, or at least some bitch he was fucking. "I need to talk to you face to face."

"Crazy bitch," Carlos muttered under his breath. Then he relented, not wanting to disrupt his customers any more than he already had. "Let's go to the back."

Carlos allowed Sabrina to lead the way and saw the nonverbal exchange between her and Sapphire. When two bitches fucked the same nigga, animosity was inevitable, no matter how much of a time span has elapsed. He pushed Sabrina along because he knew Sapphire wouldn't hesitate to beat her ass in the shop if she said something out of the way to her. And the last thing he needed in BobCutz was for another fight to break out.

Once Sabrina and Carlos were in the office, he closed the door and locked it. He stood at the door. "So what the fuck is so important that you had to come and disrupt my business?"

"I just wanted to let you know that Uncle Winkie won the lottery," Sabrina said in a hushed tone, as if others in the room could hear her.

"Fuck outta here." Carlos laughed at her. Carlos couldn't believe that Winkie, the recovering crackhead from the neighborhood, had won the fucking lottery. He remembered when he and Winkie were in the county jail together when he'd been locked up for that bogus charge with the Feds. He had taken care of the man while they were in there.

"Hell yeah. That nigga got that Pick 5 prize for $625,000, and he won playing me and my lil' cousin's birthdates." Sabrina continued to run her mouth like a faucet.

Carlos was still in disbelief. When they were locked up, Winkie was always trying to get over on some nigga. Now he

was about to be nigga rich! Funny as hell!

"So where this nigga at now?" Carlos asked as he sat down.

"Yeah, wouldn't you and everybody else like to know," she stated. "That nigga smart as hell, Carlos. He hid the damn ticket and the first thing he told me was to come and find *you*."

"Find me for what?" Carlos asked with a confused expression glued to his face.

"You already know the tax on that ticket gonna fuck up the bulk of it. On the other hand, he said that he remembered you kept talking about going legit when y'all were locked up," Sabrina reported.

"Sooooo, what the fuck that ticket gotta do wit' me?"

"Think about it. No tax for him and clean money for your ass, nigga. Lemme find out you slow." She laughed.

"Oh shit" Carlos finally realized that Winkie had sent Sabrina to him with a proposition. "He wanna sell me the ticket?"

"By George, I think he's got it," Sabrina stated sarcastically while looking up toward the ceiling.

Carlos pondered the idea of offering Winkie some dough and cashing in the winning ticket himself. This would set him straight! His money would be clean and he could finally leave the damn streets alone. *Damn*, he thought to himself, *blessings come in all shapes, forms and fashions. Even in the form of a crackhead with a $600,000 lottery ticket*!

"How much that nigga want for that ticket?" Carlos asked.

"Four hundred stacks," she stated as if she had just asked for ten dollars instead of damn near a half million. "He get the four hundred, tax free. You get the ticket with all the taxes and all

the headaches. But well worth the pain, I must say."

Carlos knew she was right and it was an offer he could not refuse. He'd gladly give Winkie the four hundred stacks for the ticket. He was going to take a small loss after taxes, but he would finally be legit! The more he thought about it, the more it made sense.

"Where my man at?" Carlos smiled.

"Oh, he yo' man now?" She laughed, then straightened her face and stated seriously, "Look, I already know how you and yo' goons get down and if anything happen to my uncle somebody already got instructions on how to handle the situation."

Carlos understood what she was saying because it wouldn't have been too hard to take Winkie on a gangsta ride and just muscle off the ticket and leave him for the vultures to feast on. "I feel ya," he stated as he nodded his head.

"So what's good?" Sabrina asked.

"Four hundred stacks . . . that's what's good."

"No doubt. He hidin' out because a few stick-up kids heard a rumor about him winning, but they not sure. They still tryna find him anyway."

"Aiight, don't worry about your uncle. I got him. I'mma give him a little somethin' on it as a down payment until the commission opens Monday morning." It was Saturday, so Carlos had two days to hide Winkie out and two days before his money would be legit. Carlos really wanted to change his lifestyle and this was his opportunity. He was going to give Winkie 25 grand to turn over the ticket, and then pay him the remainder once the ticket was cashed in. He could easily take the ticket and say fuck Winkie, but he decided he would play fair for once in his life.

"Where he at? . . . Oh, and by the way. If you ever come back in here talking all loud and shit, I'mma let Preme break your arm. You know he salty about you fuckin' Joe. And him and Face ain't got over the fact that you was the one that told me about Monk and D. C. hanging out with Cross back in the day."

"Man, fuck Preme. I had to cause a diversion and throw them nosey ass bitches in there off. And about what happened two years ago, I only told you what you asked. You asked who was with Cross and I told you. I didn't say they was the ones who had robbed Mark for yo' shit. Y'all assumed that shit and started that war on your own," Sabrina stated true facts.

"Yeah, you right. But if Preme had his way, he'd still fuck you up." Carlos laughed.

"Whatever, nigga. Look, this where my uncle at . . ." She proceeded to tell Carlos where he could find his gold mine.

***

War drove the Tahoe to the RealEyes Bookstore on 36th and North Davidson. Carlos and nobody else would suspect Winkie of being in a bookstore. The man who ran the joint didn't mind Winkie as long as he didn't steal anything.

Carlos guessed the old saying was true—if you wanted to hide something from a black person, put it in a book. And if a nigga wanted to hide from someone or a group of people, a bookstore was the safest place for him to be.

Carlos, War, and Preme got out of the Tahoe. Carlos stuck a

$5 bill in the slot to pay for the parking meter since he didn't have any ones. They walked in the bookstore to find Winkie wrapped up in a conversation with the owner about the effect of *Sweet Sweetback's Baadasssss Song* had on black film, most specifically the Blaxploitation genre. Carlos was shocked that Winkie had that kind of knowledge.

Once the conversation died down, Carlos pulled Winkie to the side. "Come ride with us for a minute."

Winkie smiled when he recognized Carlos. "What's up, big baller? Guess you and my niece had that talk, huh?"

Carlos nodded and told Winkie to follow him to the truck. She tell you about my insurance policy?" Winkie asked, making sure Carlos understood there would be consequences if anything happened to him.

Carlos laughed. "Relax, bruh. It's all love. I look at it like you doin' *me* a favor."

Concluding that he and Carlos were on the same page, Winkie followed the men out of the store and climbed in the passenger's side of the SUV.

Once inside, Carlos got straight to the point, repeating everything he and Sabrina had talked about.

"How soon can I get the money?" Winkie asked.

"As soon as you get me the ticket I'mma let you hold somethin' until I can cash it in Monday," Carlos replied as he drove down The Plaza.

Winkie took a deep breath, then undid the seat belt and dug into his back pocket to get the ticket. He handed the ticket to Carlos.

"Nigga, you walking around with a damn winning lottery

ticket stuck in yo' back pocket like a piece of lint?" Carlos fumed. Then he turned to his nephew. "War, you got that newspaper back there?" Carlos handed War the ticket and sure enough, the numbers matched with what had been reported.

Minutes later, Carlos pulled into his driveway and parked. He reached under his seat and handed Winkie a bag containing the twenty-five stacks. "This a down payment. As soon as I handle my business with the ticket, I'mma give you the rest. In the meantime, Preme gonna stay here with you and look out for you til' Monday."

Winkie opened the bag and peeped inside. He almost fainted. Carlos laughed. "Nigga, that ain't but twenty-five stacks. You might have a heart attack when you see the other three seventy-five."

The thought of having all that money made Winkie's mouth dry. He hadn't gotten high in over a year and a half and he was determined to stay clean. But with all that free money he was about to get, there was no telling what turn his life would take.

Winkie peered out the window and cleared his throat. "Who house is this?" He asked as he looked at the spacious home.

"It's my spot. At least for the next few weeks until I move into my new house."

A smile spread across Winkie's face, knowing that the deal he and Carlos had just made was on the level. Carlos felt good about bringing the man joy, and as Winkie and Preme got out of the Tahoe, he trusted that he was making the right decision. He watched Preme escort Winkie into the house as Winkie clutched that bag of money like his dear life depended on it. Carlos laughed at him again as he pulled off.

***

The news reporters had just left BobCutz after Carlos had announced the founding of the BobCutz East Charlotte Foundation, which he would use some of his "new found winnings" to fund programs that would encourage young black men to compete in local and educational programs. He felt good knowing that he was contributing to saving a community that he helped destroy with his drugs and violence. Some of the boys who were selected to pilot the program were creative to say the least, and a few of them reminded him of his and his older brother's poor upbringing.

After the last of the news reporters left the premises, Carlos retired to his office. He loosened the black tie and opened the jacket to his custom-tailored suit. His phone had been ringing off the fucking hook and his shop was bombarded with people he hadn't seen in years. News of money travels faster than the speed of light! He had chosen the shop to have the press conference so that the public could see that before 'winning the lottery' he was already a businessman.

Winkie even showed up, wearing True Religion jeans and Prada sneakers. Carlos couldn't believe that shit. Now that was funny as hell. An ex-junkie turned baller overnight!

Carlos was finally legit, but he had one final matter to attend to.

"You ready to handle yo' business?" Carlos called to check in with Tan.

The day before, he'd made his last re-up with Tan. This was the last time his hands would ever touch dirt again. He was tired of that lifestyle and determined to end it. After that last re-up was done, it was a wrap. He'd even cut off his man in Miami.

"I been waitin' for over two years to handle my bizness." Tan forced venom from her voice. "Another three days won't kill me—by the way congrats on winning the lottery. That's a smart move on your part. I like that."

"That's what's up," Carlos responded. He quickly changed the subject. "I checked out the club. Your people got plenty room by the bar to cause the commotion that would serve as your diversion." Tan had told Carlos that she had three of her cousins from Jersey meeting her in Chicago to help her pull this off. They would be driving down and bringing her the firearm she requested since she couldn't take hers on the plane. A baby 9mm with a screw on silencer.

"Justice and some of her staff will be working to make sure that the VIP room is set up for Kanye." He paused for effect. "I wouldn't recommend goin' in because if she sees you, she's gonna know you ain't come to talk, and she won't hesitate to make the first move. Plus, her security team is on point, so you'll be outnumbered."

"Well, if she's coming out the front, all I gotta do is wait on her to bail out." Carlos shook his head as if Tan could see him. She added, "Then blend in with the crowd. The plan is *way* too easy and one that can't go wrong."

"And the plan *won't* go wrong as long as you stay outside. If you go in and she spot you, it's a wrap."

"Very well then. I'll call you when I get to Chi-Town."

"Do that." Carlos pressed the END button on his phone.

Carlos let out a deep sigh as he looked at the prepaid phone he used solely for conducting business with Tan. In three more

days, he was smashing the phone to millions of pieces. Then his last connection to Tan would be severed forever.

CHAPTER THIRTY-TWO

After taking the five-hour flight from Charlotte to Chicago including a layover in New York City, Tan took a taxi to the Hilton Chicago, where she had booked the presidential suite on the twenty-fifth floor. She was glad she took the first flight out of Charlotte and arrived at a time where there were still enough hours to prepare everything she needed. Her cousins wouldn't arrive until later. She looked outside at the Chicago skyline and was amazed to see the Willis Tower and the Trump International Hotel and Tower within view.

She pulled out her phone and texted both Carlos and To'Wanda to let them know that she had arrived safely. Tan placed her phone on the bed and then went to take a soothing shower to wash away some tension. Once she stepped out of the bathroom, she heard the "Nine piece" ringtone that she designated for Carlos and picked up the phone. "I take it you got my message." Tan put the phone on speaker so she could get dressed.

"Yeah," Carlos answered quickly. "Just wanted to let you know Justice will be at Phire & Ice in about three hours to get ready for the Kanye West party."

"You spoke with her?" Tan inquired. She had full trust that

Carlos would not steer her in the wrong direction, and she knew that if anyone knew Justice's schedule, it was Carlos. She put on a black and purple blouse and black slacks that allowed her to pass as a tourist.

"Yeah. We had a nice lil' conversation this morning about me possibly surprising her and meeting her at the event." Tan rolled her eyes. Wasn't no way in hell Justice was gonna see this nigga again. "Kanye is supposed to arrive later tonight so she's planning to spend a few hours this evening to set up. All you got to do is send your people in to stage the commotion we talked about and when everybody is running out of the club, she will be in the crowd and you'll be able to walk up to her, slump her, and then follow the rest of the frantic customers into the crowd."

"This sounds too easy," Tan replied. She laced up her black leather boots with a thick two-inch heel.

"Trust me, it is *that* easy," Carlos replied. "Just make sure that you got a silencer on that monster and it ain't no reason why you can't slump that bitch without being detected. There will be so much noise and other shit going on inside and out of the club that no one should be paying attention to you. Remember, it ain't no security cameras in the lot."

Tan looked in the mirror and nodded her head as if Carlos was sitting right across from her. "You know I got a nice bonus for you on your next re-up after this shit is over with. I'm gonna show you love for my appreciation for all you've done."

Carlos took the phone away from his ear and looked at it like it had a disease. *Next re-up*? Carlos laughed to himself. *That shit's dead!* he thought. But then responded, "Yeah, good lookin', I need it," he lied.

After going over the details with Carlos, Tan ended the call and told him she would hit him before she was on her way back home. She felt confident that she would be able to get her revenge and then drive back to Jersey with her cousins for the night before hopping back on a flight to Charlotte. As she enjoyed the skyline and checked herself in the mirror to make sure she looked the part, she opened the door and walked out of the room. She had a one track mind . . . Murder!

CHAPTER THIRTY-THREE

Girl! You need to tell me how you got Kanye West to come to a damn strip club."

Toni shouted as she was sweeping the floor. Toni and Justice were in the private VIP room designated for Kanye's arrival. They were both nervous but for different reasons. They both were concerned about Kanye's impression of the place and the possibility of it becoming a place for him to hang out when he was in town. They had read in a magazine somewhere that Kanye had a thing for strippers and they wanted to make sure that he got the best impression possible. Justice had been on pins and needles, trying to call in favors to get some of the best dancers, and to get a few well-known adult entertainers to make an appearance in the club.

Justice looked at Toni and nodded her head. "I got connects."

"You got connects, huh?" Toni retorted as she swept everything in the dustpan and then dumped the contents into the trash.

"It wasn't as hard as you think," Justice began to reveal. "I knew a girl that used to work with Amber and fortunately for me, she still had her number. See, that's why I treat everybody I meet with respect because I never know when I'm gonna need them for a favor. But like I said, I knew the dancer that knew Amber, and Amber did her thing and handled everything from there."

Toni just nodded her head in amazement. "Well, I'mma finish cleaning the chairs and the tables and make sure everything is ready for him."

"I'mma go back to the office and get ready to change and take care of a few business calls. I need to reach out to his management to make sure we are on our A-game." Justice gave Toni a nod and then headed back to her office.

Justice made the walk to her office and then closed and locked the door. She took a seat at her desk and made a few calls. Once it was confirmed that Kanye was to arrive on schedule she ended the calls. Out of habit, she checked her drawer to make sure no one had snuck in and tampered with her protection.

She decided to change into something more comfortable. Justice hopped in the shower in her office and quickly freshened up. Once done in the shower she got out and walked over to her closet. She opened the closet door and grabbed a pair of jeans and a loose fitting blouse. She kicked off her knee-high Dolce textured boots and slithered out of the slacks she had on. She looked at the time on her phone and knew that in just a few hours Phire & Ice would be up and jumping.

Around 7 PM the club started getting packed. There were the usual patrons along with many new faces, who Justice knew were there to see Kanye later. Justice walked around the club to make sure everything was in order, especially the VIP. Once she was satisfied everything was up to par, she walked over to the bar and ordered her and Toni a drink.

"Cheers." Toni beamed as she held her glass high, waiting

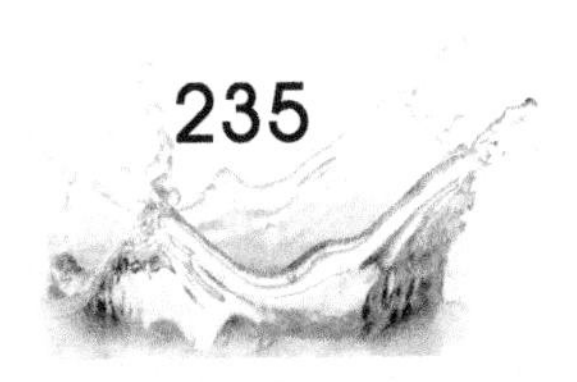

for Justice to do the same.

"What we toastin' to?" Justice asked, obliging by raising her glass as well.

"Hustlin' hard and playin' even harder," Toni stated as they clinked glasses.

After the drink, Justice decided to go back to her office and relax for a minute before shit got hectic.

***

Tan's cousins had finally arrived and after going over the plan at least a hundred times, they all left the hotel and headed to Phire & Ice. "You know where the club at?" Chico, the young man driving Tan's rental asked. Her other two cousins were riding behind them in another car.

"Not exactly, I got the address though. I'm 'bouta put that bitch's life in the GPS," she responded. Her younger cousin smirked at her ruthlessness as he watched her program the address into the system. The GPS display showed they were twenty minutes away from their destination. When they arrived at the club, Tan noticed how crowded the parking lot was. There was only one empty spot in front of the club, so she let her cousins park the car they were driving in that spot. She instructed Chico to pull around the side and park in the darkest spot he could find. They found a spot just off to the side of the club and parked there. The spot was not completely secluded, but it was dark enough for her to be obscured by patrons in front of the club.

They all got out of the cars and met near the car Tan had been riding in. Tan told them to go inside and wait for no longer than ten minutes before starting the ruckus because she didn't want to risk the chance of security coming around and telling her she had to move. She watched as her family entered the club. Once they were inside, she took out the pistol, held it down by her side, and waited for her prey to emerge.

***

Justice was ending a call when she heard a frantic knock on her office door. Toni came in and screamed, "Them niggas out there fightin'!"

Justice faked surprise. "Are you serious? Is Twin handlin' it?"

"Yeah, I think he got it."

"Aiight, good. Go ahead back out there and manage, manager," Justice teased. She waited for Toni to close the door before reaching into her desk and picking up her pistol. She carefully screwed on the silencer and checked the clip to make sure it was loaded. Satisfied her gun was ready to fire; she stood up and tucked it in the back of her jeans, gangsta style. As soon as she was on her feet, she heard what sounded like rapid gunfire emitting from inside the club area. That was her cue! She immediately ran to the door and peeped out. She saw everyone running and screaming as if they were in the middle of a terrorist attack. Justice's nerves were shot! Not because she thought someone was shooting, but because she knew within the next five minutes she would be committing her second murder . . . she hoped.

***

Within minutes of her cousins entering the club, all hell broke loose! Tan saw everybody come running out of the club just as Carlos had predicted. From where she was standing she

had a clear shot of anyone who came through that door. Half-naked strippers were struggling to balance themselves on heels while the dudes all but ran them over. Everyone she saw was irrelevant to her. She was looking for Justice, who she had not yet seen in the midst of fleeing patrons.

***

Justice made her way to the back door of the club and quickly exited into the rear alley. She pulled out the silenced pistol and held it at arm's length as she cautiously rounded the side of the club where she knew Tan would be standing. Earlier Justice had told her staff to close off the back parking lot until Kanye arrived. That way, she made sure that all of the available parking spaces would be occupied, forcing Tan to park on the side of the building where she was now headed. Once she rounded the corner, she saw a woman with short curly hair standing near a parked car. The closer Justice got, the more she became convinced that the woman was indeed Tan. At a closer look, Justice also noticed Tan was also brandishing a pistol. Tan was looking at the front door and never saw Justice coming. She was a sitting duck! Justice monitored her breathing as she crept at a slow and steady pace. When she was close enough to secure a headshot, Justice raised her gun and took aim.

***

When Tan didn't see Justice coming out of the club, she almost became impatient and wanted to run up in that bitch and start blazing. She decided she'd give her ten more seconds to come out.

At that moment, she heard footsteps behind her and she quickly spun around with her pistol raised, ready to fire.

Justice had stepped on a rock and it caused her to lose her footing for a second. That slight noise was enough to alert Tan that someone was coming. As soon as Tan turned around she was met eye to eye with her Archnemisis. It seemed as if time stood still for a split second as they both let off muffled shots.

***

Justice let out a shrill scream as a slug that hit her in the left shoulder spun around her and she almost went down. She momentarily lost her balance and ended up dropping her pistol. The gun slid across the asphalt, stopping near the gutter a few feet away.

***

Tan was not so lucky. As soon as she had let off her three rounds, she had been met with a quiet round of lead that pierced her chest. Only because of the rock Justice had slipped on, Justice's dome shot was off target. The slug knocked Tan off her feet as she let off two more shots that went wildly into the air before her gun jammed. The asphalt rushed up and slammed Tan in the face. On her way down, she saw that justice had been hit also.

***

When Justice saw Tan fall, she regained her footing and rushed to retrieve her pistol from where it had fallen. Her shoulder was bleeding and her arm had become numb, she walked over and stood over Tan. Tan was lying on her back, looking up at Justice with a shocked expression, still squeezing the trigger to no avail. Her chest was on fire and her breathing was becoming labored.

Justice kicked the jammed pistol out of her hand. "You got

what da fuck you been lookin' for, huh? " Justice spewed in pain.

Tan attempted to say something, but instead she coughed up a glob of blood. Then she managed to mumble, "See you in hell."

"Nah, no time soon bitch" Justice responded. She had tears welling up in her eyes as she heard Monk's voice in her ear telling her to send the bitch to him. Without hesitation, Justice squeezed the trigger and emptied the clip into Tan's head and torso. Tan's body jerked and spasmed as she took her last breath and began to exit this world. Justice wished she would have had more time to make the bitch suffer, but she knew she only had a few more seconds before the last of the patrons would exit the club. The entire ordeal took less than three minutes, but to Justice it seemed like an eternity.

As Justice tucked the pistol back into her jeans, she clutched her aching shoulder and ran to her car that was parked behind the club. She moved the cones that had her blocked in. So many mixed emotions were running through her mind as she climbed behind the wheel. Once again, she had taken a life and she silently thanked Carlos for guiding her through the whole ordeal and giving her the head's up. She felt as if she was now in his debt.

As she drove away from the club, she inspected her bloody shoulder and saw that it was only a graze. She sighed with relief at the fact that she wouldn't have to rush to a hospital. At a hospital with a gunshot wound would have made her an immediate suspect. She decided she would call a friend to bandage it and wrap it up once she got home. Driving down the street she could've sworn she saw a man standing on the corner who looked just like her brother, Monk smiling at her. He slowly nodded his head in affirmation of what she had just done, and at that instance, she knew her brother's death had been avenged. Justice closed her eyes for a moment, and when she reopened them, the man had disappeared. Through the pain in her shoulder, she looked out her window, toward the sky and smiled. Just then, Sapphire came to mind and Justice silently thought, *now* I can forgive.

CHAPTER THIRTY-FOUR

Carlos smiled like a proud father when he stepped before his baby. The mostly brick, one story, 2,500 square foot masterpiece was almost complete. With its large trees out front along its elegant brick driveway, Carlos's dream house was coming alive from the pages of a *New Home* magazine. The flowers planted in the flowerbed on the right side of the house and around the base of the mailbox easily put it in the running for "Yard of the Month." A white picket fence bordered the house and encircled his property in the back. With its address right on the edges of Ballentyne, Carlos was proud to see his dream come true.

"Just a few more days, and I'll move in completely," Carlos said aloud as he watched the people from DISH setting up to install their satellite. The Rooms 2 Go crew would be bringing in his living room, dining room, as well as some of the guest room sets within the next hour or so. Later on, he was going to have his master bedroom set taken from his current residence to the new place, as well as some of the mahogany and sable pieces he'd been collecting over the years. As the days drew closer for him to move into his new home, he enjoyed the comforts of staying at The Westin in downtown Charlotte.

Carlos had seen the news briefing about Tan's death on Chicago's news website and had assumed that Justice had done her thing. A part of him was worried when he called her and she hadn't responded—but he knew she wasn't dead because that would've been mentioned. When Justice finally reached out to him, he was beyond happy. He was concerned when she had told him that Tan had gotten off a lucky shot but he was put at ease when she told him it was only a graze. Her blouse and her front seat were ruined but she was ok.

Carlos's excitement tripled when she had accepted his offer of coming to stay with him in the new house for a while. He could not wait to bring Justice to his new home. Carlos was about to enjoy the fruits of his labor and be out of the game for good.

As Carlos walked around the property, inspecting the new home for slight imperfections and coming up with ideas for what could be done to improve the house; he began to think about new business ventures. BobCutz was good, but he knew that being in a barber and beauty salon day in and day out would run him nuts. The thought of having a club ran across his mind, but he didn't want to take the chance of competing with existing clubs like Fifth Element, Lux and Nine Three Five. A Laundromat or a car wash could be lucrative in the right neighborhood, but Charlotte was in the middle of a drought and they were prone to water restrictions that would greatly limit his business. He thought about having his own convenience store or a gas station, but gas was just as high as dope these days. Yet he knew that upon his retirement from the drug game, it would be a good time to diversify his business holdings. BobCutz was making a good profit and would serve as the perfect cornerstone to his legal ventures, but he knew that another business or two would round out his portfolio and keep all of his eggs out of the same baskets.

Carlos was easing War into position of "Boss" so he could start commanding his old empire. He had done what many drug dealers dreamed of but few have accomplished; he was going legit after having a successful run on top. Nothing seemed to be standing in his way as he stepped into his future.

Carlos's phone vibrated in his pocket. "'Sup." He answered after verifying Preme's number on the screen.

"You ain't gonna believe this shit."

Carlos cursed to himself—he knew he wasn't gonna like what Preme had to say next. Every time Preme started his conversation with those six words, what came afterwards was never good. It seemed like every time he tried to enjoy a little piece of *sugar* in his life, some twisted act of fate tried to stuff *shit* down his throat. "Two of the houses on Tuckaseegee got robbed."

Carlos wanted to throw his phone at the side of the house. "The fuck!" *War needs to be handling this shit,* Carlos thought. *That nigga the one runnin' shit.*

"Yeah, bruh, doors got kicked in and plenty work got took. I'm still looking into it."

Carlos shook his head as if Preme could see him. "Okay. I'll handle it in a minute." Carlos didn't wait for a response before he hung up the phone. "Fuck, fuck. FUCK!" Carlos was frustrated. It seemed that every time he wanted to take a step or two out of the game, he was getting knocked back a couple of feet into it.

He thought about the fact that the Westside was Lil' Joe's

stomping grounds and if anybody knew something about this he would be the one to contact. After the bike party at BobCutz, Joe had told Carlos that he was about to start grinding for himself. Carlos was cool with that because he himself was about to be out of the game. It was understood that Joe was not to step on any of Carlos's team member's toes and if that line was crossed, it would be consequences and repercussions of great measures. Joe said that he understood but deep down, Carlos knew Joe wouldn't respect that when it came to Preme. After Joe's split from the crew, Preme was assigned to the Westside.

Some of the unresolved issues with Joe and Preme came to mind. The near fight with the two of them, the murder of Dave, and the murmurings on the street kept rising that Lil' Joe had gotten a team of young niggas who was slanging on Tuckaseegee Road also. Carlos entertained the thought for a second, but then decided not to play into that. "Nah, I know that nigga ain't crazy," Carlos stated aloud.

Carlos thought back to the altercation between Joe and Preme, and he had almost regretted not letting the two handle that shit right then and there. He knew when it would've all been said and done, Preme would've been the one to emerge from the smoke still breathing. Joe talked a good one but Preme was a black-hearted killer with no conscious whatsoever. Preme had also wanted to body Joe shortly after they had bodied Dave in Opa Locka because he said he didn't trust that nigga. Nevertheless, unlike a lot of niggas in the game, Carlos knew Joe wasn't a snitch and Carlos didn't see him as a problem at the time so he gave him a pass. A certificate of life so to speak.

Now he had to deal with *this* shit!

Carlos scrolled for Joe's name on his contact list and he touched the CALL button on the screen. After getting Lil' Joe's voicemail, he hung up the phone, mad as hell, but he didn't want to let Lil' Joe know he was pissed. He decided to call back a few minutes later, after a few rings he got the machine again, and he left a message:

"'Sup, my nigga, this Los. Hit me when you get this message, it's important. One."

Carlos put the phone back in his pocket and thought it had been a minute since he and Joe had talked. He wanted to give Lil' Joe the same opportunity that he'd given Dave; the chance to clear the air. He knew that Joe was most likely to tell the truth, and whatever that truth was Joe would hold true to it like a man. Carlos had decided he'd not accuse Lil' Joe of anything until he had a chance to talk to the man and hear what he had to say.

CHAPTER THIRTY-FIVE

Justice was fucked up at the thought of losing Kanye West's party to a rival club a few blocks from her spot. But she knew there was no way in hell that Kanye, or anyone else on that level, or even a few steps under him would be coming to Phire & Ice after Tan's body had been discovered leaking in her parking lot.

She knew that the possibility of her murking Tan would happen, but deep down, Justice had hoped that she wouldn't have to do it at the club—but it seemed there was no other way. Detectives had concluded that Tan's murder had been a direct result of the altercation that had gone down inside the club between the three Spanish men. Witnesses had collaborated the fact that a fight had broken out minutes before Tan had been reportedly murdered. No one even looked in Justices direction as a suspect. Her wound was so insignificant that no one saw it. She kept it bandaged and wore shirts with sleeves until it healed. Justice felt no remorse for how she handled her business. She felt good knowing that Tan went out the same way she had sent Monk out, face down on the cold asphalt.

After a couple of weeks of waiting for the news of the shooting to die down, Phire & Ice was back in business. Justice walked past the dressing room where the girls were changing and she felt good not seeing Precious and Virgin, and not having to deal with their scandalous asses. The ladies seemed to be getting along better and being more cooperative about all the bitches making money instead of the dollars being chased by a "select few." The dressing room and the atmosphere in the club hadn't been this calm since before the day she made the mistake of putting them two bitches on.

"Boss lady," Toni called out from inside the dressing room. Justice didn't even see Toni in the room with the girls. In fact, Toni should've had her ass in her office making sure things were being prepared for one of the minor league baseball players, who'd agreed to host a bachelor's party for his friend at the club. Justice knew that after the shooting she was going to have to take baby steps in order to land someone on the same level as Kanye back at the club again. Pulling off this bachelor's party without a hitch was a first step in the right direction. "Boss lady!" Toni yelled again, interrupting her thoughts.

"Damn girl, I heard you the first time."

Justice saw Toni was wearing a pinstriped black vest and blue silk tie with matching slacks and some heels. Her newly dyed sandy-brown locs had been pulled back into a ponytail that she loved to whip around like a white girl. "Anyway, boss lady, I just wanted to get up with you to say thank you for the opportunity."

Justice hugged Toni from the side. She understood what it meant to be a black woman giving another sistah a chance to shine, and though that was not the intention, she was happy to give the girl an opportunity many had to fight for. "You don't have to do all that. All you've got to do is make sure the club stays packed. Continue to network with the dancers and the promoters to keep the bitches interested in dancing in the joint because flying them here ain't gonna make them dance. They have to see the potential of them doubling or tripling what you are paying to bring them here."

Toni took notes in her mind. She had a level of respect for Justice being a woman of color in a predominantly male world. The fact that Justice could wheel and deal with the best of them was a plus. Her years of being in the streets, as well as being affiliated with niggas like Carlos and J.T. had served its purpose and prepared her well as she dealt with the men who handled most of the strippers and other issues that came with running this business.

"And when a bitch get outta line, you nip that shit in the bud the moment it becomes a problem. That way, the other bitches will stay in line and know not to try their luck."

In reality, Justice shouldn't have had to tell her that, but she knew there were distinct differences between herself and Toni. Justice was a street bitch; she knew how to get down for hers whether it be setting a nigga up to be robbed or finessing a nigga out of his wallet. Toni didn't like niggas like that, and she'd also had a sheltered upbringing—she'd hardly gotten into trouble in school because she knew her parents would kick her ass. She graduated from college and held down legit jobs damn near all of her life. In addition, at heart, she could never be a street bitch. Therefore, Justice knew she could trust Toni long enough to make their partnership work, and she was willing to give Toni room to grow to be her own boss. Furthermore, Justice was secure with the thought that she would be coming back to Chi-Town often, so nothing would get so far out of hand that she couldn't handle.

After killing Tan, Justice had decided that it would be safe for her to return to Charlotte on a more permanent basis. With no one chasing her or having a reason to, there was nothing keeping her from enjoying the familiar stomping grounds as she had years before. She and Carlos were rekindling their romance, and she felt at ease being in his presence. Justice wanted to see how far she and Carlos could go. He had invited her to stay with him in his new house with no pressure at all. However, the way Justice was starting to feel, a little pressure might have ended up turning her on. The fact that he helped set Tan up ultimately erased any doubt about how sincere he was in his apologies for how everything had gone down with Monk and D. C.

The idea of hanging out with Sapphire whenever she wanted to without having to catch a flight appealed to her as well. It had been a minute since she and her girl made some bitches envious at a club, and now that Sapphire was back to her old self, it was time to get out and do their thing.

"Everything is set up for the girls coming from D. C.—they should be arriving in the next thirty minutes or so," Toni said as she followed Justice out of the dressing room and back to the office.

"That's what's up. I'mma be in my office for a few minutes and you make sure they are taken care of."

Toni nodded her head and then went to the back entrance the girls used when they were arriving to perform at Phire & Ice. Justice couldn't wait to get to the Queen City and get shit popping. It was the end of February and almost time for CIAA! Not only were some of the best black college basketball teams competing for the championships, there were step shows, concerts and mad parties. Not to mention networking opportunities to meet new dancers and most importantly, celebrities she could host parties for at her club. It didn't matter whether you went to one of the schools in the CIAA conference or not, when the championships were in town, it was time to unwind and get your party on. She was looking to take a break and couldn't think of any other place she'd rather be.

CHAPTER THIRTY-SIX

Lil' Joe was pissing Carlos off and he was getting closer and closer to making Carlos send Preme to see his ass. Carlos was so vexed he wanted to pull the trigger himself. He had tried for the fifth time after moving all of his furniture into his new house to get in contact with Joe, but the man was ghost. All the calls were going straight to voice mail. Carlos had hoped that Joe hadn't gotten picked up, but that would have been the first thing a nigga would have heard if it was true. Niggas would have immediately put that on the wire. And there weren't any rumors that the nigga was dead either.

What the fuck? Carlos looked at his phone with Joe's number on the screen and he couldn't figure out why the man wasn't answering.

Carlos scrolled down and found Sapphire's number. He had almost forgotten that *he* was the reason the two of them had started fucking on a regular. Sapphire had proven her loyalty to him, and he figured he could count on her. He figured if anyone knew where this nigga was at it would be her.

After listening to J. Cole spit some lyrics on Sapphire's ring back tone, Sapphire picked up the phone. "Hey, big bruh."

"'Sup sis, how you?"

"I'm good. Justice is coming back and a bitch excited as hell. I'm tryna figure out what I'mma wear to that day party at Prevue."

"See, ya' already tryna to cause trouble," he teased. "Listen, you seen Joe?" Carlos got straight to the point. He would call Sapphire socially at another time, but for the moment he needed to handle his business.

"No—he left for Philly to take care of some medical emergency that came up with his son," Sapphire spoke as if it were common knowledge. "His baby mama called two weeks ago, and Joe literally dropped me off at my place and told me he'd be back in a few weeks."

Son? Carlos thought to himself as he tried to remember Joe's family tree. *I didn't know the nigga had a son. Damn, I'm fuckin' up.* "Aiight, when you talk to that nigga, tell him to contact me ASAP. I really need to see him. Give him the address to my new spot and tell him to come through."

"No problem."

"And I hope ain't nothing wrong with the little man." Carlos tried to sound caring. He didn't want to seem completely heartless—children were innocent no matter whose seed they came from. Plus, he wanted to stay on Sapphire's good side.

"Okay. As soon as I hear from him, I'll definitely tell him to hit you up."

"Good look. Peace."

Carlos ended the call and the thought that Joe had a seed fucked with him. That was another thing the big house was missing . . . Justice and a few kids that came from his spawning. Carlos almost could not believe he'd gotten so far in the game

without a baby mama or two. Face, Preme, and Ali all had kids. Even Dave had left two little girls fatherless. For a minute, the fact that he did not have any kids had him feeling some kind of way.

Fuck it. I still got time. I'm still young. He looked out the window and imagined Justice walking in the front door with a couple of little ones harassing her at her side. He smiled knowing that in the many days ahead, his vision could become a reality.

***

Justice had arrived and Carlos was beyond ecstactic. The house was ready and all the furniture had been moved in. When he saw Justice's reaction after arriving to the house from the airport, Carlos knew that all the frustrations and headaches with the builders, inspectors and everyone else had been worth it.

Within an hour of being situated and enjoying a light meal, Carlos and Justice wasted no time christening the place as they got it in from wall to wall. The sexual frustration between the two was at a fever pitch and with all of the murder, deceit and greed they faced day in and day out, they both had some pent up frustration to release.

When morning arrived, Carlos greeted Justice with breakfast in bed. Very few people knew he could burn in the kitchen. The aroma from the chicken and vegetable omelet and buttered toast helped Justice gather her senses as she sat up in bed. One of Carlos' old Carolina Panthers T-shirts covered her nude frame. She admired the way the gray wife beater fit snuggly on Carlos's chest and the cotton pajama pants highlighted all of the parts she liked.

"Wow! Carlos—I never—" Justice responded in shock. She could not believe that Carlos stood before her with a tray of food for her to eat in which he had prepared.

"Kinda figured you hadn't," Carlos smirked as he placed the folding tray at her waist. Justice dug into her food and when she realized that Carlos didn't have a plate, she swallowed the bite of omelet quickly, "you not eatin'?"

"Naw, I just fixed enough for you. I'll be eating later on." He snaked his hand beneath the t-shirt and stroked her hairless vagina for a second while biting his lip and staring into her eyes. Justice's body tingled as she very well understood what he was referring to eating later. He pulled his hand away and tasted her juices. "Lemme stop," he smirked. "Go ahead and enjoy your breakfast, babe," he said as he stood to leave the room.

Justice watched this thugged out gentleman exit the room and her stomach fluttered with butterflies of passion. "Damn, I missed that nigga," she mumbled before digging back into the food before her. As she savored the taste, she knew in her heart she could get used to this. No man had ever cooked her breakfast in bed before nor treated her like a lady in the manner that Carlos had done. In fact, Carlos, in a short period of time had demonstrated the true balance of being a gangsta and a gentleman and this was something that Justice could come to appreciate.

CHAPTER THIRTY-SEVEN

Tan's one-year memorial service was bright—everyone at the Mendoza estate was dressed in their finest. The smell of barbeque chicken, ribs and other delectables permeated the air as children ran across the spacious living room Tan used to call home.

It had been a year since Justice had gotten her revenge and Papa Mendoza had finally decided that he would call the family and friends together so they could help him celebrate her life. The funeral and subsequent cremation had been private as Tan had chosen to be cremated before death. Her ashes were sprinkled all over the flowerbed that lied south of the estate.

Within days after Tan's death, her family had completely renovated the house and was looking to convert it to the likings of Papa Mendoza, the true owner of the house. Pictures of Tan when she was young lined the walls and some of her favorite childhood toys and games were kept in various rooms. Papa Mendoza never spent much time in Charlotte but in his grieving, he'd come to develop a fondness for the Queen City—and he didn't mind making her old house his new home. And after a year, he'd come to visit the place often as he felt this was the only way he'd get to spend time with his daughter.

As Papa Mendoza passed the plate for everyone to get their helpings, To'Wanda sat next to Papa Mendoza in her rightful place as Tan's lover. Next to her sat Chico, Fontaine and Tico—

the three cousins who had attempted to help Tan on her mission to kill Justice. Marques attended but kept his distance as he too had come to pay respects to the family. Tan's cousins' hearts were heavy because even though they delivered the gun to Tan and followed her instructions to a tee, they felt they had failed their older cousin by not staying with her or even watching her from a distance to make sure that the job was done.

"I hate them Asian fucks!" Chico gritted through closed teeth as he pounded his fist on the table. The teardrops were newly tatted on his face and had a double meaning besides their obvious implication. He towered over his other two cousins by at least six inches.

"No son," Papa Mendoza spoke softly—contrast to the man that they'd known him to be. "It is not a race of people you hate; it is a person who happens to be of that race."

"Justice is a dead bitch!" Chico vowed.

"No!" To'Wanda said weakly. Her place as Tan's lover had been respected and she felt the courage to speak up as if she were blood. "No more killing. Killing Justice is not going to bring Tan back just like I'm sure when she murdered my baby it didn't bring her brother back."

Papa Mendoza took off the shades that had been concealing his tears and his own passion for revenge. He was shocked because in all of the years he'd known To'Wanda, he'd never heard her speak up like that. Even though he knew that To'Wanda was developing a fondness for Marques and he'd given her his blessing to move on, a part of him was happy that she'd made Tan happy in her last years. However, a small part of him wanted to slap the shit out of her because after all, he had buried his daughter and not the other way around. Nevertheless, because of his love for Tan, he would behave.

To'Wanda looked into the older man's eyes and she knew she'd said something foul that he didn't agree with—her first in all the years she'd known him. She reached up with a glove-covered hand and forcefully wiped the tears from her face. "I loved Tan," she said barely above a whisper and forced her opinions through her tears, "I don't want this no more."

Papa Mendoza slowly nodded his head. To'Wanda reached over and kissed the salt and peppered man on the cheek. In return, he hugged her in the manner in which he hugged Tan and in To'Wanda's heart, she knew that regardless of what she said, she was safe.

"I want you to go to Paris," Papa Mendoza said as he pulled out the tickets that he'd just purchased the day before. "And take Marques with you."

"What?" To'Wanda looked on confused.

"My once daughter told you to go to Paris and to take Marques with you. A year has passed and you haven't honored her wishes," "Papa?"

Before To'Wanda could get the final thought out, Papa had shaken his head no and To'Wanda knew it was wise for her to keep her mouth shut. "Go" He ordered.

To'Wanda took the tickets out of his hands and found that she and Marques would be boarding the plane tomorrow morning. Her eyes popped, wide. "Thank you."

She reached over and hugged the man. To'Wanda got up out of her seat and she went to Marques to share the news. Chico scooted down to her seat. He'd wanted to sit next to his beloved uncle and this was finally the moment he'd get a chance to speak his piece.

"Are you really gonna let that Justice chick ride like that?" He asked boldly, knowing that To'Wanda was not within earshot.

"I have something special planned for Justice—and that maricon traitor." Papa Mendoza almost spoke Carlos' name but couldn't bring himself to say it. He knew in his heart that Carlos had somehow helped Justice with the murder and part of the confirmation were the phone records indicating that Tan had talked to Carlos when she'd arrived in Chicago.

Papa Mendoza seethed every time he thought about Carolos living and breathing while his daughter was scattered out back like fertilizer. This motherfucker was enjoying a legitimate life out of the game as if everthing was all-good. If it weren't for Papa Mendoza and his steady supply of cocaine through his daughter, Carlos wouldn't have anything to enjoy. Nevertheless, given the number of years Papa Mendoza had been at the top, he knew that in time, all major problems took care of themselves one way or another. As he looked around at his nephews, he hoped that Chico, Fontaine and Tico lived long enough to understand that concept.

CHAPTER THIRTY-EIGHT

"When you gonna take this blindfold off of me?" Justice asked, wanting to reach up and pull the cloth from her face.

"When I get ready," Carlos said sarcastically as he pulled into the shopping center. He found the parking space that had been reserved for him for the day and he cut off the ignition. He opened the door, walked around and opened Justice's door and he helped her step out of the Tahoe. Carlos silently oooh'd and ahh'd at the tight, form-fitting dress that he had specially designed for her. He was looking dapper with a new Prada suite with a matching fedora. "We almost here." Carlos whispered in her ear as he led her into the shopping center. As he approached the door, he looked out over the parking lot and saw two men parked in an Impala, the same two Hispanic men he'd seen earlier at the mall while picking up his shoes from Neiman Marcus. He didn't think much of it as he proceeded with his date.

Carlos had Justice blindfolded, as he wanted to surprise her for their dinner date. He had gotten War and Luther to help him arrange to have Amélie's cater a special dinner and desert in the atrium of the NoDa @ 28th building. At first, the owners of the building weren't feeling the idea of shutting down the whole building to set up a romantic candlelight dinner, but once Carlos wrote a five figure check paying all the tenants' rent for the next month, needless to say that all the business owners were happy to take a day off.

Once Carlos opened the door, he escorted Justice inside and he slowly lifted off her blindfold. Justice saw small white candles burning brightly in a single line that led to a trail where their table sat. In the middle of the table was a bucket of chilled Rosė.

"Oh wow!" Justice exclaimed. "I didn't expect this."

"With me, learn to expect the unexpected." Carlos boasted confidently as he walked hand and hand with her to their table. He pulled out her chair and helped her sit down comfortably. As he went to his seat, a waiter appeared with a single rose in his hand.

"For the beautiful lady," he handed her the rose and bowed. He left and reappeared with a pad to take their order. Carlos ordered two steak and lobster plates along with vegetable soup. The waiter then put the pad back in his pocket, uncorked the champagne, and poured their glasses.

"This is really nice." Justice complimented. She watched the waiter disappear and a live band started playing a medley of Sade's greatest hits off in the distance. It had been a minute since she'd heard any of her songs and knowing that her mother was a huge Sade fan, she definitely appreciated the gesture.

While enjoying the music, the waiter returned with their food and they took turns feeding each other. After eating their meal and enjoying their drink, Carlos got on his knee and pulled out an engagement ring from his pocket.

"Justice, we've been through a lot together—as friends and as enemies—but from this moment forward, I know in my mind

and in my soul that I want to spend the rest of my life with you. They say you never know what you have until it's gone. But I say I knew exactly what I had when I had you. I just never thought I'd lose it. They also say if you love something, set it free. If it comes back it's yours to keep. If not, it was never meant to be. Well, here we are baby. I don't wanna lose you again for no reason whatsoever." He paused, and then asked, "Would you do me the honor of being my wife?"

With tears in her eyes, Justice quickly nodded her head yes before verbally indicating her answer. Carlos got off his knees and he hugged Justice tightly before kissing her passionately. The band began to play "Spend My Life" by Eric Benet and Tamia and that was the perfect song to define how Justice and Carlos intended to spend the rest of their days.

EPILOGUE

It was a beautiful Sunday evening and Justice and Carlos lay side by side in the hammock Carlos had assembled in the backyard two days prior. The sun had set and they were enjoying the cool summer breeze. It had been exactly one month since Carlos had proposed, and Justice was relishing in the thought of finally becoming his wife. After all the trials and tribulations she had endured, she finally felt like her life was meaning something.

"Did you ever think the day would come where we would be here? When I say 'here,' I mean right here in this day and time together. I mean, we done been through a lotta shit." Carlos gently traced with his forefinger, the fading scar on Justice's shoulder from where Tan's bullet had grazed her. He was gazing in her slanted eyes while he waited for her response.

Justice took a deep breath and looked towards the sky, "Honestly?"

"I'm almost scared to say, but yeah, *honestly*." He chuckled.

"Hell no!"

They both laughed at her truth.

Just then, the doorbell rang.

"Damn, saved by the bell," Carlos muttered while slowly climbing out of the hammock so it wouldn't flip.

"You expecting company?" Justice was disappointed. She had just gotten comfortable lying next to Carlos a few feet in the air.

"Yeah, I finally caught up with a nigga I need to holla at. I need to dead a issue. I'm tryna make amends with old friends." Carlos looked at his watch. *Joe right on time, too,* Carlos thought. Sapphire had contacted him and told him that Joe was back in town and he was willing to meet him. Carlos wanted to let him know that he didn't care about what had happened in the past and all that bullshit was behind them now. At this point, he honestly didn't give a damn about what was going on in the streets anymore. He just wanted peace. Reconciliation was going to start with this meeting with Joe. "I'll be back in a few minutes aiight?"

Carlos leaned in and kissed Justice on the cheek. She watched with admiration as Carlos walked toward the back door and disappeared into the kitchen, headed toward the front door. While lying back in the hammock, Justice closed her eyes and began to reflect on her life. It is said that everything in life comes full circle. And at that moment, Justice truly believed every word of that proverb with all her heart. Just a few years earlier, she was living in Charlotte, and in an on-off relationship with Carlos. After running to Chicago, she ended up right back in Charlotte with the same man she had subsequently run away from. *Hmmm, I could get used to this,* Justice thought, relishing in the fact that she was in love and it felt oh, so, sweet. After a few minutes without Carlos returning, Justice was wondering what was keeping him. She sat up in the hammock and called out, "Carlos! Who was at the door?"

No answer.

Fuck they in there doing? She thought to herself while

climbing out of the hammock to be nosey.

Justice entered the kitchen through the back door and noticed the house was eerily silent. She assumed Carlos had stepped out onto the front porch or out in the driveway to speak with whoever was at the door. “Carlos,” she called out while walking through the living room. Still no answer.

Once she entered the foyer, she noticed the front door was open. She started to approach the door, but a guttural sound to her right caught her attention. She couldn’t make out the noise, but it resembled a wounded animal struggling to breathe.

She followed the sound toward the dining room and saw what appeared to be blood smeared on the wooden tiled floor. Immediately, her hand flew up to her mouth to cover whatever sound was trying to escape her lips. Being so keen to violence, her mind instinctively clicked into survival mode. If someone had hurt her man and was still in the house, she was damned if they were getting out alive! She had already lost too many people in her life. There was no way she was letting someone rob her of the only joy she’d ever really had. She ran to the bedroom where she knew Carlos had one of his many pistols stashed. After retrieving the gun she slipped back downstairs, slowly approached the dining room, and saw a trail of blood so thick that she was almost sure no one could have survived whatever had taken place. She dry heaved from nausea because the smell of blood was so overwhelming. Tears of confusion and rage clouded her eyes as she slowly entered the dining room with the pistol cocked and loaded.

She was shaking so badly she could barely keep the pistol steady. As she entered the dining room in a blind rage, she couldn't believe her eyes!

"OH MY GOD! NOOOOOOOO!" she screamed at the top of her lungs. The scene before her was unbelievable!

There was so much blood! The floor, the counter and the walls were all splattered with it. On the floor lay Carlos with multiple gashes, which Justice knew to be stab wounds. She ran to his aid, but already knew there was nothing that could be done for him. From the loss of so much blood, Justice knew he would soon be on his way to the afterlife. Other than Carlos's struggling breaths she didn't hear a sound in the house, so she assumed that whomever the assailant was had fled. She dropped to her knees and cradled his limp head in her lap while crying uncontrollably. She couldn't believe that someone had done Carlos like that. Nevertheless, she also knew that Carlos had done so much dirt in his past that maybe it had finally caught up with him. "Baby, breathe . . . please breathe." She cried as she rocked back and forth with his head still buried in her lap.

Carlos opened his weak eyes and attempted to open his mouth to speak, but no words came out, only globs of blood. "Baby, who did this to you?" Justice screamed, her mind now bent on revenge! Carlos couldn't answer but Justice noticed he cut his weak eyes as a warning toward the door that led into the sunroom before he took his last exasperated breath and exited this world. "No baby . . . Nooooo . . ." Justice pleaded while still cradling his lifeless body. His still eyes were fixed on the sunroom as Justice gently ran her trembling hand from his forehead to his mouth, shutting his eyes once and for all.

Still in shock, Justice gently lay Carlos's lifeless head back onto the floor and slowly arose to her feet with the pistol aimed

in the direction of the sunroom.

Justice screamed into the sunroom. "Muthafucka, you got two seconds to show yo' face before this pistol start spittin' lead at yo' ass!" She knew there was only one way in and one way out of the sunroom, and the killer would have to exit past her to get away. And that was definitely NOT happening! As far as she was concerned, whoever was in the sunroom was already a dead man because murder was inevitable.

"One, muthafucka . . ." Justice counted. "Tw—" Before Justice could finish, out stepped the killer with the bloody knife still in hand.

"What the f—" Justice started. She was in unbelievable shock by who she saw standing there covered in Carlos's blood. She glared at the killer in disbelief while slowly lowering the pistol to her side. She could only manage to utter one word, "Why?"

Sapphire dropped the bloody knife to the floor and looked down at her crimson colored hands before speaking barely above a whisper, "He—he, almost had me killed, Justice. And for what? For what he *thought* I did. That nigga . . ." She pointed a bloody finger at Carlos's corpse. "He had no value for human life! He killed without hesitation and with no remorse!" Sapphire began crying. "I had to learn to walk, talk, and function like a normal human being all over again because of that monster." She was still pointing at Carlos. "They declared me partially brain dead at one point . . ." Then her tone changed, "I warned you that I was capable of doing shit that your mind could never conceive."

Justice was confused as hell because she remembered all

that "forgiveness" shit Sapphire had preached to her.

Sapphire had never gotten past the fact that Carlos was the reason she had been scarred for life. Carlos had told Sapphire too much throughout the years. She knew his strengths and she had also learned his weaknesses. She knew Dave was a weak nigga and that was why she had tipped off the Miami police as to what Dave would be driving with the kilos in it. In fact, it was one of the detectives who had called her phone for a follow-up while she and Justice were in the limo on the way to her mother's burial.

She knew Dave would snitch and Carlos would do what he had to do. She also knew Dave's death would cause beef with Carlos and Joe. She was also the one who had paid two young goons to run up in Carlos's trap houses on the west side so the beef could escalate. She was antincipating Joe, Supreme, Face and Carlos killing each other off sooner or later because of all of the ongoing conflict. That would have gotten rid of everyone who had been involved in her brutal attack. But to her dismay, Joe never stepped up and handled Preme and Face like she had planned. Joe and Carlos both had gone soft and wanted to "talk". Sapphire became fed up and decided to handle the shit on her own. After killing Carlos, her plan was to escape unnoticed and unsuspected and let the situation die down before going after Supreme and Face herself.

Joe had wanted to go to Carlos and talk to him like a man and let him know that he didn't have anything to do with the robberies, but Sapphire could not have that so she had convinced him to let her talk to him instead. "He listens to me," she had told him. "Don't speak with him until I talk to him."

"Aiight, but if you ain't talked to him before I get back from Atlanta I'mma talk to him." Joe had told Sapphire.

"Don't worry. When you get back everything'll be back to normal," she said, convincing Joe.

Once Joe was in Atlanta, Sapphire began baiting Carlos for deception. When Justice moved back to Charlotte, Sapphire knew Carlos would have his guard down. She had called and told Carlos that Joe was back in town and he was ready to meet with him. When Carlos opened the door to greet Joe, he was surprised to see Sapphire standing there. "What's up, girl? I thought you was Joe," he had said before turning his back to walk back through the house to rejoin his fianceé. "Justice in the back—" was all he was able to get out before Sapphire plunged the knife deep into his back, puncturing his kidney and slightly severing his spine causing instant paralysis. She kept plunging the knife into his back until his body went limp. Once on the floor, she continued to stab him until she heard Justice's voice. It was then when she hid in the sunroom.

Sapphire had played everyone! Out of all the players in their crazy ass circle, Sapphire was the one who had exacted the ultimate revenge.

Sapphire was still rambling on like a mad woman, but Justice didn't hear a word she was saying. It all sounded like gibberish because her head was so clouded with confusion and shock, to the point in which she felt like she was spinning out of control. Her thoughts were all colliding into one another. Her man was lying dead on their dining room floor, and his killer was her best friend who had slain him because of a vendetta. A unsettled score Sapphire had begged Justice to settle and one of the reasons why Carlos was her man again to begin with.

Justice grabbed her head with both hands in an attempt to stop the cyclone that was swirling through her brain. She shook her head uncontrollably as the tears fell in droves, staining her chiseled cheeks.

This *couldn't* be real! Justice had finally found happiness and now in a blink of an eye it had all been taken away from her! Why did this world continue to treat her so cruelly? Why didn't anyone want to see her happy? Why when every time she thought her life was about to be on the correct path, somebody did something to cause it to spiral out of control again? She couldn't understand it! Truth be told, at that instant she couldn't understand *anything*. Her understanding was ZERO!!

She heard a voice but could not decipher the words as she pointed the pistol at the cause of her latest despair. Justice heard what sounded like pleading, but had no regard for Sapphire's words as she closed her swollen, bloodshot eyes and squeezed the trigger six times in rapid succession.

DISCUSSION QUESTIONS

(1) Do you think Carlos truly loved Justice or was his conscious for his past actions beating him down and he felt obligated to right a wrong?

(2) Do you think Justice should have forgiven Carlos and allowed him to re-enter her life again as her lover after all that transpired in the past?

(3) Do you think Carlos's death was Justice's karma for the murders of J.T., Tan and the abortion?

(4) Was Carlos's death his own karma for Tan and Dave's murders and the murders of so many others he was responsible for in his past?

(5) Do you think Sapphire should have told Justice about her plan to exact revenge on Carlos so Justice wouldn't have fallen back in love with him?

(6) Overall, do you think Justice made rational decisions throughout the book, i.e. the situation with Precious and Virgin? The decision of not telling her father about J.T.? Deciding to move back to Charlotte?

(7) Who did you think was hiding in the sunroom before the killer revealed herself? Lil' Joe? Tan's cousins?

(8) Do you feel as if Sapphire's motives for revenge were strong enough for her to take the extreme measures she had taken? Were her intentions well enough hidden throughout the book?

(9) Was Justice wrong for shooting Sapphire? If so, how do you think she should have handled the situation with Sapphire at the end?

(10) Who do you think was the THIRSTIEST character in this book?

WAHIDA CLARK PRESENTS BEST SELLING TITLES